Awakening Rayne

(Natura Series Book 1)

Cover Art by Kerry A. Sandoval

Lellow Merote Press

ISBN 978-1-7341972-0-4

Facebook.com/AwakeningRayne

KerrySandoval.com

For my real-life Klara, the true water goddess.

Prologue

"I'm so sorry." A whisper in the dark. The woman sits alone her fiery red hair blazing. Her face weathered from age and unspoken pain, memories threatening to consume her. She looks down at her palm where she holds three small, silver charms delicately, staring as though they may disappear. They shimmer in the darkness a reminder of what could have been, what should have been. She wipes away the sting of a tear from her eye. A soft knock at the door draws her from her sorrow. Her fist closes tightly around the charms.

"Come in."

"I'm sorry to disturb you love, but we've found her."

The woman turns abruptly, eyes now alight with a spark of hope.

"Where?"

"A small police station in Georgia."

"Finally, sixteen years…"

"Shall I assemble a team to go and extract her?"

"No…I think it best if I handle this myself. I don't want to frighten her."

"Yes, of course, she may not know who she really is."

"…or what she is capable of…"

∞∞∞

Klara Rayne wished she was normal.
She wanted to blend in with the crowd…fit in
with the crowd…avoid the crowd.
The problem was she couldn't be further from normal.
She had always known this day was coming, the
day her whole world would change, but is anyone
ever really prepared to face their destiny?

Chapter 1

It started out like any other spring day in Georgia. Blazing hot. The sun threatened to turn her already tan skin a shade or two darker. Her long dark hair was pulled up into a ponytail because she couldn't stand to feel the sweaty strands against her neck. She was making the short walk to school like every other day for the past three years. She could do it with her eyes closed. Klara didn't take the sidewalks along their suburban streets like everyone else did. She had fashioned her own secret path to school through the forest behind her house.

Today the air was thick, and the gnats were swarming as usual. They buzzed in and out of her ears and nose like little explorers, it was second nature to swat them away but it never really did any good. Georgia gnats will always win the battle. Anyone else would have begged their parents to drive them to school but not Klara. She loved these woods. She could spend hours here in her secluded sanctuary, away from the world of people looming outside. She knew every tree, every flower, every hidden gem. They were her friends, these trees. The woods were the only place she felt safe, felt…free. She could escape here to the quiet sounds of the forest, birds chirping, wind blowing through the branches, the water flowing softly over the rocks in the little creek. Here there were no people to bother her, no emotions threatening to overwhelm her, no expectations burdening her, no insane future awaiting her. Here she was just Klara. Here she could pretend to be a normal teenage girl with normal teenage problems.

Klara walked along her small path to school thoughts stuck on the day she had ahead of her. It was the day before spring break and she knew all the students would be brimming with excitement. The teachers would show movies in class because nothing they taught today would be remotely retained. This simply meant idle time. She hated idle time, not just because she genuinely loved to learn but because idle time meant Mallory and her clones would have more opportunities to pick on her.

Mallory's pointy-nosed face popped into her mind. Klara shook it away. Why did Mallory like to torture her so? Klara never bothered anyone. She kept to herself, head in a book, never voiced an opinion in class, never stuck her nose where it didn't belong. Still, Mallory had made it her mission in life to seek Klara out and ruin her day...every...single...day.

"Well Chip, maybe today will be lucky and Mallory won't be at school?"

"Meow." the sleek tomcat rubbed his body against her leg affectionately. He looked up at her with his bright eyes that matched one of the shades of orange in his fur. He was large for a cat and extremely intelligent. Klara was certain he understood every word she had ever told him. Which had been quite a few. She had spent the past sixteen years pouring her heart out to the furry feline. There had been several instances of crying into his side and leaving a smear of tears and snot in her wake. He never seemed to mind. He was the best sort of friend in her opinion. He was a great listener and he never judged her. Unlike her parents. She could feel the disappointment coming off them in waves.

Klara's parents were hard people. Sure, some kids had stern parents who rode them about their grades or behavior, but Klara's parents could care less about grades. From the day she was born, they had been grooming her. Apparently, Klara had a destiny. She was supposed to be someone special, someone powerful. According to her mom and dad, Klara was from some mystical world, where magic existed, and people have powers. It sounded like the ravings of crazy people and under normal circumstances Klara would have called child protective services to rescue her from the madhouse. The only problem was Klara knew what her parents told her was the truth. At least the bit about the powers was true, she had seen her parents use their powers many times. Her mom could produce little balls of light with her hands and her dad could heal animals.

Chip had benefited from her dad's power a time or two. One time when Klara was five, she lost control of her bike and went rolling into the street, she heard a horrible screeching sound and the smell of burnt rubber permeated the air. When Klara turned around, she saw that Chip had run after her and he was lying prone in the street, a woman had gotten out of her car and was apologizing repeatedly. Klara had been hysterical. Her parents sent the woman on her way and calmly brought Chip inside. They laid him on the kitchen table and her dad held his hands over the cat's center. A faint purple glow came from his palms and spread into Chip's body. The next thing she knew, her kitty was sitting up on the table like nothing had happened.

Up until that day, Klara thought her parent's stories were just make-believe stories they told her to fill her little imagination. As she got older the stories turned into lessons and lessons turned into training sessions. Those training sessions had become a great source of stress and animosity between her and her parents. She tried to remember a time her parents had spent time with her for anything other than training but came up empty. She honestly couldn't even remember ever having seen either one of them smile.

Since Klara was destined to be some "superhero", her parents were constantly pushing her to figure out her power. The best she had been able to do was read the emotions of other people and even that had been hit and miss except when it came to Chip. She could read him every time. Empathic abilities that only worked on your cat did not exactly scream "Wonder Woman is here to save the day."

Klara shook her head.

"What does it matter Chip? I will never be able to live up to their expectations, why do I even try?"

"Meow."

Chip sat down on the trail. They had reached the edge of the woods and she could see the school up ahead, looming like a prison. Klara wasn't sure what Chip did all day while she was at school, but he was always right here waiting for her when the final bell rang. She imagined him chasing birds in the woods or sunning himself on the rocks of the stream. His silky orange fur glistening in the warm rays. Such freedom he had as a cat; Klara wished she could switch places with him. Get lost in the woods never to return. It sounded perfect.

"I bet you would make a better superhero than me wouldn't you boy?"

He just stared up at her.

Klara bent down to pat him gently on the head before making her way across the schoolyard.

Klara's high school looked the way one might expect a small-town school to look. It had been built in the late sixties and was a mass of red brick with some trailers scattered about where the student body had grown over the years and the school had to improvise for more classroom space.

Klara navigated the busy walkway that led to the side door of the school like a ninja in stealth mode. She held her head low and weaved in-between students, careful not to bump shoulders with anyone. If only her power could be invisibility, now that would serve her very well. She breathed a sigh of relief when she made it to her locker with no one paying her any attention. Her book bag was heavy, and she was happy to drop it to the ground beside her locker.

As she had predicted the other students were buzzing with anticipation. She could hear the kids around her discussing their plans for spring break. Some of them were going to the beach, others were headed to one theme park or another. Klara knew she would be spending her spring break in the basement of her house going through training exercise after training exercise while her parents argued about the best way to bring her powers to the surface. If she was lucky, they would get going at each other hard enough that she could slip away and escape into one of her favorite books.

Klara was jolted from her thoughts by a boney elbow stuck in her back.

"Watch it you little freak." A nasal voice came from behind.

Klara didn't need to turn around to know that voice was coming from a very blonde, very condescending, Mallory.

"Sorry." Klara said avoiding eye contact and staring down at Mallory's feet.

"Sorry? I don't think sorry is good enough Klara, what do you think girls?" Mallory smirked at her friends.

Mallory grabbed Klara's book bag off the ground and dumped the contents all over the floor.

Laughing Mallory and her cronies continued down the hallway leaving Klara with a mess.

"Well she let you off easier than normal, must be feeling generous with spring break around the corner." The boy to her left said. Steven was his name maybe? She wasn't sure. Klara thought she felt a brief feeling of sympathy coming from him but then he slammed his locker shut and walked off with a shrug.

Klara bent down to gather up the contents of her bookbag. She could feel the tears welling up in her eyes and she pushed them back down. If her parents saw her acting like this, they would call her weak. She was weak, why couldn't she ever stand up to that witch Mallory. What was wrong with her. Klara let out a sigh and stood up, she shoved her bookbag into the tight locker. She considered grabbing her textbooks but reached for her favorite teen vampire novel instead. As she slammed her locker shut the bell rang overhead. Klara made a mad dash for her first-period class.

As she had predicted yet again the teachers were showing movies or allowing free periods today. The morning had passed by quickly, Klara had managed to avoid Mallory and anyone else for that matter. During lunch, she grabbed a small insulated bag out of her locker and headed to the girl's bathroom. She let out a sigh of relief when she arrived to find it empty as usual. Everyone else would be in the cafeteria right now. She chose the stall furthest from the door, it was the handicap stall and it had a small counter with a sink in it. She locked the door behind her and climbed up on the counter to eat her lunch. This is how she had eaten her lunch for the past three years, alone, hiding in the girl's bathroom. Pathetic.

Klara unzipped her lunch bag and pulled out a hummus wrap, some edamame beans and a bottle of water. Klara preferred a vegetarian diet, it wasn't because she cared to eat super healthy or anything, it was just that the thought of eating an animal turned her stomach. As she took a bite of her hummus wrap, she cracked open her book. Klara escaped into a world of vampires and romance. She loved to read, the books took her to places far far away. She liked this particular book because she could relate to the main character. Someone who felt like she didn't belong anywhere, someone who always felt inadequate.

"I know I saw her come in here."

"I don't see any feet in the stalls"

"She must be hiding, try the handles"

"Klara! Come out Come out wherever you are!"

Klara could hear Mallory and her clones wiggling the door handles one by one. She felt panic growing in the pit of her stomach. What could she do? There was no way out of there, except right past them.

Mallory's head popped under the door of the stall. "Here she is!"

"Open the door, Klara, we just want to talk to you."

Klara could see a pen push through the slit in the door and push the latch out of place. The door swung open. Mallory and three of her friends waltzed into the small stall.

"OMG! You eat lunch in here?! That's nasty!"

Klara climbed down from the counter and was about to try and dart past them when Mallory grabbed her by the ponytail.

"Oh no you don't, not until we get a picture of this, it's so going on Instagram."

Mallory pulled Klara by the hair back over to the counter where her lunch box still lay, she took Klara's face and shoved it down into the half-eaten container of edamame beans.

"Quick get a picture of her eating like the dog she is, I bet you drink out of that toilet when you are done too."

Still clutching her hair, Mallory and her friends pulled Klara over to the toilet and slammed her down on her knees, they smashed her face up against the cold porcelain and began laughing hysterically at her.

"Quick, take the picture, this is great!"

They took their picture and Mallory let go of Klara's hair.

"Thanks for the laugh, dog."

They stopped in front of the mirrors to check their hair and then left the bathroom.

Klara placed a shaking hand to her head and rubbed her scalp, it was tender from Mallory's cruel grip. She didn't get up off the floor of the bathroom stall, instead, she sat there and let the tears fall this time. She trembled as the sobs came out one after another.

By the time Klara stopped crying and cleaned up the remains of her lunch it was time for the bell to ring signaling fifth-period classes. Klara exited the restroom and made her way back to her locker; she placed her lunch bag back inside and slammed it shut. It just wasn't fair, why Klara, why always Klara. Surely there was some other poor soul for them to pick on? Klara felt a pang of guilt, she didn't really mean that. She didn't wish this on anyone else. She just wished she could be brave enough to make it stop.

Klara's fifth period history teacher showed the Manchurian candidate in class for the fourth time that year. They only ever had enough time to see the first half of it, but no one seemed to care. After the first time he showed it, Klara had gone home and downloaded it online, so she could see how it ended. She thought maybe there would be a quiz or something over it and she wanted to be prepared but there wasn't one.

At the end of class, Klara headed to the door to leave when her

History teacher approached her.

"Klara, could I speak with you for a moment?"

"Yes, Sir?"

"I was really impressed with the essay you wrote comparing the roles of women in the sixteenth century to women of today."

"Thank you, I enjoyed researching it, you know women of that time frame had so many challenges facing them but still had huge impacts on history, even if they had to be hidden behind the face of a man, take…"

He cut her off. "Yes, I agree and I thoroughly enjoyed reading your essay. Klara have you thought any about your future? What colleges are you interested in?"

Now Klara understood where this was going. He mistook her for a normal girl. He thought she was going to get to go to college and have a career someday. If only that could be true.

"Actually, I have put a lot of thought into my future and I plan to go into the family business, but I'm so glad you enjoyed my essay. Thank you for telling me, it really made my day." She gave him a smile and left the room before he could question her further.

Klara was trying so hard to get out of there that she didn't pay attention to where she was going. Of course, her luck had her slam right into Mallory.

Everything happened in slow motion. Klara turned just in time to see Mallory's face a few inches from hers, Mallory had just raised her drink to her mouth when they crashed into each other, Mallory's drink spilled down her face and onto her clothing, ruining Mallory's outfit.

"Ahh! You little bitch! You did that on purpose!"

"Language Mallory, it was clearly an accident, now go get yourself cleaned up and I will give you a hall pass to be late to sixth-period." And the history teacher shooed Mallory on her way.

"This isn't over." Mallory threatened. Klara could feel Mallory's anger loud and clear.

By the time Klara entered her sixth-period class, the photo Mallory had posted on Instagram had made its rounds. Kids were staring at her, pointing, laughing. She wanted to crawl under the desk and disappear. It took every ounce of inner strength she had to hold back her tears during class. When the bell finally rang, she grabbed her book and ran to the door. She didn't bother stopping at her locker for her bookbag. Her lunch bag would probably be pretty ripe by the time she came back from spring break, but she didn't care. She just wanted to get out of there. She fled as fast as her feet would carry her out the side door of the school and straight for her secret path.

As always Chip was waiting for her.

"I'm so happy to see you boy! It was awful, just awful!"

Klara walked a few feet into the woods making sure she was out of sight of the school campus. There was a large tree stump to the side of her path. It was covered in bright green moss with little mushrooms growing out of the sides of it. Klara took a seat and Chip hopped up into her lap. She lifted him in her arms and held him close to her. He began to purr, and Klara buried her face in his fur. She let all the tears come out that she had held back during sixth-period.

Klara was so consumed with her grief that she didn't hear Mallory and two other girls approaching.

"So, this is where you disappear to after school. Your family too poor to get you a car?"

Mallory walked closer to her with a sneer on her hateful face.

"Do you see what you did to my favorite shirt? I told you this wasn't over."

Klara stood up and Chip jumped down off her lap to the ground. Klara began to back up and was preparing to run.

Chip let out a hiss and got into a pouncing position.

"No, Chip let's just go!"

"What's this your little bodyguard?" Mallory turned toward Chip and kicked hard. Her booted foot connected with his little head and he went flying towards the tree stump.

"Chip!!!"

Klara watched his body hit the stump and go limp. She filled with rage.

She turned towards Mallory her eyes blazing with fury. Klara could feel the hair in her ponytail began to float around her. Energy started to grow from somewhere deep inside and spread through every inch of her skin until it pooled, a light blue glow, in her palms waiting patiently for her to direct it. She lifted her hands and pointed them straight at Mallory. Large, strong streams of water shot out of them and lifted Mallory off the ground, surrounding her. Mallory barely had time to scream before the water covered her face and she was thrashing about. Her friends backed away in fear and ran towards the school. Klara's rage was consuming.

She focused the energy at Mallory even harder, letting the water envelope Mallory in a watery cocoon. Klara felt strong, she felt powerful, she felt vengeful but then she felt something else pierce through…fear…not her own but Mallory's fear had pierced through the water and Klara felt the terror the young girl was experiencing. Klara forced her hands shut and the energy drained away. Mallory dropped to the ground in a pool of water and gasped for air. She locked eyes with Klara and started to back up on her hands and knees terrified. Klara stared at the girl for a moment. This girl who only moments ago was torturing Klara was now cowering from her.

What had she done? Had she almost killed someone? Klara scooped up Chip and ran towards home never looking back.

Chapter 2

Klara reached the back door to her house in record time. She practically ripped it off the hinges and burst inside. She found her parents in the kitchen, her dad preparing dinner and her mom folding laundry at the table.

"Chip is hurt!"

She rushed over to the counter where her dad was standing and laid Chip gently down.

Her dad set down the knife he had been using to chop potatoes and placed his palms over Chip's body.

"What happened?" Her mom came up to stand beside her.

"He was trying to defend me.... I...he..." Klara felt the panic well up inside her. Her head was spinning. What had happened? What had she almost done?

"Klara you need to calm down and stop acting like a child. Tell me what happened." Her mother's voice was calm but laced with annoyance.

Klara took a deep breath and began again.

"I was attacked in the woods by some girls from school. Chip was trying to defend me and was injured. I'm not sure what happened but when they hurt him, I felt a surge of power and the next thing I know water is shooting from my palms. I wasn't trying to hurt her...I think she will be ok..." Mallory's terrified face popped up in her mind again.

"What!?!" Klara's mom grabbed her by the arm forcing her to face her directly.

"You used your powers on a human!" she spat, clearly angry.

Klara didn't need to be an empath to tell that. There was no concern for Klara coming from her mom. She could feel her mothers' fingers digging into her arms painfully.

"Klara what were you thinking. Haven't we told you over and over again that you must never expose us?" Her dad seemed only vaguely interested in the conversation. He was busy running his hands over Chip, his healing powers slowly working to bring her best friend back to her.

"It wasn't on purpose; I was so upset it just kind of happened and as soon as I realized I was hurting her I stopped." Klara pleaded.

"You have been exposed; don't you know what this means? You're not ready to go back but now you will have to." Her mother dropped her arm and walked out of the room.

Klara rubbed the spot her mom had just clutched; it was red and painful to the touch. Klara knew it would be bruised in the morning but she had received worse from her mother in the past. Her father never physically hurt her. He criticized her when he felt like taking an interest but he was usually just detached. There was this one time. One good memory she had, she was maybe 3 or 4 and she could remember him singing a song to her but over the years she thought maybe she had just imagined it. Her mother however made sure Klara knew how she felt about her both verbally and physically.

"Nothing I do is ever right"

"Well, you better get it together, they won't take it easy on you like we did once you get back to our world." her dad finished up with Chip his hands returning to their natural color. He picked up his knife and resumed cutting the potatoes like all this was just a normal everyday occurrence.

Chip opened his eyes, sat up and began grooming himself.

"What did she mean by I'll have to go back now?"

"I think you know what she meant. You will have to return to our world, it won't be safe here any longer, Mallory will tell her parents what happened, and the humans will come for us." Her dad seemed very nonchalant about the whole thing.

"Meow." Chip looked at Klara with his head cocked slightly to the side. She sensed his confusion.

"If I have to go back there, will I be able to take Chip with me?"

"Yes, what reason would he have to stay here, you will be his problem there now not ours."

"What does that even mean?"

Her parents always talked in riddles like that and hurtful statements. It's like they resented her for existing. They never told her anything useful about her future either. She felt like they were setting her up for failure.

Her dad didn't even bother responding to her last question. She wasn't surprised.

Her mother reentered the room with a small duffle bag in her hand.

"Go upstairs and pack your things, only necessities, you will have no use for your human trinkets where you are going." She shoved the bag into Klara's arms.

Klara took it and turned towards the stairs that led to her bedroom. Chip hopped down off the counter barely making a sound and followed her. As she climbed the stairs, she heard her parents conversing.

"Are you sure we can send her back without making contact first?" Her dad asked tentatively.

"I don't care...I'm done helping them. What have they ever done for us except punish us? She has exposed herself, there was never anything in the deal about having to risk exposure to the humans. They banish us here to live in the human world but then make us babysit for them. She can go back and they can deal with it." Her mother answered bitterly.

Klara's mind was racing as she packed her bag. She threw in a few pairs of clothes, hairbrush, toothbrush, toothpaste, deodorant, lotion, her three favorite books and a small stuffed cat that resembled Chip. She had won it out of one of those crane machines in the supermarket years ago, her parents had scolded her for wasting her money, but they let her keep it. She didn't care what her mom said about human trinkets, if she was expected to save the world, she could at least be permitted to take a few things with her. Klara sat down on the bed and Chip hopped up next to her. He nuzzled her side and purred as she stroked his head. She looked around her room one last time. There really wasn't much to note. Her parents weren't the type to shower her with gifts so anything she had she got on her own and that wasn't much.

"I guess this is really it." She looked down at Chips little face, he looked up at her with his sparkling orange eyes, blinking slowly the way cats do.

"At least I have you, my little man." She kissed him gently and he rewarded her with a soft head butt on the chin.

Klara stood and walked toward her bedroom door, Chip close behind her. They ascended slowly down the stairs to find her parents waiting by the back door. Her mother impatient and her dad indifferent.

While she had been upstairs her father had cleaned up the kitchen and thrown the cut potatoes in the trash. He held a granola bar and a protein shake out to her. Dinner of champions she thought to herself.

Her mother snatched the duffle bag from her hands.

Please don't take anything out. Klara hoped to herself, but she needn't worry, her mother only added a few items to the bag. A canteen of water, a bag of what looked to be trail mix and some fruit leather.

"You have a long walk ahead of you." She explained. "Let's go."

Klara followed her parents to the back yard where they began trekking towards the woods. Klara's woods.

"Where are we going?" she didn't like the idea of them going into her sanctuary. These woods were her special place, her escape from them, from everything.

"We are taking you to the gateway." Her mom reached up and removed her locket from her neck. Her mom wore the necklace every day. It was silver and delicate with an engraving of a tree on the front. Klara had admired it over the years and couldn't recall ever having seen her mother take it off.

As her mom opened it Klara couldn't help but try and sneak a peek. She had often wondered what picture her mother kept inside. She never for once thought it would be a picture of her, her mom didn't seem to care about her enough for something that sentimental but maybe it was a picture of her dad?

Instead what Klara saw inside was a tiny moving arrow floating on a background that shimmered and glittered under the sunlight. It looked like some sort of mystical compass except there were no marks indicating north, south, east or west.

"What is it?" Klara's curiosity won out.

"It's a gateway compass, it will point us to the path home." Her mother stated simply. The little arrow began to move and pointed towards the forest.

Klara followed her parents deep into the woods. They walked in silence, which was not uncommon. They rarely had anything to say to her unless it was criticism.

Chip kept pace with them eagerly, his paws moving swiftly and silently through the underbrush. Klara could swear she picked up on excitement mixed with a nervous feeling coming from her feline BFF. That seemed odd to Klara, what would a cat be nervous about?

They continued to walk for what felt like hours. Klara had explored these woods many times, but this was the furthest she had ever been. They had been following the path of the little creek for some time now and it had been steadily growing in strength and depth until it was now a strong river. Klara could hear the sound of rushing water up ahead. She could feel energy in the air all around her. The energy felt familiar and wonderful. She had a sensation of tingling on her skin causing goosebumps to pop up all over her body.

As they pushed through the dense foliage, they stepped out onto the bank of the most spectacular waterfall Klara could have ever imagined. It stood over 100 feet tall and the water came bursting over the cliffs above. At the base of the falls was a pool of crystal-clear water. The shore of the pool was lined with all manner of flowers. Colors everywhere, bees buzzing, birds chirping. It was truly breathtaking. If only she had known it was there, she would have journeyed to it daily.

"We're here." Klara's mom pointed to the falls.

"You will follow that path and jump."

Klara glanced in the direction her mother had indicated. There was a pathway of rocks, each higher than the next that led directly to the front of the falls. The last one stood at least 50 feet high and was very intimidating.

"I don't understand?"

Klara's dad spoke up this time. "You will need to jump from rock to rock until you reach that last one there and then you jump straight into the waterfall. When you come out the other side you will be in our world."

"You are not coming with me?" Klara was growing concerned now. It's not that she didn't want to leave her parents. There was no love lost between them now, but she couldn't be expected to journey to this place alone. She didn't even know what she was supposed to do when she got there.

"No, we have fulfilled our part of the bargain and you can tell them I said that." Her mother's response was so cold and uncaring.

How could they do this? After everything they had put her through, they were just going to walk away. What kind of parents do this to their child?

"How can you just leave me alone like this? Don't you care even a little bit about what happens to me?" she asked flatly.

Her mother looked her straight in the eyes with no remorse, no feeling at all. "No, we really don't care what happens to you."

Klara felt the tears well up in her eyes again. No, she would not give them the satisfaction of seeing her cry. She turned her back to them and walked to the water's edge. Chip was already waiting for her on the highest rock. She focused on him and jumped. She leapt from rock to rock until she stood next to Chip, facing the falls. Chip looked up at her. "Meow" and without hesitation, the brave little cat lunged through the water as if he knew exactly where he was going. Klara watched him disappear behind the falls. She didn't bother looking back at her parents, she didn't care if they were still waiting below or not. She took a deep breath and jumped towards her destiny.

Chapter 3

Klara briefly felt water all around her and then fell face-first onto the ground. She could taste dirt and grass in her mouth. Sputtering she used her hands to push herself into a sitting position. She began brushing herself off and realized her clothes and hair were dry. How could that be? She had just jumped through a waterfall? She looked behind her and saw nothing but open meadow, as she turned her head to view her surroundings, she saw it was more of the same. She was sitting in the middle of a large meadow. The sun shined brightly above, the aqua blue sky was crisp and clear. She could see flowers blooming all around her. In the distance in each direction was the tree line of what looked to be a very large forest. Moments ago, she had been in a very hot, very muggy Georgia but now the air around her was cool and light. There were no gnats flying up her nose either, only a gentle breeze ruffling her ponytail.

An urgent-sounding "Meow" came from the ground next to her.

"Hey boy, I bet you landed on all fours with no dirt in your mouth." She reached over to stroke his soft orange fur and he slowly backed away from her eyes locked with hers.

"Chip? What's wrong? It's only me?" She stood up and took a step towards him.

"Meow." Chip took another step back and arched his back low to the ground.

Later Klara would tell herself she always knew there was more to Chip than just your average housecat. There were little clues like a trail of bread crumbs that had led her to the conclusion that she stumbled upon years ago. Chip was special. Chip was her best friend. Chip understood her like no person ever had. Chip had more evolved feelings than her parents ever had. Especially when it came to her. She knew this to be the undeniable truth because where she struggled to use her empathic abilities on people, she had always been able to sense Chip's emotions loud and clear. Their feelings connected with each other like two magnets snapping in place.

Perhaps that's why what happened next didn't shock her as much as it should have.

She looked down at his slender orange frame backing away from her. His body language was off, it didn't line up with the emotions she could feel emanating from him. His emotions were screaming excitement, anticipation, freedom and a strong sense of relief. Yet he appeared agitated and defensive?

Klara took a step closer to him and Chip planted his hindlegs firmly in place. His torso hoisted itself upright like a tiger in a circus doing tricks for a raw piece of meat. His transformation spanned only seconds, but time seemed to slow to a crawl while her most trusted confidant revealed his shocking secret. She looked on as the fur covering his body began to ripple and pulse, matching the rhythmic beat of Klara's heart. His limbs stretched forth and his midsection elongated. Where a mass of fluff and fur had once been now a defined abdomen topped with an impressive array of chest muscles and broad shoulders appeared. His arms and legs once slender and delicate now strong and capable. Instead of looking down at her feline companion she had to raise her line of sight to peer up at a boy not much older than herself. His fur was gone leaving only a messy mop of hair atop his head. Like his fur had once been the hair on his head had several shades of orange striped through it. He was wearing a fitted pair of shorts. No not shorts but capris? They were very odd-looking, like the pants you saw men wear in movies about fairy creatures. She realized she had been staring too long at his lower half, embarrassed she lifted her gaze to his face. It was fierce and feral looking. Their eyes met, and she gasped. They had not changed one bit. He still had his golden-orange eyes, a shade of liquid fire with the diamond slit pupil's characteristic of a cat. Right now, those eyes were staring intently at her. It was Klara's turn to take an agitated step back.

"Klara, please don't be frightened. It's still me." His voice was husky but unsure and pleading.

Klara's throat felt dry, she felt a sudden desperation for water.

"I…" she began but words escaped her. She just stood there blinking at him. Say something, anything she demanded of herself, but what? What does one say when something impossible happens right before your eyes?

"Please sit, take a moment, I know this is…unexpected." Chip motioned to a nearby rock. It was smooth, just large enough for her to sit down and try to pull herself together. She steadied herself and walked slowly over to the rock all the while keeping her eyes locked on Chip. "They should have told you about me. I never understood why those idiots never explained what I was." He was rambling.

Chip picked up her duffle bag and pulled out the canteen of water her mother had provided. Should she even still be thinking of her as her mother? It was all too much, her parents weren't really her parents, her cat wasn't really a cat, what next? "Here take a drink, you don't have to say anything, just listen and I will try and explain OK?" he passed her the canteen, she took it, nodded her head yes and placed it to her lips tentatively. The cool water soothed her dry mouth and throat.

Chip lowered himself to a seated position on the ground in front of her, his movements swift and graceful.

"As you can see, I am not an ordinary cat." He stated calmly, but she could sense the worry he was experiencing. Somehow it was comforting to her that she could still sense his emotions so easily, that they were still so in tune with one another.

"I am your MoChara. We are bonded, since the day you were born. It is my most sacred duty to be your guardian and protector, but I have failed you already, the magic in the human world was too weak and I was forced to remain in my animal form. Time after time I wished for nothing more than to be able to take my true form and defend you from that evil little rat Mallory-isss." He said Mallory's name with a little hiss at the end like it left a bad taste and in his mouth.

Klara felt a giggle escape her and some of the anxiety she had been feeling drained away. Chip tilted his head to the side like a question and stared at her, a smile crept up on his face. Klara felt the worry he had been holding start to melt away as well. It was like their emotions were playing off each other. Not just her reading his but hers affecting his and vice versa.

"It was torture waiting at the edge of our forest everyday knowing what you were going through inside that school building." Klara liked the way he said *our* forest like it meant something to him the way it had meant everything to her.

"I'm so sorry I lost my temper and went for Mallory. None of this would have happened if it weren't for my actions." He hung his head low avoiding eye contact with her. She felt his guilt piercing through.

Finally, she found her words again, seeing him beat himself up, it was too much, she had to comfort him, reassure him.

"Stop, this is not your fault. I'm not sorry this is happening, not one bit. You lived in that house with me, you saw how awful it was, I'm glad to be free of them. Yes, I'm scared, terrified even, of what's going to happen next. I'm not gonna lie, you morphing from my sweet little kitty cat into some hot guy is a lot to process."

She felt the blood rushing to her cheeks and heat creeping in. Had she just called him a hot guy? OMG, he was her cat for crying out loud! What was wrong with her?

If he took note of her comment, he didn't show it.

"So, you're not mad at me?" he looked like a scolded little boy asking if he was in trouble.

"No...surprised, confused, maybe a little self-conscious but not mad."

He looked at her with that head cocked to the side confused

look again.

"Why self-conscious?"

Klara could still feel the heat on her cheeks. What could she say? Of course, she felt self-conscious. Chip knew her every thought, her every secret, her every hope. She had cried into his furry little body more times than she could count. Laid all her insecurities and self-doubt bare for him to see. She thought back to the many pity parties she had, using him as a snot rag. Now she understood why he had always looked like he was listening to her intently. He really had been! She played back every embarrassing moment from the past 16 years and Chip was there for each of them, never leaving her side. He must think her a useless child. What had he said? He was bound by duty to protect her? What a burden he must think she was. He was stuck watching her every pathetic little move. Then, a thought popped into her mind.

"I've undressed in front of you!" now her cheeks were burning like they were on fire.

Chip stood up abruptly.

"No, No, No, I never looked! I swear to you I always averted my eyes, always. I would never disrespect you like that." She could feel him willing her to believe him. He was so genuine, so offended that she could think that of him. Klara knew in her heart he was telling the truth. Chip would never hurt her, he would always protect her, be there for her. Maybe all these years of friendship really had meant something to him and not just to her. Logically, she knew she should be more alarmed by this but honestly, she felt relieved not to be alone for what was coming next.

"I know Chip, I believe you."

Chip let out a sigh of relief and at the same time his stomach let out a loud growl of hunger.

Klara laughed in spite of herself.

"Some things never change, its way past your dinner time."

Klara stood up and stretched her legs. She took another cool sip of water and screwed the cap back in place. She didn't know how long their journey would be and she may need to conserve the water.

The sun was setting, and she could see hues of orange, pink and purple on the horizon.

"It really is very lovely here."

Chip looked off into the distance at the setting sun.

"I agree, this place puts even our little forest to shame, doesn't it? But wait until you see Natura."

"Natura?"

"Yes, this place is called the Meadowgate. It's a gateway between the human world and Natura...our homeworld."

"This is a pretty big gateway."

"Actually, it's a lot smaller than it looks. Once we pass through that tree line over there, we will be in Natura. The horizon you see is only an illusion."

She smiled. "I'm starting to think my whole life has been an illusion. You know, they never told me what our world was called. *Natura*...that's the first I've heard it."

"Yes, they often spoke in riddles your guardians, didn't they? Never giving you the answers, you needed. I failed you there as well. They were so cruel to you and there was nothing I could do. I have a feeling though that they will suffer the consequences of their actions in the not so distant future."

"It's ok, they were frustrated with me, I get it. I was weak. I never got the training exercises right; I'll never be what everyone expects me to be." She felt the doubt crawling in, consuming her.

Chip stepped closer to her and took her hands in his.

"That stops now. All the self-doubt, all the second-guessing and beating yourself up. You forget, I have known you your whole life and you are strong and brave and kind. You will be everything they expect you to be and more."

The way he said it with such certainty and passion she could almost believe him.

"Wait you called them my guardians?"

"Yes, I did because they are not your parents. They were chosen hastily to watch over you and keep you hidden until you came into your powers. Your real parents were kind and gracious people." Chip seemed lost in an old sad memory when he said it. "I guess I should be shocked but honestly...they never felt like parents...in fact, I'm quite sure they hated me. In a way, it's a relief to know they aren't my parents." Klara had so many questions she just didn't even know where to start or what to say.

Chips stomach growled again and this time hers answered his with its own loud growl. They both laughed.

"Ok, we really do need to get going now. It will be dark soon." Chip was still holding one of her hands and he tugged her along behind him. He reached down and scooped up the duffle bag flinging it over his shoulder with ease.

"Where are we going?"

"After we pass through the Meadowgate, I know somewhere not far from here where we can get a hot meal, a warm bed, and where you will be safe for now."

Chapter 4

Klara was still very aware of Chip holding her hand as he dragged her along behind him. They arrived at the forest edge and Klara looked up at the trees looming before her.

"You said we are going somewhere I will be safe, is my safety in question?" she tried her best to sound brave, but her voice cracked slightly.

He turned to face her. "I'm afraid so, every moment you spend in Natura you will grow stronger and the risk of him learning you are here increases."

Klara didn't think she was ready to learn who "Him" was. Instead, she decided to focus on keeping up with Chip.

They entered the forest and the trees towered above them. She kept pace with Chip, he was walking fast but it wasn't tiresome, not yet anyway. With each step, she took the forest floor cracked and crunched beneath her shoes. Chip had dropped her hand and was now walking in front of her clearing a path. She could still feel the warmth on her palms where his hand had been in hers. Chip moved through the forest with the quiet elegance of a cat. His footsteps were silent, light, almost springy. He looked at home among the trees.

Klara was by no means as graceful as Chip but from the instant they had stepped into the woods, she felt a tingling all over her body and a sense of being at home came over her. There was a majestic feeling all around, as though these trees had been here since the dawn of time. The air was cool and crisp. It smelled of nuts and pine needles. Klara looked in every direction and she did not see a single sign of mankind. No littler thrown carelessly about. No notches made in the bark of the trees or worse, trees chopped down. She glanced behind and saw that where the meadow should have been now there were only dense trees in every direction. They had crossed into Natura. She knew this, she felt this in her core. She felt instantly connected, rooted in this place. She could feel Chip's emotions of relief and bliss pouring off him. He was happy to be here too.

"Stop where you are!" a voice demanded of them.

Several men dressed from head to toe in grey and black uniforms with some sort of insignia on the chest came out from behind the trees. They were heavily armed and looked like they very much knew how to use their armaments.

"What is this, who are you? What sort of abominations is this to be holding such violent devices here in our homeland?" Chip had moved in front of her, shielding her from view.

"We will ask the questions, identify yourself and submit to inspection. These are dire times traveler."

"Who are you to demand that of us? We are Naturians, we have every right to be here."

"Well if what you say is true, then you have no reason to object and nothing to fear from us."

Chip's emotions were on fire, Klara could feel his anger boiling over.

"What else could we possibly be? Only Naturians can pass through the Meadowgate and if we were one of the banished, we would dare not cross back unless we were suicidal."

"How long have you been gone, traveler? It seems you are very behind the times."

The man seemed to sense Chip's sincerity and lowered his weapon to approach. However, his comrades kept their weapons pointed in place.

"If you insist on knowing, it has been sixteen years since we have been home."

The man arched his eyebrow in surprise and quickly switched his expression back to stoic.

"That does explain your lack of knowledge then friend. Please allow us to scan you and we will allow you to be on your way."

"Fine, complete your scan. We are tired from our travels and eager to return home to our long-overdue reunion with family."

The man pulled out a device that reminded Klara of something she saw on Star Trek once. He scanned them both and the device made a beep each time.

"What is that? Since when does the Natura guard use tech devices?" Chip inquired.

The guard simply turned an eyebrow up at him like he was crazy.

"You both check out fine. Shifter and Wielder. No humans. You are free to go."

"Like I said, every right to be here." Chip placed his arm protectively over Klara's shoulder and ushered her past the guards and deeper into the forest.

"What was that about?" Klara asked.

"I'm not sure. I worried for a moment that they were there looking for you but clearly not. Or if they were, they didn't do a very good job did they?"

"The guard said, not human. What did he mean by that? I thought you said no human could pass into Natura?"

"Yes, I caught that too. As far as I always knew…no human could but it seems things have changed since we've been gone. Don't worry Klara. There will be answers to be had where we are going, I promise."

Light from the setting sun peeked through the dense canopy overhead like little spotlights on a stage. They walked in comfortable silence for a while, Klara was thankful for the opportunity to take in the beauty around her. How was it that she felt so at ease here? So, at peace? There was a gentle hum of energy all around, flowing from the trees, the rocks, the plants, and the flowers. It was almost tangible like she could feel it creeping up her fingertips, entering her veins. In that moment, she felt strong, powerful, like she could take on the world.

"What is this feeling? It feels as though the forest is alive?"

Chip slowed his pace to walk beside her.

"In a way it kind of is alive I suppose. You are feeling the magic of nature, here in our world it flows freely all around us, it powers us, fuels us. I imagine you feel pretty spectacular right now. Like I did when we entered the Meadowgate and I was finally able to take my true form. For you, it must feel like your battery is recharging after being drained for years. The humans have destroyed so much of the nature in their world that the energy, the magic there is difficult to feel or tap into. It's a bit easier in places of nature like our forest which is why we felt so safe there, more at home. It was as close to our real home as we could get."

"I do feel stronger here, connected to this place, that's strange though isn't it? I've never been here before, that I can remember at least."

Chip smiled at her. The sun had gone down now and was replaced by the soft glow of moonlight. Chip's eyes were even more dazzling in the night, glowing like hot embers in a fire. Above their heads the trees were still dense and tangled up with each other, embracing one another, blocking out a lot of the night sky, but every so often a hole opened up and the stars could be seen shimmering through.

"I don't think it's strange, you are very much connected to this place, you were born here. As was generation after generation of the women in your family. Each of them drew their strength from the energy you are feeling right now."

Generation after generation. Why then did they choose to send her away from here. Was she damaged somehow? Did her parents know when she was born that she would grow up to be weak and useless?

"Why did they send me away? My real mother…didn't she want me? Did they see some flaw in me when I was born?" it was such a soft whisper that Klara couldn't be sure she even said it out loud.

Chip reached over and took Klara by the hand again.

"No, Klara, it was nothing like that. Your family sent you away to protect you. At the time, there was simply no other choice. Though I only met your mother and father once, I know that they loved you and your…loved you very much."

"Chip, what aren't you telling me? You forget I can sense your emotions better than anyone else and I know you are holding back, but why?"

Chip looked down at the ground as they walked not meeting her questioning gaze.

"Come on, I've really had my fill of half-truths and unanswered questions, don't treat me like they did, tell me what I need to know. I can handle it." She didn't mean to sound sharp, but she was tired, hungry, and frustrated with everything and everyone right now.

"It's not that I'm trying to hold things back from you and I do know you can handle it, you can handle anything, I'm sure of that, but some stories are not mine to tell and I don't want to overstep."

"Chip, screw that! You're my best friend and the only person in this world I can trust, who better to tell me?"

Chip continued walking silently beside her, she could feel mixed emotions and she was certain he was about to crack and give in to her demands.

"What about a compromise?"

Klara's eyebrow arched with suspicion. "I'm listening?"

He gestured to a thicket of trees twenty or thirty yards ahead.

"Just past those trees, we will be in view of our destination. Can we table this discussion until we get there, get settled, and have a plate of hot food in front of us? This is really a conversation best had with full bellies, clear minds, and seated bottoms." He tried to make a joke, but it fell flat. However, at the mention of food Klara's stomach roared with agreement. She placed her hand over her midsection willing it to hush.

"Well, even if I don't fully agree it seems my stomach does so I will go along with it, but I better get my answers mister."

Chip smirked, happy with the win.

What was he so hesitant to tell her? She thought maybe it had to do with the *him,* the man he had mentioned before. Who was he and why was she in danger from him? Who would want to her hurt?

"Halt! Identify yourselves!" an unseen voice bellowed from somewhere up above them.

Chip stopped abruptly, placing one hand in the air and the other in front of Klara to stop her in her tracks.

"Not this again." Klara mumbled.

"It's ok Klara, this time is different." Chip reassured her.

"My name is Cosantoir, I need to speak with Mystic."

It hadn't even occurred to Klara that Chip's name wasn't really Chip. Of course, it wasn't…she named him that when she was a little girl. Klara didn't have time to dwell on it long because she was suddenly bombarded with emotions…curiosity…fear…sadness…and…hope, a lot of Hope. She felt herself step closer to Chip, if she could shrink away and disappear behind him that would be great, she thought.

Klara could hear the hushed voices, whispers coming from the treetops. "At ease, my friends." A booming voice bellowed from above. In a flash of silver and black, a man leapt down from the branches. He landed lightly on his feet, one hand to the ground in a crouch. He straightened himself and came closer to them each step like a flourish of wind. He was taller than Chip by a foot or so and was lithe. His limbs moved like the branches of a willow tree, graceful and breezy. His wild, untamed hair a tangle of silver and black stripes. His beard was short, cut close to his face. His clothing was detailed, intricate patterns woven delicately into the black material with a shimmering silver thread. A black cape was strewn over his shoulder haphazardly clasped in place with a silver pendant, the image of a fierce cat engraved upon it. The man had a regal look about him, a kind face but also something that screamed: "I can rip your throat out in one swift move if I need to." His most striking feature, however, were his eyes. Where Chip's eyes blazed orange and red like a burning campfire, this man's eyes shimmered like tiny silver stars on a sea of black.

Beside her Chip dropped to one knee head down in a show of submission. The man approached Chip first, stopping in front of him he placed his hands gently on each of Chip's shoulders.

"Stand my son."

Chip stood slowly the man's hands still on his shoulders holding him at arm's length. The two of them stared at each other for a lingering moment and then the man quickly pulled Chip in for a strong embrace, slapping Chip on the back.

"How I've missed you!" The man radiated with joy and Klara felt it loud and clear.

"Sixteen years was far too long son, I'm so happy to welcome you back home!"

"Father, though I am overjoyed to see you, I've come to seek sanctuary and your assistance." Chip turned to Klara he reached for her arm, pulling her closer.

"Let me introduce you to…"

"Let me stop you there, son. We shall say nothing else until you and your companion are fed and sheltered."

The man's eyes bore into her, curiosity and questions lurking behind the sparkling orbs. This man was not one to be toyed with. Klara could see that easily. Although he appeared gentle and friendly, she knew without a doubt that he could probably turn lethal in a moment if necessary. She wasn't sure how she knew this, it could be the energy she felt swirling around him or maybe it was her empathic sense.

"Yes of course father, Thank you."

Mystic held out his hand and Klara took it, he had a firm handshake and Klara could feel the power lingering under his skin.

"Any friend of my son is welcome among my people." He said and gave her a slight nod of the head.

"Thank you, Sir, that is very kind. "

"You both must be tired and hungry; I will accompany you back home and we can speak there."

They followed Mystic towards a thick curtain of vines several yards away. Chip went through first, gently pulling Klara along behind him. The vines were a dense tangle of harsh green leaves and thorns. The thorns snagged at Klara's clothing and she was very thankful Chip went through first because his bulky frame was keeping the worse of it from touching her. He pushed forward like it was nothing, like he had done it a thousand times and she guessed he probably had since this was his home. It was so strange for her to imagine Chip's home being somewhere other than her own but then wasn't it strange that her cat was really a walking, talking, human being. Klara caught herself staring at Chip's glowing eyes again. Perhaps human being was not entirely right either.

After several feet, the thorns were less dense and, in their place, delicate purple and white flowers started to spot along the length of the vines, even the leaves growing along them began to take on a gentler appearance. Whereat first it felt as though they were walking through a tangle of hanging snakes now it was a stunning array of hanging gardens, soft and colorful. She held her hands out to either side of her letting the strands fall delicately against her fingers. The smell was amazing, she inhaled deeply savoring the sweet perfume. She thought she could hear the rushing of water somewhere near, she closed her eyes and took it all in. Chip looked back at the sound of her breath and smiled. He moved beside her now and pulled a small purple flower from one of the vines, he reached over tucking it softly in her hair.

"I've always wanted to do that but it wasn't possible when I didn't have thumbs." A crooked smile forming at his lips.

Klara chuckled and gave him a gentle shoulder bump; she could feel heat tingling on her cheeks.

"Your names not Chip…I'm sorry…of course it isn't…I just didn't think to ask?"

"My name became Chip the day you gave it to me, and it will remain thus until the day I die. You have nothing to be sorry for besides look…. We are here."

Klara followed his line of sight through the curtain of vines, she could see lights just beyond the edge. They stepped through the last of the vines and found themselves in front of a serene river. Though it was lovely Klara was confused. How could this be home? The only semblance of life she could see here were two torches standing lit near the edge of the river bank.

"I don't understand?" Klara said.

"Of course! I'm sorry, it's been so long I almost forget." Chip waved his hand in a flourish in front of her face. She could feel a spark of something, energy, magic?

Klara's eyes widened, not believing what she was seeing. She now stood at the foot of a massive stone bridge, it sprawled out in front of her providing safe crossing of the no longer serene river. It had been replaced by a raging flow of water that poured off the side of a high precipice of bedrock to her left. To her right the river went on without any end that she could see, curving off into the distance. The two torches still stood in place, but they now framed the entryway of the bridge. Two towers of smooth white stone connected to each other forming an arch-way. Ivy crept up the sides of the stone, swirling around, giving it an ancient appearance. Klara could see guards standing high in the towers, eyes shimmering in the torchlight. On the opposite side of the river, there was yet another dense curtain of vines blocking from view whatever hid on the other side of the bridge.

"Amazing…"

"Wait until you see what's on the other side." Chip said.

Chapter 5

S he could feel the anticipation coming from Chip. How wonderful it must be to be coming home after such a long time. Klara wondered if she would ever have somewhere, she longed to return to, to call home. She certainly didn't feel that way about the house she had spent the last sixteen years in. The group made their way across the bridge and Klara couldn't help but run her fingers across the smooth stone that spanned the sides of the bridge. It was cool under her touch. As they approached the curtain of vines waiting on the other side, she saw fireflies dancing in the air around them. This place was magical, there was no doubt in her mind about that.

"This place is amazing, I'm half expecting fairies to come flittering about in the starlight." She mused.

"Nah, they don't really hang around this part of the forest and besides they tend to keep to themselves." Ship answered seriously.

Klara just shook her head in disbelief. "What's next? You will tell me trolls like to have tea parties on the riverbank?"

Chip stared at her wide-eyed. "How did you know that?"

"What? I... didn't...I was just..." Then Klara gave him the evil eye. "You are messing with me."

Chip laughed. "Sorry couldn't resist."

This time it was Mystic who stepped forward to open the tangle of vines. Klara stepped through and where the bridge had been amazing, the sight she now saw was absolutely enchanting. Before her stood a village, no a city, but not a city like any she had ever seen. It rose up before her carved into the bedrock of the same beautiful white stone as the bridge. Layer after layer gently sloping up to a magnificent structure standing at the top. The only word she could find to describe the structure was a palace.

The city was bustling with activity. As they walked along the cobblestone streets, Klara tried to absorb it all. The ground level of the city held a marketplace of sorts, small shops and open-air vendors lined the streets. They displayed a variety of wares, clothing made from the most delicate of silk, embroidered with intricate patterns. Handmade jewelry glittered in the soft glow of torches. Klara could smell a mixture of perfumes on the air, soft floral scents. Plants and flowers littered the buildings and ground all around her. The place looked like a secret garden of hidden treasures. Although it was a city with man-made things all around, they were almost melded into the nature instead of replacing it. Trees were still growing strong all around them and the structures just wove through not wanting to damage any of the existing plant life. It was a perfect blend, a perfect balance.

A shimmering of light caught Klara's eye and she found herself wandering over to a stone table displaying delicate silver jewelry. An elderly woman sat beside the table her hands busy, expertly etching into a small trinket. She looked up at Klara as she approached and gave her a soft smile, her eyes glowing in that catlike manner she was starting to get used to.

"Hello, young one, do you see something you like?"

Klara carefully picked up a tiny charm from the table. It had the most intricate designs carved into it, the tiny lines were so perfectly done, Klara couldn't imagine how someone could manage such a difficult design by hand. She turned it over in her hand admiring it.

"Ah, a protection charm. Are you expecting a wee one love?"

"Oh, what? No, I'm sorry, I was just admiring your work, it is so lovely." Klara handed the charm back to the woman and their hands brushed.

"Thank you ch—" the woman's eyes went white and she was as still as death. Her hand clasped Klara's tightly.

"Ma'am, are you alright?" Klara shifted uncomfortably and tried to gently pull her hand away.

The woman began to speak her voice eerie and unsettling. *"Though there is strength in the one, only united as three can the answers be found, and the light set free."*

It ended as quickly as it had begun and the woman's eyes were normal again, her grip released. Her gaze lingered on Klara thoughtful. She reached for a small wooden box on the table and retrieved something from inside.

"Klara of the Maithar, please take this, inside you will find three items, one belongs to you, child, the other two you will know who to give them to when the time is right." She pressed a small satchel into Klara's hand.

"How...how do you know my name?"

The woman only smiled and turned her head down to resume her handiwork.

"Klara, I turned around and you were gone—" Chip must have noticed the expression on her face.

"Is everything ok? What happened?"

What had just happened? Klara was too tired and too hungry to even process it.

"I...nothing, I'm fine, I just stopped to look at this booth. She's very talented. Anyway, I'm starving let's go." Klara tucked the satchel into her pocket and darted off to catch up with Mystic leaving Chip to wonder what was really going on.

They wandered through the winding streets of the city, slowly approaching the palace at the top. People here walked with such grace and seemed light on their toes. Even the children running and playing in the streets. A young girl pounced playfully after a ball thrown by her small companion. Laughing, she lept off the ground and swung her feet around a nearby tree branch, hanging upside down she caught the ball easily and hopped down from the tree landing soundly on her two feet. She threw the ball back towards her young friend and they both ran after it.

As they passed, people would nod respectfully at Mystic and look at Klara and Chip with curious eyes.

Suddenly Klara felt very insecure. She averted her gaze down and stared intently at the pathway below. However, that couldn't last long, as they approached their destination curiosity won out and Klara had to look around her.

The palace stood before them a giant mass of carved stone, it towered over them beautiful but intimidating. The entryway alone was larger than the home she had grown up in. Klara looked like a child, eyes wide in wonder trying to see every little detail she could and log it away in her mind.

"What is this place?"

"Home." Chip was almost giddy, and it was infectious. Klara couldn't help but smile for her best friend's homecoming.

At the entrance to the building, there were two large wooden doors. The wood was impressive, smooth and solid but the best part was the carvings on each of them. One side was a carving of a fierce creature, mouth wide showing barred teeth, two glowing jewels in place of the eyes. She couldn't quite tell what type of animal it was. On the other side was a woman with long flowing hair out to her sides almost floating, her hands were held up to the sky and three jewels floated in-between them, one red, one green and one blue. Ivy wrapped all around her body in place of clothing. She looked like some sort of goddess, powerful, just as fierce as the creature in the carving next to her. Klara founded herself gently touching the carvings, drawn to the woman and her unbridled power.

Chip moved to stand beside her and he reached out to touch the other carving.

"A reminder of where we come from." Mystic's voice was solemn.

"How so?" Klara asked without looking away from the carving.

"This is Chara, the first shapeshifter companion. She was unique, neither cat nor dog nor any other animal but a combination of them all. She was MoChara to Maithar, the woman you see carved here." Mystic spoke with such reverence.

"What do the jewels represent?" As Klara touched each one, she felt a small spark of energy. She lingered on the blue jewel, clearly, this carving had been here for ages, yet the jewels still gleamed in the torchlight as if new.

"Maithar's power was the strongest ever to have existed, she could manipulate the earth, produce the burn of fire and control the flow of water, among other things. You have heard stories of her in the human world as a child, I am sure, but I believe there she is referred to as mother nature and thought to be a fairy tale, correct?"

Klara turned to face Mystic her trance on the carvings finally broken.

"Wait? You're telling me that Mother Nature was a real person?"

"Yes, she most defiantly was a real person." He smiled at her.

"I heard a woman in the market say that word…Maithar…"

"Father, it's been a long journey and I'm afraid our stomachs may decide to start eating these stones here soon." Chip interrupted.

"Yes of course! Come inside both of you, follow me."

Mystic stepped forward pushing open the heavy wooden doors. Klara stayed close to Chip as they entered the massive palace.

"If you don't mind, I will be right back. I'm going to go see about getting some dinner served for you and arrange some rooms, I will only be a moment." Mystic excused himself and left through a door at the far-left side of the room.

The entrance hall was as wide as her school's gymnasium. The walls were lined with an assortment of paintings, tapestries, and artifacts. Each one was more fascinating and beautiful than the next. Klara imagined she could spend days examining each one and still not unlock all their secrets. Chandeliers hung from the ceiling throwing light across the grand room. As she looked closer at them, she realized it was not fire that lit the chandeliers but dazzling white orbs dotted the tips of each chandelier prong.

"What is that?"

Chip followed Klara's wide-eyed gaze.

"Beautiful isn't it? We call it diamond light, but it's a form of light magic, it will never burn out as long as the one who cast it still lives."

"Wow, even the lights here are unbelievable, and look at this staircase!"

In the center of the room, there was a magnificent staircase, it was wide enough to fit twenty people side by side on each step. It led up to a landing and then split off to each side leading to a second level of the palace.

Klara stepped toward the staircase and ran her hand along the smooth railing. "If someone had told me yesterday, I would be standing in a palace today, I would have called them crazy."

Chip chuckled. "It's not exactly a palace, it's a training center. We provide training here for my people and your people alike. Even some of the canine clan come here to train, though they do have a center of their own and a leader of their own."

"Canine clan?"

"Yes, there are two different types of shifters, Canine and Feline. There have been other animal shifter types in the past but they are extremely rare and the stories surrounding them are always the stuff of legends."

"Chip, can I ask you something?"

"You know you can Klara, it's great to be able to actually answer you now."

"Yeah, it makes our conversations much more productive." Klara smiled.

"So, what do you want to know?"

"I was wondering…How old are you exactly Chip? Regular cats only live what, like fifteen to twenty years or something and I know you have been alive at least sixteen but you definitely look…. healthy and fit."

Klara felt embarrassed by her words and could feel her cheeks betraying her.

Chip smirked at her.

"Well actually I'm 17 I guess…well kinda."

"How can you be kinda 17?"

"We spend our childhood growing with the love of our families around us, aging the same way you do. We attend the training academy to prepare us for whatever path we choose, much like humans attend school. When our Maithar announces she is excepting a child, a select few of us who are of the age 17 begin training to become MoCharas. Right after the young Maithar is born we go to the castle for a special ceremony where the powers of our earth let it be known which of us is to be bonded with the infant Maithar."

"Wait…so if MoCharas are only bonded to Maithars and you are my MoChara does that make me a…oh no no no…I am not some kind of mother nature….I can barely control whatever this water thing is that I have….I am not a leader…I…I…I can't breathe" Klara sat down hard on the bottom of the staircase and gripped her stomach.

Chip kneeled down beside her and placed his warm hands on her shoulders. "Klara deep breaths…you are going to be ok…you can do this…I will be with you every step of the way." He leaned in and kissed her gently on the forehead.

She could feel the burn of his kiss lingering on her skin and she began to inhale slowly, calming her racing pulse. Get it together Klara she heard her fake mother's voice in her head.

"I'm sorry, it's just a lot to take in." She said quietly.

"I know it is and you don't have to process it all right this second ok?" Chip squeezed her shoulder and then moved to sit next to her.

"No, it's ok, I need to know the truth. I need to understand what's going on. Please finish telling me, you said that you were bonded to me when you were 17?"

"Well yes but that's not exactly how it's supposed to be. See that first ceremony at age 17 is meant to only identify the bond. The Shifter is then supposed to go home to resume training and when the Maithar reaches the age of 5 the Shifter is then bonded to her. By that time the shifter is meant to be an adult and would have had five years of intense training to become a MoChara."

"So why were you bonded to me too early?"

"I'm not sure I'm the one who should be telling you this besides wasn't your original question about my age anyway?" He smiled teasingly at her.

She knew he was intentionally changing the subject but she decided to go with it for now anyway.

"Yes, I did ask about your age and something doesn't add up. If you were 17 when you were bonded to me and I was only a newborn then how are you still only 17?"

"We stop aging once the bond is made. It's for our benefit and yours really. We age the same way humans do normally but if we become a MoChara we stop aging for the length of our bond. We stay young and healthy to be a perfect protector for our Maithar."

"So, you are immortal?"

He smiled and shook his head. "No, we only stop aging as long as we are bonded. Once the bond is broken, we begin to age again which allows us to then live a normal life, get married, have kids should we choose too."

Klara didn't like how that sounded; the bond being broken. She didn't want to lose Chip, she valued having him by her side even if it was only because he was honor-bound to be there. She also didn't like the idea of him getting married to someone but she wasn't ready to think about what that meant to her.

"So, the bond can be broken? You can choose to leave your MoChara?"

"No Klara, not by choice, the only way the bond is broken is by death, no one would ever choose to leave their MoChara, the bond is too strong, it would destroy them both."

Klara couldn't speak for Chip's feelings, but she was certain he was right about that part. She knew it would destroy her if he ever left her. She had always relied on him even when he was just a regular cat, he had been her best friend and kept her sane, kept her from feeling alone. Over the few short hours they had been in Natura her feelings had become increasingly strong. It was almost like Chip was a part of her she couldn't imagine being without. She wouldn't dare tell him that and just thinking about it made her go red in the face all over again. She wondered what sort of feelings he was having? She tried to reach out with her mind to read him and she felt the same things she usually picked up from him...contentment...confidence...anticipation...hunger. She shared that last one with him for sure.

Mystic couldn't have had better timing. "Who's hungry?"

"ME!" They both replied in unison.

"Great, follow me."

Mystic lead them to the dining hall. Klara had thought the entrance hall was impressive, but this room was insane. It was twice the size of the entrance hall. The ceiling was also lit by the glowing diamond lights and they illuminated the six long tables throughout the room. Each table had a combination of benches and chairs with them, some were simple wooden creations, some stone, and some were lined with plush fabrics. They were all mixed up around the tables giving the room an almost comical effect. Windows lined the side of one of the walls and they too were all different. They seemed to be placed completely at random and all different shapes and sizes. Klara though it looked like something out of a kid's cartoon but she liked it. No one could feel uncomfortable in a room like this, it was just plain fun.

There were a few people seated at some of the tables. Most of them kids. One group was playing some sort of table game and they were talking animatedly with each other. Some were reading alone, absorbed in their stories. Klara could relate to that but the books they were reading looked strange like stone tablets that shimmered when touched. She reached for her duffle bag, safely at her side and felt the comforting spine of one of her books inside.

Mystic lead them to one of the tables where several platters had been laid out still covered keeping the contents warm for them. Klara chose a chair lined with a velvety blue fabric. When she sat down, she sunk into the chair letting her muscles finally relax. She hadn't realized till then just how sore her legs and feet had become. Chip sat down next to her and began to uncover the platters in record time.

"Sorry, father but hunger wins out over manners today."

"I understand son and I'm just so happy to have you home that I can overlook you eating like a canine instead of a feline today." Mystic teased.

Chip gave his dad a brief look of insult but then quickly returned to the feast in front of them.

Klara liked watching Chip with his dad. It was nice to see what a loving parent-child relationship looked like, but it also made her feel sad for what she had never known.

She decided to turn her attention to something she could have...food. She reached for the platter closest to her and uncovered it to find an array of fruit, cheese, and bread. Klara decided she could forget her manners as well and just dug in greedily.

"Try one of these, you'll love it."

Chip passed her some sort of savory looking pastry.

"Is it vegetarian?" Klara knew Chip probably knew she was a vegetarian but he had been in cat form all these years so she couldn't be sure exactly what he paid attention to.

"Yes, of course, it is, everyone in Natura is a vegetarian. We would never intentionally harm a living creature unless it was self-defense."

"Really? Everyone is a vegetarian here just like me?"

"Yep—" chip said as he stuffed his face with another pastry.

Klara had always been teased by her classmates for being a vegetarian. It was comforting to know that she would have one less thing to draw attention to herself here.

She took a bit of the pastry Chip had handed her and it was delectable. She could taste peas, potatoes, and a hint of curry inside.

"mmmm...so good—" she said as she took another bite.

"Sorry to interrupt you two from your...intense food eating contest you have going but son we need to speak privately. Perhaps you two could fill your plates and come with me to my

KERRY SANDOVAL

office?" Mystic asked.

Klara and Chip both piled their plates up as much as they could and followed Mystic as he led the way to his office.

Once inside he motioned for them to sit down and he locked the door behind them. He came and sat down behind his desk and studied Klara for a moment before turning to look at Chip.

"Son, am I correct in assuming your companion is a Maithar?"

"Yes, father...let me officially introduce you to Klara of the Maithar and I am her MoChara."

Mystics glowing eyes dilated ever so briefly. Klara reached out with her abilities and could sense a strange combination of fear and...was it hope, coming from Mystic.

"I knew you had been sent away to guard over one of them but none of us knew whether the bond had been properly made. It seems it has and that is joyous news but you cannot tell anyone who she is, son. Not yet anyway. It is too dangerous."

"I understand. Father, I was hoping we could stay here at the training academy for now. Klara needs somewhere safe to train and we need time to try and locate Karina. Do you have any idea where we should start looking for her?"

"Of course, you can both stay here. I trust our clan and none of the foreign students here are old enough to recognize you, son and Klara was just an infant when she was last here so I think we can come up with a cover story for now. As for the teachers here, I trust them all with my life so there will not be an issue in telling them the truth. It would be an honor to train a Maithar and it would be a blessing to spend time with my son. As for Karenia, she left several weeks ago suddenly and with no explanation but that is not uncommon for her. She has been searching for many years for what was lost." Mystic said cryptically.

"Thank you, father, I knew coming here would be the right plan."

"Umm...I don't mean to interrupt this father-son moment but could you maybe explain who this Karenia is?" Klara was confused.

Chip laid his hand over Klara's.

50

"Karenia is a Maithar like you, she once ruled Natura until she passed the crown down to her daughter...your biological mother."

Chip's eyes were searching Klara's for recognition.

"If her daughter was my mother, that makes her...my grand-mother?"

"Yes, Klara...Karenia is your grandmother...and she is the only one who can reunite you with your sister."

"Sister! What sister?"

"You are one of three Klara. A triplet. It had been foretold that you and your sisters would be the most powerful force Natura has ever seen, but then.... well that is a story for Karenia to tell you."

Klara remembered the old woman in the market place...

"Though there is strength in the one, only united as three can the answers be found, and the light set free."

Klara pulled the satchel from her pocket and emptied the contents into her hand...three bracelets fell out. All made of the same beautiful silver she had admired at the woman's booth. The strands of silver had been woven together to look like little vines of ivy. Each bracelet held a single charm on it and each Charm was the figure from the wooden doors, the powerful woman Mystic had told her was Maithar...mother nature. In each charm, Maithar was holding a small gemstone close to her heart, each a different color. The woman had said one was meant to be hers and she would know which one. Without hesitation, Klara chose the one with the blue gemstone for herself leaving a green and red. She placed the bracelet on her wrist.

"The woman in the marketplace knew me somehow...she gave me these and said I would know who they belonged to. Don't ask me how or why but I know these are meant for my sisters."

She placed the other two back into the satchel and tucked it away safely in her pocket.

"I may not know what I can do, or who I am meant to be...but I know I want to find them...my grandmother...my mother and father...my sisters...I want to find my family."

"I'm so sorry Klara but your mother and father…they…"
Mystic interrupted Chip. "No son…this is Karenia's story to tell……"

Chapter 6

"Name?"

"Rosaline but you can call me Rosie"

"Ok Rosie, Last name?"

"Don't have one"

"Don't be smart, everyone has a last name kid"

"Well, I can make one up if you want"

"Give me a break here, you look like a nice girl, can you just cooperate?"

"I'm not...a nice girl that is...and I don't have a last name."

"Fine have it your way, Rosaline no last name, you are under arrest for criminal trespassing and vandalism. You have the right to remain silent. Anything you say or do will...." Rosie half-listened to the officer read her Miranda rights. Rosie knew them by heart. This was not her first rodeo with the law.

The officer handcuffed her and led her to the back of the police cruiser. She opened the door and gently pushed Rosie's head down to load her into the seat. It smelled strongly of alcohol and urine inside but Rosie didn't care, she figured she probably didn't smell much better.

A bark followed by a growl came from behind them.

The officer turned to see a large grey and white dog with teeth bared. She quickly pulled her gun ready to fire.

"No! please wait, don't shoot her!" Rosie pleaded.

"Daisy, heel."

The dog obeyed immediately.

"She has to come with me, she is my.... service dog. I have....

a seizure disorder and she can identify the seizures before they happen. If I don't have her with me, I could die and it would be on you officer." Rosie thought her lie sounded pretty decent.

"Look, kid, I don't believe a word you just said but it's the end of my shift and I just want to go home to my kids so tell the dog to get in."

Rosie gestured for Daisy to get in the cruiser and the dog hopped up into the seat next to her. Rosie felt kind of bad because this cop really had been nice and had tried her best not to arrest her but Rosie had left her no choice.

The cruiser pulled out of the parking lot and merged on to the highway towards what Rosie assumed would be the city police station.

Rosie settled herself into the seat and leaned up against Daisy. Daisy laid her head down on Rosie's leg and looked up at her with big brown eyes.
"You're such a good girl." she cooed quietly.

"So, what were you thinking? Why did you do it, you had to know they would call the police?" The officer inquired from the front seat.

"I couldn't just stand by and do nothing, could I? I mean they are torturing those poor animals in there. Someone had to do something." Rosie snipped.

"Yeah, but you realize that it's a chicken factory, right? I mean that's what is supposed to happen in there. Releasing all the chickens and flooding the place won't change that. They will just gather them back up and clean up the water. Business as usual by tomorrow for them but now a night in a jail cell for you. Was it really worth it?" The officer replied.

Rosie didn't respond. She knew everything the officer said was true and maybe she didn't really think it all through. That's how she always landed herself in trouble, she would get all worked up about something and the next thing you know she was flying off the handle by the seat of her pants. She had a temper that could burn the devil himself and she knew it.

She really didn't care though. So, she was arrested. Wasn't

the first time and probably wouldn't be the last. At least it meant she would get a hot meal, a warm bed and if she was lucky a shower. She couldn't remember the last time she had a real shower. Sink bathing at the gas station did not count in her book. Daisy let out an annoyed groan as the cruiser went over a speed bump. Luckily Rosie had convinced the officer to let Daisy come. She could care less what happened to her but if she could give her best friend a warm bed for the night it would all be worth it.

Daisy was more than a dog to Rosie. The big grey and white canine had been there for Rosie time and time again. She provided warmth on cold winter nights under the bridge they called home. She was a fierce protector; Rosie knew there was no way she could have made it all these years on her own without Daisy by her side scaring away all the creeps out there. Rosie was a tiny little speck of a girl. She may be Sixteen but she looked like she was 12. She only stood about five foot one and she weighed next to nothing. Years on the street not knowing where her next meal would come from had given her a very slim and boney appearance. Her features were very defined and not an ounce of padding could be found on her small frame. She had straight, silky dark brown hair, deep brown eyes, and a tanned complexion. She guessed she could have been considered pretty but it was hard to tell under the layers of filth on her skin and in her hair. Her clothes were a mismatched combination of things she had found in the donation bins outside the goodwill shop. They hung loosely on her petite body.

Rosie looked down at Daisy wishing she could pet her soft fur but the handcuffs made it impossible. It would be nice to sleep soundly tonight. Daisy would have a break from guarding her and Rosie could sleep knowing she was safely behind bars. She needed a good night's sleep.

"Don't you have anyone I can call? Parents or something?" Rosie could tell the cop was concerned, she guessed she was probably thinking of her own kids and was imagining them in the shape that Rosie was in right now. She could tell her heart was in the right place, but she knew the cop should forget it, Rosie was a lost cause.

"No, there's no one, thanks."

Rosie had been on her own since she was 5 years old. She had fuzzy memories of her parents, a mom who used to hug her tight. A dad who used to read her stories and sing to her at night. As the years passed by, she wondered if those memories were even real. One thing she knew for certain was that she was on her own, except for Daisy. She had to take care of herself because there was no one else out there that would. Daisy provided her protection and companionship, but it was up to Rosie to feed and shelter them both. Sometimes she would go to the public park and watch the children play, they would fall, skin their little knees or elbows and a mom or dad would come running from a bench somewhere, scoop them up, hold them close and all would be right in their little worlds. Rosie wondered what that would be like, to have someone to run to, to count on.

"Alright, here we are kid, let's get you processed." The officer opened the door to the cruiser and led her into the police station. Daisy followed behind them.

They approached a woman at a desk with large glasses that made her eyes look comical.

"Ah, I see miss Rosie and her sidekick Daisy have graced us with a visit again." "You lucked out with this rookie cop Rosie, letting the dog tag along." She winked at Rosie as she spoke.

"I thought this one might be a repeat offender, said she has no last name." The officer explained.

"Well, she does have a last name. She's been in and out of the foster system, every time CPS gets her placed, she runs away and we lose track of her for a while. I'll call her social worker. What's the charge today?" The big-eyed woman asked.

Before the officer could respond, Rosie quipped. "Chicken liberation."

The woman shook her head with a smile. "Rosie, with that wit of yours you could do so much more hun. Alright, take her back to processing."

"What about the dog? She says it's a service dog." The rookie cop asked.

"Service dog? You fell for that one, did you? It's ok. They all know Rosie and Daisy back there, let her tag along." Big eyes said as she reached down to scratch behind Daisy's ears.

"Thanks" Rosie offered with a sideways smile.

The officer led her back to processing and handed her over. They took her pictures and fingerprints, she was a pro by now.

"Alright kid, all finished, let's get you to a cell, anyone you want to call?" an officer questioned.

"No, there's no one, but do you think I could take a quick shower before you lock me up?" Rosie pleaded.

"Sure kid, it's slow tonight, come with me." He led her through the barred doors that would take them to the holding cells. They passed a security desk and turned to find a door with a plastic woman's bathroom sign on it. The officer unlocked the door and handed her a towel, orange jumpsuit, and a bar of soap from the nearby shelving unit.

"Ok, you get 10 minutes and then we have to get you to your cell ok? Take the dog with you, she smells like she could use some of that soap too." He stated while fanning his nose.

Rosie and Daisy entered the bathroom and heard the officer lock it behind them.

"Just knock on the door when you're done" she heard him call to her.

Rosie took in her surroundings. She had the place to herself. She was in a large room with several shower stalls separated by tiled walls but no curtains. Each stall had a small bench built into the wall. On the opposite side of the room there where several toilet stalls built in the same manner. At the far end of the room were the sinks and a large wall-length mirror.

Rosie walked towards the mirror and took in her reflection briefly before turning to Daisy.

"Well, girl it looks like we both are long overdue for baths."

Rosie chose a shower stall and set down the items the officer had given her on the bench beside her. She turned the shower faucet on and a strong but ice-cold jet of water came spilling out. Daisy jumped back with a yelp.

"Sorry girl!" Rosie tried to adjust the temperature on the faucet, but it would not get warm. She turned it off and went to the next stall to find the same issue.

"Hmmm. Looks like jailbirds like us can't get warm water. I tell you what Daisy girl, we are alone in here and I don't see any cameras. You think I could do my thing and no one would be the wiser?" She asked Daisy.

Daisy looked up at her with a questioning look, if a dog could understand a human, Rosie knew it was Daisy.

"Don't worry girl, it will be ok, we deserve a hot shower, it's been too long. I will be careful, I promise."

Daisy let out a whine.

Rosie ignored it and turned on the water, she placed her hands on either side of the faucet. She closed her eyes and concentrated hard on the water inside it. Her hands began to burn, and she felt a familiar energy coursing through them. She opened her eyes and could see her hands glowing bright orange and red in color. Heat radiated from them, gently warming the water that was coming out of the faucet.

"Ok girl, you first." She pulled Daisy under the stream of water and wet her down. She grabbed the bar of soap off the bench carefully to keep one glowing hand in contact with the faucet. She scrubbed Daisy thoroughly with the soap and rinsed her off.

"All done."

Daisy walked to the middle of the room and shook out her fur the way dogs do and then sat down to wait for Rosie.

"Rosie quickly undressed with one hand and got under the showerhead. The warm water felt amazing on her skin. She stood there for a moment and let it run down her body. Then she remembered she didn't have long before the office would be unlocking that door and she could not let him catch her like this.

Rosie began to soap up her hair and body, scrubbing away all the dirt and grime of the past few months.

Her thoughts wandered back to the last time she used her power. It had been two years ago. She had been staying at a foster home in Los Angeles. She hadn't tried to escape from there because they had actually been decent to her. Even allowed Daisy to stay inside the house and sleep in her bed. Usually, the foster homes would not allow dogs and Rosie refused to go anywhere Daisy couldn't so she would always give them the slip. This time however the lady Khloe and her husband Rick had been kind-hearted people who loved animals. Rosie had been staying there for several months, She and Khloe had become close. Rosie was finally beginning to think there may be some hope for a future with them. She was clean, fed, and had a whole room just for her and Daisy. It felt like she was living like royalty compared to what her life had been until then.

One evening Khloe asked Rosie to sit down at the kitchen table with her.

"Rosie, Rick and I have been doing a lot of thinking and…we would like to adopt you and Daisy permanently. How do you feel about that?"

Just as Rosie was about to answer her with an enthusiastic yes, two men busted through the kitchen door. They wore ski masks over their heads and were brandishing handguns.

"Do as we say, and no one will get hurt!" they demanded.

Daisy sensing danger lunged from beneath the table at one of the men. She knocked him down quickly and went straight for his throat. At the same time, Khloe stood up and reached to the drawer behind her grabbing a taser she kept there. She went to fire it at the other man but was not quick enough. The man fired his gun hitting Khloe in the arm. He turned and was about to fire at Daisy when Rosie felt her power grow from the pit of her stomach. Her hair flew wildly around her and her toes lifted off the ground. She felt the energy course through her arms and down to the palms of hands. She knew exactly what to do and she aimed her hands at the man. A stream of hot fire shot from her hands straight at the man causing him to go up in flames within seconds. All that was left was a pile of ash where he stood. Khloe screamed behind her and Daisy returned quickly to Rosie's side having left the other man in a pile of blood on the floor his throat torn open.

"Rosie! What have you done! What are you!" Khloe screamed at her backing up towards the door.

Freak! What is she, call the police, dangerous, not normal, run Khloe run now or she will turn on me next.

It was strange, Rosie could hear words coming out of Khloe's mouth, but she could hear the other things as well, almost like she was hearing inside her mind. What she heard in that moment broke her heart and shattered any chance of hope that had begun to grow inside her for a normal happy life.

Before Khloe had a chance to run or call the cops, Rosie got out of there as fast as she could, Daisy by her side and she never looked back. She caught a ride with a truck driver that very night and he took her all the way to Georgia.

Rosie shook her head, not wanting to think about that awful night. This was different, no one was here and there was no danger in using her powers. As if Daisy could read her mind, she let out a concerned groan again.

"Don't worry Daisy, no one can see me here, and besides I'm almost done anyway."

It felt good to use her powers again after so long, it was like a release of pent up energy.

Prior to that night, she had used her powers here and there with no notice. She discovered her ability when she was seven years old. It had been a particularly cold, wet night and she had not been able to scavenger anything for her or Daisy to eat in several days. Usually, Daisy never left her side but this night they were both so hungry and so tired that Rosie couldn't find the strength to go any further. She collapsed next to the dumpster in an alleyway. She had been trying to search the dumpster for something, anything to eat but had no luck. Daisy whined at her side when she fell and Rosie looked at her with pleading eyes.

"I'm sorry girl, I can't find anything and it's so cold." It had been raining hard that night and the temperature was frigid. She had begun to slip in and out of consciousness and in her state of delirium she thought she heard Daisy's thoughts.

Don't worry child, I know I swore to never leave your side, but I must find you food and drink or my promise to your mother will not matter by the morning.

Rosie knew now she must have imagined it due to her condition, but daisy had left her side that night for the first and only time ever. She returned shortly after and she was drenched from the rain and freezing but in her mouth, she carried a paper sack containing food and water. The dog gingerly set it down in front of Rosie and nudged her awake with her snout. Rosie gathered what strength she had left and sat up.

"Thank you, girl, you are the best puppy in the world." she opened the bag and greedily ate the contents. She reached over to share her food with Daisy but the dog had collapsed next to her. Her chest rising and falling slowly. Rosie held her little hands out to pet Daisy and try to wake her to eat but when she touched her, she could feel that she was freezing. The wet rain and cold wind had frozen her best friend to a point that was dangerous.

I'm so sorry I failed you little one. I will not last the night.

"No Daisy, you can't leave me, we have to take care of each other!" Rosie buried her face in Daisy's fur and began sobbing. As she cried, she felt the energy for the first time growing somewhere deep inside her. It radiated from her core, up into her arms and to the palms of her hands. Rosie didn't know what was going on or how to control it but somehow, she knew she needed to keep her hands on Daisy's body. Her hands began to glow that now-familiar red-orange color and Daisy's fur began to warm up. The heat spread out all across Daisy's body and in mere moments the dog was dry and her body temperature had returned to normal.

Thank you, you have saved my life this night.

The dog looked deep into Rosie's eyes. Even at only seven years old Rosie had known that moment was significant for them.

Rosie remembered that night like it was yesterday. She had discovered that she was different. That she was strong and that she could survive. She never heard Daisy's thoughts again after that and as she grew older, she knew she never really did, to begin with. It was just a dehydrated and hungry child's imagination. Still, she considered how impossible it was that she had this power of hers so who knew what else was possible. Maybe... just maybe she really had heard her loyal companions' thoughts that night.

A loud pounding came from the door snapping Rosie back to the present.

"Alright kid, times up! Gotta get you to that cell now." The officer called from the hallway.

"Ok, I'm ready" Rosie replied.

The officer unlocked the door, Rosie and Daisy followed him back the way they came and he led her to a cell for the night.

As he locked the cell door behind her he said. "Try and get some sleep kid, we will figure out what to do with you in the morning."

Rosie walked over to the small cot against the wall and crawled under the covers. She patted the bed with her hand and Daisy jumped up next to her. Rosie covered them both up and laid her head on the pillow. She breathed a deep sigh and fell asleep quickly.

 When Rosie woke up the next morning, she felt rested. Daisy was still curled up next to her but she was already awake and watching Rosie.

"Hey girl, did you sleep ok? I sure did. Maybe they will let us stay another night"

Rosie stood up and walked over to bars of the cell. She peered to the right and saw an officer sitting at the desk eating a doughnut.

"I don't suppose I could have one of those could I, officer?" she asked.

"Oh, you're finally awake. They said to let you sleep but I have your breakfast tray over here." He said as he stood up. He walked over to the counter near his desk and retrieved a green plastic tray with a covered dish and cup of something on it.

He walked it over to her, unlocked the cell and handed it to her, then locked the cell back and went back to his desk.

Rosie carried the tray over to the bed and sat down next to Daisy. She uncovered the tray to find eggs, bacon, oatmeal, and some toast. She took a bite of the Bacon and held it out to Daisy. Daisy turned away from it.

"Daisy, I will never understand how a dog won't eat meat? As hard as it is to find food, I will eat just about anything."

Rosie started on the oatmeal. She held the plate out to Daisy and daisy took a small bite of the eggs.

"It's ok, girl, eat a little more, there is still plenty here for me." Rosie pushed the plate further under Daisy's nose.

Daisy took another few bites of the eggs and then hopped off the bed over to the toilet bowl in the room. She began lapping up the water in the bowl.

"Yuck, thank goodness there is some orange juice on this tray because I really don't want to drink from that toilet with you Daisy." She laughed.

Rosie took her time enjoying the hot meal. She liked this police station. They had always been kind to her here. They usually would bring her in, feed her a meal and call child protective services. The caseworker would arrive and take her to a foster home where Rosie would quickly give them the slip. She couldn't ever let herself get close to anyone again. If they found out her secret, she may not escape next time and who knows what would happen to her.

Rosie heard the phone ring at the officer's desk.

"Ok, I will bring her out now."

He got up and walked over to Rosie's cell.

"Ok Miss Rosie, your family is here to get you."

"No, it must be my social worker, I don't have any family."

"I don't know, the front desk called, said your grandmother is here to get you."

The officer unlocked the cell and led Rosie back to the squad room. Daisy lopped happily after them.

Rosie was confused. What was he talking about? She didn't have a grandmother. Maybe they had her confused with someone else.

When they reached the squad room Rosie saw a woman waiting at the desk talking with the big-eyed receptionist.

"Oh, there you are Rosaline! I've been worried sick about you!" The woman said as she approached Rosie and pulled her in for a big hug.

"Just go with it" she whispered into Rosie's ear.

Rosie stood there shocked. She didn't know what to say. Who was this woman? She looked the woman up and down. Well dressed. Early to mid-sixties. Bright red hair cut short in a funky pixie cut style. She had a bright smile and eyes that seemed to change color slightly as she spoke. Something about her seemed safe and familiar but Rosie couldn't for the life of her figure out how that was possible.

"It looks like she's shocked you found her Grandma. Take care of this one and try and keep her out of trouble." Big eyes said. Something was off though. Big eyes was speaking but she seemed in a daze, her words were robotic sounding.

The red-headed woman signed some paperwork and turned to Rosie.

"Alright are you and Daisy ready to go?" as she said it Daisy bounded right up to the woman and licked her hand. The woman reached down to pat Daisy's head.

"It's been a while old girl." She said to Daisy as if they were long lost, friends.

Daisy and the woman started to walk out of the police station. Rosie hesitated a moment but then decided to go along with it. She trusted Daisy's judgment and Daisy seemed to trust this woman. The dog had never led her wrong in the past so why would she now.

They walked through the front doors of the station and out into the warm sunlight of a spring day. The air smelled fresh and the rays of the sun felt nice on Rosie's face. She followed the woman down the steps of the station to the curb where a sleek black car was waiting for them. The driver got out and came around to open the door for them.

"Thank you, Fred." The woman said as she climbed in the car. Daisy hopped right in and the woman gestured for Rosie to follow.

Rosie slid into the seat beside the woman and the driver closed the door behind her swiftly.

"I imagine you have a lot of questions. I promise in time I will answer them all but right now you need to know something important." The woman explained.

"Your life is about to change drastically and everything you thought you knew about this world is wrong, but the most important thing I want you to remember is…I love you and I will never leave you again…ever."

Chapter 7

"Nice shot!" Chip dodged just barely missing Klara's water jet.

"Not good enough, I still haven't been able to hit you." Klara sat down on a bench in the training room frustrated. It had been three months since they had arrived in Natura and she didn't feel like she had made enough progress.

"What good will my powers do me if I can't aim them at anything, when I need to?"

"Klara, stop being so hard on yourself, you will get there I promise." Chip sat down beside her and threw his muscled arm over her shoulder. He always seemed so sure; Klara wished she had his confidence.

"Look how far you've come already? You can call upon your powers in an instant now and the strength behind your water is much more forceful. Wasn't it you who knocked down the practice dummy yesterday or was that some other water goddess?"

Klara couldn't help but smile, Chip was so good at building her back up.

"I'm no goddess Chip, but thanks for the ego boost." Klara laid her head casually on his shoulder and Chip's arm tightened around her shoulders as if it was second nature.

"I have to learn to aim better, what good is this power if all I can do is take out a hay-filled dummy. Somehow, I don't think Raphe is going to send an army of dummies after me and I need to be able to defend myself, you said so yourself." She shuddered at the mention of his name, Raphe was the man who had murdered her real parents.

Mystic had not yet told her much more than that. He had said he wanted Karenia, her grandmother to share the story with her but they had not been able to make contact with her yet and there were some things Mystic had to tell her for her to be able to understand the purpose of her training.

Over the past three months, Klara had learned a lot though, about her powers and about the way of life in Natura. Mystic had insisted she enroll at the academy and she didn't argue with him. In fact, she was the happiest she had ever been. She fit in easily here with the other students, some were shifters like Chip and some were Wielders like her. Shifters could manipulate magic on themselves to transform into animals whereas wielders could manipulate magic outward to do a variety of different things but could not use their magic on themselves the way shifters did. She had also learned her power was unique because of her heritage. Only the Maithar line had the power to control the elements. Some of her ancestors had been able to wield water like her and some fire or earth. Maithar the first of her lineage had been able to wield it all, she was the most powerful wielder to have ever lived. Klara had soon learned she was also the most beloved. Klara and her fellow students spent every Tuesday and Thursday morning in history class learning everything there was to know about Maithar and Natura. The other students had heard these stories their whole life so a lot of them were bored listening to Master Lucien lecture about the past, but Klara absorbed every word like a sponge. She had always been a good student in the human world and loved to learn but here...learning about this amazing place and her family's history...it was so exciting and wonderous for her.

She had fallen into a comfortable schedule each day. The day Mystic had given her the class assignments she had been so nervous, everything on the schedule seemed so foreign to her.

Mondays and Wednesdays:
9:00am-10:45am: Human History with Mistress Curchio (Classroom Level Rm #14)
11:00am-12:45pm: Zoology with Master Lolas (Outer Gardens B)

1:00pm-1:45pm: Lunch
2:00pm-3:45pm: Wielders studies with Mistress Helenia (Tower #3)
4:00pm-6:00pm: Defense Training with Chip (Training gymnasium #5)
<u>Tuesdays and Thursdays:</u>
 9:00am-10:45am: Natura History with Master Lucien (Classroom Level Rm #22)
11:00am-12:45pm: Botonny with Master Zuchee (Green House #12)
1:00pm-1:45pm: Lunch
2:00pm-3:45pm: Power Classifications with Master Tuxiene (Classroom Level Rm #4)
4:00pm-6:00pm: Defense Training with Chip (Training gymnasium #5)
<u>Fridays:</u>
9:00am-10:45am: Maithar Studies with Master Mystic (Underground Level, chamber #1)
11:00am-12:45pm: Tonics and herbal healing with Mistress Brienne (Hospital Wing, Classroom #4)
1:00pm-1:45pm: Lunch
2:00pm-3:45pm: MoChara Studies with Mistress Seraphina (Classroom Level, Rm #15)
4:00pm-6:00pm: Defense Training with Chip (Training gymnasium #5)

Mystic had started her out with the younger students, but Klara had proven a quick study and had already moved into classes with students her own age for Human History, Natura History, Zoology, and Botany. She was still slightly behind in Tonics and Herbal Healing, and Power Classifications. The two subjects were just so different from anything she had ever learned that is was taking some time to understand the content. The best part was she had yet to meet a single bully at this school. People here genuinely cared for each other and were respectful of each other. Sometimes Klara felt like it had to be too good to be true. As for the rest of her classes, wielders studies she was excelling in and had surpassed the students of her age. It was the one good thing her fake parents had given her with their brutal training sessions to discover what her power was. MoChara studies and Maithar studies were both one on one classes she was taking and could progress at her own pace. She truly enjoyed all her classes, but she looked forward to 4:00 every day the most. It meant she got to spend her time alone with Chip.

"Do you want to call it a day?" Chip asked.

Klara had let her mind wander again; it was so easy to do with her head resting comfortably on Chip's shoulder.

"No, let's give it one more try for today, your pep talk got me hyped back up." Klara winked at him.

"Alright but I'm not going to take it easy on you." Chip teased. He hopped up from the bench and strolled confidently to the center of the gymnasium.

Klara gave a snort and stood up.

"Do your worst cat-boy."

"I always do water-goddess."

Klara smiled, she held her hands casually behind her back still facing the bench and felt the energy burst into her palms, she spun quickly to her left and threw one arm out in Chips direction, he darted to the side anticipating her jet of water but Klara quickly spun back the other way, crouched low and shot water from the opposite hand. The strong burst hit chip squarely in the gut and soaked his shirt.

"You know cats hate water, right?" He laughed.

Chip pulled his soaked shirt over his head and began wringing the water out of it. Klara felt her cheeks go red at the sight of his bare chest. Chip looked away from his wet shirt to meet her eyes.

"Everything ok?" he asked, and Klara could swear there was a mischievous glint in his eye. She reached out with her mind to read his emotions and all she found there was contentment, pride, and…hunger. Klara laughed. Chip was nothing if not predictable.

"Yeah everything's fine, I'm starving, and it seems you are too, want to get changed and head to the dining hall?" Klara offered,

"Why Miss Klara you haven't been reading my emotions again have you?"

"Guilty as charged." She answered as they started their walk back to the living quarters.

"How is that going by the way? Has my dad been able to help?"

Klara had been taking a one on one class with Mystic for Maithar studies. Klara could learn the history of her family in the Natura history classes with the other students, but Mystic said she needed to learn other things that were meant for her only. He told her that if her grandmother were here, she would be a better teacher for her because these things were passed down from one Maithar to the next but since they had not been able to find her Mystic vowed to teach her what little he knew. Although it seemed to Klara that he knew a lot more than he gave himself credit for.

"He has helped me immensely; I can turn my empathic powers on and off at will now which is fantastic. I don't have all the anxiety I used to have in large groups now because I'm not getting slammed with everyone's baggage all at once. It is so freeing."

"I'm glad to hear it."

"Chip can ask you something?"

"You know you can."

"How does your father know so much about the Maithar?"

"I'm surprised he hasn't told you yet but perhaps he feels there are other topics more important for him to go over with you first. My father knows a lot about the Maithar because he was MoChara to one."

Klara was shocked. How could Mystic think that wasn't worth mentioning?

"What? He was? Who? was it my mother?"

"No, it was your great aunt but she passed away at a young age from illness. She was Karenia's sister. My dad and your grandmother became close friends after that, they both could relate to each other's shared grief, I guess. Your mother's MoChara was a canine and no one has seen her since your mother's murder. Many people believe she died broken-hearted. To lose your MoChara in such a brutal way is unthinkable."

"Yes, I think I understand." Klara couldn't imagine what she would feel if Chip was stolen from her like that.

"I don't know that you do, not fully. Our two races are a gentle, peaceful people. Until Raphe our world had not experienced that kind of violence and evil first hand. Those of our people who chose to go into the human world have had some taste of it but it had never entered Natura until that night."

Klara didn't know what to say, she had grown up in the human world and saw the evil in the world first hand. She felt the sting of violence from Mallory and people like her. She saw the horrors on the news, war, children starving, families ripped apart over race, religion or politics. She was still trying to get used to the idea that a world existed somewhere without all that.

"Shifters who choose the path of MoChara know that one day we will be parted from our bond but it is meant to be after a long and natural life. Death of old age and yes sometimes sickness but even that is rare. For your mother's MoChara it must have felt like her heart was ripped out of her chest, the pain both mental and physical would have been shattering. A MoChara bond to a Maithar is said to be unbreakable, unending…I can't even think about what I would do if you…"

Klara put her arm around Chips waist and pulled him closer to her as they walked.

"Don't be silly…you're stuck with me forever cat-boy."

Chip looked at her with a sad sort of smile. "That's right my water goddess…forever." And he kissed her gently on the side of her forehead.

Chapter 8

The dining hall was full of life when Klara arrived as usual. Students were gathered at tables in groups busy eating and socializing. Klara made her way to her regular table where her new group of friends sat waiting. Chip had not made it down yet. He had been pretty soaked after their training session and probably needed extra time to dry off. She smiled to herself proud of the day's accomplishments.

"Klara! Finally! Maybe you can help us end the debate." Kenna called.

Kenna and Klara had become fast friends. Kenna was a chatty girl. She had long flowing red hair that she usually kept in a French braid down her back. She was short and plump. Kenna called herself fat all the time but Klara didn't like that term. Kenna didn't care though, she was very confident, and people here didn't seem to get hung up on body image like they did in the human world. Besides, Klara though Kenna was a very pretty girl, her eyes were bright blue and she had a heart-shaped face covered with cute little freckles. She was as lovely on the outside as she was on the inside. Her mouth was quite large and that worked well for her because when she laughed it helped to create a sort of air horn for her. When Kenna laughed, everyone around her couldn't help but laugh too. Kenna was a wielder and she had the ability to bend light. People with her talent produced the diamond light Klara had grown so fond of. They could do other things too like produce sunlight from nowhere and direct it where they wanted. Essentially, they were a walking flashlight which Klara thought was pretty cool. Kenna and Klara Shared a bathroom in the living quarters. The younger students all had roommates but when you reached your final year at the academy you were granted private rooms that shared a bathroom between two. Even though Klara wasn't technically in her final year at the academy having only just arrived here Mystic felt it was still appropriate that she have the privacy of her own room. Klara was very very thankful for that decision. Although she was quickly learning to make friends and connect with people, she still valued her privacy and alone time. After all, until three months ago she had spent her whole life alone save for Chip.

"What's the debate?" Klara plopped down in her favorite green plush chair. Her friends were kind enough to notice she liked it and always saved it for her. She had never even voiced the preference out loud, that's just the way people here were. Kindness and courtesy for others just came naturally for them.

"Dante thinks we should go to the human picture show festival in the square tonight and I think we should go to the diamond light tournament," Kenna said.

"We can go to the tournament anytime, but they only have the picture show once every couple of months, come on Kenna, the only reason you want to go to the tournament is so you can stare all googly-eyed at Milo." Dante pleaded.

Dante was right. Klara may not have known her friends long but between her ability to read emotions and her good observation skills, she had already deduced that Kenna had a crush on Milo and Dante, unfortunately, had a crush on Kenna. Dante was quiet and shy, a lot like Klara. He had green eyes that reminded Klara of an owl, always wide and watching. His hair was always a wild mess making it look like he just rolled out of bed. He had a dark complexion and was very tall. He usually stood taller than anyone in the crowd which was useful for him since he liked to watch everything. Dante was a shifter and he had not yet made his first shift which he worried about all the time. Everyone else his age had already shifted and it did not sit well with him that he had not yet. Kenna always told him to stop worrying because good things come to those who wait and she felt that the reason he was so late is because he would be the fiercest Canine shifter ever. Kenna liked to lift people's spirits. She could be everyone's personal cheerleader all she needed was some pom poms.

"Picture shows should only last about two hours, right? Or at least they did when I was in the human world. So, wouldn't we be able to go see the show and then go catch the second half of the tournament?" Klara offered.

Her friends all knew she had spent time in the human world. The story as far as the students were all concerned was that Klara was the daughter of two wielders who had been living in the human world as suaders. Suader's were wielders with the ability to sway human emotions in the directions of nature and animal conservation. They played an important role in trying to save the humans from themselves. Klara's "Suader parents" had decided Klara needed a formal Natura education and sent her to the academy to get one. People here were so trusting and they just took the story as fact since it came from Mystic. Chip's story was just that he was Mystics son who returned home from studying with the Canine clan. It created a little bit of a buzz in the student body that Mystic had a son no one had known about and that he had spent all these years among dogs, him being the son of the cat leader but people speculated that maybe Mystic had sent him away because it was too hard after having lost his other children in the rebellion years ago. The rebellion being the murder of her real parents but that was a story Klara didn't want to dwell on right now. Instead, she thought of how quickly the talk had died down and everyone had accepted Chip. How could they not Klara thought to herself, he is amazing after all.

"There's my girl always the voice of reason and compromise." Chip came up next to Klara and sat down. He immediately grabbed a loaf of sourdough bread and stuffed it in his mouth. Klara couldn't help but laugh at him.

"Chip, are you sure you are not a canine?" Klara said.

"What?" Chip asked confused.

Kenna and Dante both laughed.

"Old habits there Chip? Too many years with the dogs?" Kenna teased. "Anyway, I think I can live with missing the first half of the tournament. What picture show is it tonight?"

Klara half-listened to her friends as she looked around the table to see what tonight's offerings were. Meals at the academy were always wonderful to her, so many choices and all of them vegetarian she was living in a dream life now. Klara settled on a delicious looking BBQ tofu kabob with broccoli, zucchini, tomatoes and purple onion on it. She also helped herself to a large helping of couscous with peas. She had just taken a bite of her tofu when she spotted a bowl of juicy strawberries and she grabbed a few of those as well.

"Klara, have you?"

Dante's question snapped her back to the group's conversation.

"I'm sorry what was the question.?"

Kenna laughed. "Now who is the canine? You and Chip both eat like you've never seen food before. Didn't they feed you in leechville?"

Klara winced at the word. Soon after starting classes at the academy she had learned that humans were often referred to as leeches due to their "leeching off" of planet earth and sucking her dry, so to speak. It was definitely a derogatory term and it was used often by the students and adults alike. The teachers refrained from its use and would scold kids that said it in class, but it didn't lessen anyone from using the term. Having grown up among humans the word made her uncomfortable. Sure, she could understand the point of view that people in Natura had about humans but Klara also knew that it wasn't right to stereotype an entire race. There were so many wonderful humans out there but that was not a view shared by many at the academy.

"I asked you if you had ever seen the picture showing tonight it's called Avatar?" Kenna repeated.

"Yes, I have, and you'll love it." Klara knew they would all enjoy the nature-loving race depicted in Avatar. She was willing to bet they wouldn't be seeing it in 3d like she had though. That was the one thing Klara missed about the human world. There were some technological things there that weren't available here like computers and cell phones, but it was a sacrifice well worth it she thought. Plus, they had other ways of doing things here that worked better than the tech world of humans. They didn't need cell phones because they had sound orbs. You could speak your message into it and it would sound out of an orb in the other location, Klara had watched Kenna use one to call her parents before. They were very tiny and could be held in the palm of your hand with you wherever you went. Klara doubted they ever lost their signal like a cell phone sometimes did. Now computers, Klara had not found an equivalent for yet. She missed having the vast knowledge of the internet at her fingertips. Here you had to go to the library to research something, but Klara had always loved books and didn't mind it too much. Klara was really happy she had brought some of her books with her too because they didn't have many copies of human literature.

"The picture starts at 6:45 so we better head out soon." Dante was clearly eager to get there.

Klara stuffed one more spoonful of couscous in her mouth and got up to follow her friends back to the living quarters. The boys headed towards their wing of the academy and Klara continued beside Kenna up the stone staircase towards their rooms.

"Kenna? This is my first picture show here, how exactly do they show it without all the gadgets we had back in the human world?"

"I'm not entirely sure but I think I heard Mistress Curchio say that it's a combination of Human tech and light wielders power."

"But I thought there was no Human tech in Natura?"

"King Raphe has allowed some exceptions over the years. He believes we should embrace some of the Leeches tech as long as it doesn't hurt Natura."

Klara winced when Kenna said Raphe's name with a twinge of admiration in her voice.

 It wasn't common knowledge that King Raphe had murdered

her parents. Only a small fraction of people truly knew. The story that King Raphe had put out there was that it was a rebel extremist group that had murdered the royal family and he had been the valiant hero who had held Natura together in the wake of such a tragedy. He had supposedly graciously volunteered to run things until Karenia could be found to resume things after the death of her daughter. Raphe had been a trusted advisor to Karenia and then Klara's parents as well so the people felt it only natural that he should take over everyone held out hope that Karenia would turn up one day. There were so many rumors circulating that Karenia had lost her mind with grief and disappeared or that she had died of a broken heart. No one seemed to question the lies that Raphe fed them, the people here were just so trusting and naïve. Mystic had told her that he knew Karenia was, in fact, alive and had been in hiding trying to find Klara. Klara hadn't been given the whole story as to what had happened the day her parents were murdered but she deduced that Karenia had played a part in hiding her away in the human world. Mystic had warned it wouldn't be long though before Raphe found out she was alive and in Natura. Secrets have a way of making themselves known he had told her and Raphe although very evil was also very cunning.

"…Klara…earth to Klara?" Kenna's voice pulled Klara back.

"Sorry Kenna, what did you say?"

"Where do you go when you check out like that Klara? It must be someplace wonderful." Kenna giggled at her.

"I said this picture better be good if I'm giving up half the tournament to see it." Kenna rolled her eyes.

"Don't you mean giving up time staring at Milo?" Klara teased her friend.

Kenna pretended not to hear Klara.

"I'm going to go get cleaned up then I'll meet you in your room. Get that cute little brown dress out, it will be perfect for tonight."

"Yes, ma'am whatever you say." Klara laughed.

Kenna gave a triumphant smile and headed into her room.

Chapter 9

The marketplace was more crowded than usual that evening with the influx of visitors for the picture show festival. In the past Klara would have avoided scenes like this, situations where she would be bumping shoulders with strangers in the crowds but not anymore. She had made several trips to the marketplace since arriving in Natura and she found that she enjoyed visiting each booth and admiring all the handmade treasures on display. She could feel the weight of her silver charm bracelet around her wrist. She had tried several times to locate the old woman again to ask her what she knew of her and her sisters but she had not been able to find her. Mystic had the village security ask around for her as well but no one recalled the woman or knew anything helpful. It was all very odd and mysterious.

"Oh! Klara Look at this! It would go perfectly with your dress!" Kenna squealed and was holding up something she had found at one of the booths.

Klara laughed to herself as she made her way over to see what Kenna was so excited about. Kenna had taken it upon herself to try and dress Klara like her own personal Barbie doll. Kenna loved fashion and pretty things. Klara didn't have anything against that, she enjoyed looking nice and feeling feminine but years of living with only the necessities, as her fake mother had liked to put it, had always limited Klara's options and contributed to her daily torment at school.

As she approached, Kenna grabbed her arm pulling her in close and wrapped a braided belt around Klara's waist.

"Isn't it perfect? You just have to get it."

The belt was made of silk and it was a light green color that reminded Klara of the color of the inside of an Andes Mint. The belt was delicate and thin, there was a shimmering silver thread woven in between the green silk giving the belt a sparkling quality. It was meant to be tied at the side and Klara was fumbling to adjust it right.

"Here let me help…. there we go, that looks perfect." Kenna expertly tied it in a little loop with the excess draping down her side.

Klara's dress was a light brown spring dress with little green leaves sewn in at the neckline. It was form-fitted at top and middle then billowed out just above the knees. The belt matched wonderfully with the green leaves and made the dress pop.

"You are right as always Kenna, it's really cute."

Klara purchased the belt handing the young woman behind the table a few coins.

"Please keep the change, your work is lovely."

"Thank you miss," The woman nodded graciously and accepted the coins.

Klara still wasn't used to being able to spend money without consequences. Mystic had given her a large satchel of coins and informed her that she should not feel strange about spending them how she saw fit. Her grandmother kept the bulk of her assets here at the village treasury and Mystic assured her that her grandmother would provide her with anything she desired if she were here. Klara was not used to that sort of generosity and having never met her grandmother she still felt awkward spending her money. So far, she had only bought things she really needed, some clothing so that she would not stand out so much in her human attire. She had purchased some supplies she needed for her classes and that had been an adventure. She should have known they didn't use paper and pencils here, such a blatant waste of trees. They had these fascinating tablets called Knowledge Keepers or "Keepies" for short that you wrote on using a pen powered by light magic. The tablet is framed in stone and has a glass center, like a little window. The pens would etch into the glass whatever you wrote or drew with it in any color you chose and then save it. It was like having an iPad with unlimited data storage. The best part about the Keepies though were what they could do to books. So, because the people here chose to limit their use of paper when a book is published only one traditional copy is produced. People take their Keepies and press them on top of the original to copy it into their personal Keepies, then they can take their Keepies and share the copy to anyone else's Keepies as well. Klara had purchased herself a Keepie and light pen right away and had already copied every book she could get her hands on. She had also purchased several pair of sturdy boots for training and some sandals for leisure time. Luckily her room at the academy had already been furnished and even though Chip assured her she could make any changes she wanted to it she had chosen to leave it the way it was for now. Meals in the dining hall were included in tuition at the academy but Klara had gone out with her friends a few times to eat in the marketplace and spent some money there. Mystic had refused to accept any money for her tuition at the academy stating that under normal circumstances a Maithar would be trained at the castle by private tutors and he did not feel right charging her tuition. Klara hoped when her grandmother arrived, she could convince him to change his mind and accept the money. The people here lived simple lives, they were all generous with each other and you could tell some people may have more funds than others but no one wanted for anything, no one was poor or hungry or in need of the basics. Neighbors took care of neighbors and friends took care of friends.

Klara readjusted the belt comfortably on her hips.

"I suppose it wouldn't hurt to make one frivolous purchase, right?"

"Klara that belt is not frivolous, it is a necessity."

"Kenna to you all fashion is a necessity." Klara laughed.

"Hey, what did I miss?" Chip joined up with them as they continued towards the village square.

"I turned my back for a moment and Kenna has kidnapped you."

"Sorry, even though the weapons booth you have spent the past fifteen minutes at is very fascinating, I was easily distracted by Kenna's great taste in belts." Klara did a quick turn for Chip to see her new belt.

"It looks great Klara, but then you always look great in whatever you wear." Chip took Klara's hand like he often did.

Klara felt the heat return to her cheeks. Why did Chip say things like that to her? Was it just an attempt to build her up like always, ever the good coach and guardian or did it mean something else? Klara shook her head. It's not like she was going to ask him that. Besides she wasn't even entirely sure if wielders and shifters were allowed to be romantically involved anyway.

The three of them arrived at the village square and began searching for Dante. He had insisted on leaving ahead of them because he wanted to get the best seats. Klara was surprised to see how much the square had transformed for the festival. All along the cobblestones were row after row of chairs, the huge fountain that was normally the focal point of the square was drained of water and stood quietly unused.

Along the outskirts of all the chairs were booths selling a variety of snacks and drinks for people to enjoy. One booth, in particular, appeared to be very popular and the line of people waiting snaked out around the square.

"Come on we better get in line if we want to get any snacks before the show starts." Kenna grabbed Klara's free hand and pulled her and Chip along behind her to join the line.

"Kenna? How do we watch the show? I don't see a screen or projector anywhere?"

Chip and Kenna both smiled suspiciously at her.

"I think you will just have to wait and see." Chip said.

Klara didn't bother questioning them further, they clearly wanted the suspense to kill her. Instead, she turned her attention to the growing crowd of people getting settled in the chairs. She saw families with small children, young and old couples alike, even some single viewers dotted the crowd. Shifters and wielders all mingling about. One couple caught her attention. A young woman with striking feline eyes was holding hands with a light wielder. She knew he was a light wielder because he was producing a small orb of light in his palm and twirling it between his fingers in what looked like an unintentional habit. She had noticed a lot of light wielders did this, Kenna, for example, had a habit of producing an orb and rolling it around on the table with her pinkie finger when she was nervous. It wasn't the action of the man's orb that caught her attention though, it was the way he was looking at the young shifter. They were deep in conversation and had leaned in very close to one another. The young shifter giggled softly and tucked her hair behind her ear. They were clearly into each other; it didn't take cupid to tell that. Klara reached out with her mind to the young shifter and picked up a very strong very undeniable feeling of desire. The wielder leaned in further and kissed the shifter right on the lips. As he did so the orb in his palm brightened significantly enough that the people around him turned to take notice but then upon seeing the couple turned back to what they were doing.

"What's caught those eagle eyes of your Klara?" Chip said turning to follow her line of sight.

Klara turned back around quickly not wanting Chip to realize what she had been watching.

"Oh, it was nothing, I was just taking in the crowd."

"Are you uncomfortable? We don't have to stay if you don't want to. I know how you feel about crowds." Chip squeezed her hand tighter.

"No not at all, I'm excited to see the show. Besides crowds aren't so bad now that I can control what I take in and don't take in."

Chip smiled and turned to say something to Kenna and Klara snuck another look at the young couple. They were still locked in a passionate kiss, fully embracing one another. Maybe, wielders and Shifters were allowed to be with each other after all? Surely if it was forbidden the couple wouldn't be in the middle of the picture festival making out with each other. Klara felt butterflies in her stomach. Maybe, just maybe the idea of her and Chip together wasn't so crazy after all.

"Penny for your thoughts water goddess?" Chip leaned and whispered in her ear, it sent shivers through Klara's whole body and she jumped a little.

"Sorry didn't mean to startle you, you sure are jumpy today, you sure everything is ok?"

"I'm fine Cat-boy don't be such a worrywart; it's almost our turn anyway so let's see what all the fuss is about in this line."

Klara turned her attention to the booth in front of them and had to stifle a laugh. The booth was selling movie theater snacks you would find in every theater in the human world. There was popcorn, nachos, a variety of candy and carbonated drinks. The people were going crazy for it like it was all something so rare and different. Klara realized to them it really was. Since she had arrived here none of the food she had seen or eaten was packaged, processed or commercialized in any way. So, all of this must seem pretty strange to them and a novelty.

"Klara you have to tell me what to get! There is too much to choose from, you have probably had all of this stuff before, haven't you? Lucky!" Kenna was squeaking as she talked from excitement.

It didn't take much to get Kenna going but Klara loved her new friend's positive nature. Always chipper and viewing the glass as half full. If the human world had more Kenna's in it perhaps it wouldn't be so bleak.

"Well, you can't see a movie…err picture show without popcorn and I personally like to get these little candy-coated chocolates here and dump them into my popcorn. Then choose your poison with the drinks, my favorite is the root beer."

Klara chose a large tub of popcorn, a pack of M&M's, and a large root beer.

"We can all share this, it should be more than enough." Klara offered.

"Ok, I trust your taste in food, after all, you and Chip seem to be professional eaters." Kenna teased.

Klara went to pay for her purchases and Chip had already beaten her to it.

"My treat today ladies."

"You don't need to do that Chip; I can get it."

"Hush, Klara, it's the least I can do and It's nice to finally be able to do something for you for once."

Klara smiled and let Chip pay. He added two more root beers to the order.

"I think I see Dante over there." Kenna pointed towards the center of the crowd.

Klara and Chip let Kenna lead the way and they found Dante easily.

"Cutting it close, the picture is supposed to start in three minutes." Dante motioned for them to sit in the chairs he had saved.

"Here Dante, have a root beer and relax." Chip passed a drink to Dante and one to Kenna.

"I didn't think you would mind if we shared one." He whispered to Klara.

Klara was starting to think maybe this was more than just a night out with friends. Could Chip have feelings for her or was she reading him wrong? Klara of three months ago would not even consider the possibility that he could like her that way. This new Klara was trying to be more confident, more assert-ive and Chip was always telling her to trust her instincts. She checked in on Chip's emotions just a peek to see what was in that head of his and she found the same thing she always did… contentment…always contentment…what did that mean?

A noise from the center of the square drew Klara's attention. The huge fountain began to split open and a large orb of light began to float upwards to the night sky. Klara felt a jolt and the chair she was sitting in began to recline slowly so that she was laying back comfortably facing the sky above. Her feet were elevated and her head back, it was like laying on the beach in a lounge chair. The orb paused in the sky above them about fifty feet up and began to expand so that a large rectangular sheet of light covered the length of the village square forming a spectacular movie screen.

"Wow, this is so neat. I think I like movies here better."

"I wouldn't know, they never let cats into the theaters back there." Chip whispered.

Klara thought about how hard it must have been for Chip to be trapped in his cat body for sixteen years, not being able to speak or see his family. He had sacrificed so much for her.

"I'm sorry Chip."

"For what?" He turned his fiery eyes on her.

"It's just…you gave up so much for me and for what?"

"Are you kidding…for what? For the most amazing girl in the universe that's for what and I'd do it for another sixteen years if it meant being by your side. When will you believe that?" He put his arm around her and pulled her close.

The movie sprang to life on the magic glowing screen and the picture was clear and crisp, the sound bellowed all around them. It was like being at a drive-in theater that was on steroids, it was truly epic.

Klara settled in next to Chip and was enjoying the movie, it was like seeing it for the first time. She looked over at her friends and noticed Kenna jump at something on the screen and she absentmindedly grabbed Dante's hand. Poor Dante looked like he was going to have a stroke. Klara made a note to herself to try and talk to Kenna and see if she realized Dante's feelings for her without breaking his confidence of course.

Klara was sitting there happy and thinking about how much her world had changed in the past three months for the better. Then suddenly the screen went white. She could hear everyone around her questioning what happened?

"What's going on? Is this normal…is there some sort of intermission or something?" Klara asked Dante.

"Not that I know of—"

Attention Citizens of Natura…

A man's face appeared on the screen. The first thing Klara thought of when she saw him was… a bird. He looked like a creepy man bird. His nose was long and pointed with a light curve at the end. His eyes were too large for his face and had big black pupils with only a thin white line circling the edges of them. His skin was taut and stretched looking and his hair stood up around his head like an angry bird's feathers. His voice was sickly smooth and frightening. Klara instantly disliked the man. She felt Chip tense up next to her.

I am sorry to disrupt this evening's events.

Klara looked around and saw that many people had pulled out their pocket orbs and his face was plastered all over those as well.

I will be brief…It has been brought to my attention that one of our beloved Maithar triplets has returned to us. Such a blessed day this is to find that she is alive and well!

Oh no Klara felt the dread rising from the pit of her stomach. "He knows I'm here." She whispered to Chip. He held her closer to him, tighter, she could feel his pulse racing. She couldn't tell if it was her emotions or his she was sensing. Panic…fear…anger… determination.

I wish to welcome her back to Natura and have sent an envoy from the castle to go and collect her. It has long been our tradition that the Maithar reside in the castle and receive proper training. Let me assure the citizens of Natura that I will do my best to prepare her for her destiny. Klara…I look forward to meeting you soon.

The man gave a sick smile and disappeared from the screen his face replaced with the blue creatures of Avatar.

The next few seconds happened in a blur.

"Klara lets go…now."

Klara felt Chip pulling her away, pushing through the crowd, all eyes trained on her instead of the movie. Kenna and Dante stood up confused. They could see the panic in Chip and instinctively followed to make sure Klara was OK.

"Klara…did you know? Why didn't you tell us who you are?"

Dante looked hurt but Klara didn't notice she was still staring at the screen even though Raphe's face had been replaced by the movie already.

"What is…who was…was that him? Was that the man who murdered my parents?"

"Murdered your parents!? What are you talking about?" Kenna squeaked.

"We have to get back, my father will know what to do, we need to make sure you are safe." Klara heard the urgency in his voice and snapped out of it. She looked from Chip to her friends and then to the crowd of students and villagers. Klara could see one by one the people in the crown slowly realizing the truth. All eyes on her now confusion and curiosity in their faces. Then Suddenly she was running.

Chapter 10

The streets were eerily empty and dark. Everyone was still gathered in the village square trying to figure out what was happening. Chip was tugging Klara along behind him like a rag doll. Kenna was directing a light orb floating along in front of them lighting a path. Dante's eyes were huge and she could tell her friends were concerned and unsure. Regardless of that here they were by her side anyway and that meant something to her.

"Chip, what does he want with me? How did he know I'm here?"

"I don't know but the best thing we can do right now is get you to the academy and let my dad know what has happened if he doesn't already."

"I don't understand? Why are we running? What do you mean King Raphe murdered her parents?" Dante questioned.

"Dante…Kenna…I need you to trust me. Klara is not safe with Raphe. We have to get her to my dad and we have to do it now." Chip spoke firmly.

"Ok Chip. I trust you. If you say this is what we need to do then you can count on my help." Dante said.

"Me too." Chirped Kenna. "Besides I don't want Klara leaving me to go live at the castle anyway." She took Klara's hand and squeezed it as they quickly made their way back towards the academy.

As they rounded the corner, a voice sounded in the darkness.

"Stop right there shifter."

Their path was blocked by a group of soldiers, they were armed and dressed in uniforms that Klara knew to be the castle colors. One of the soldiers stepped forward a woman with a nasty sneer on her face.

"We will take her from here shifter, Klara please come with us." The woman demanded.

Chip stepped in front of Klara blocking her from view. "She's not going anywhere." His words were more of a growl than words.

"Let's not make this difficult, children. I would hate for one of you to get hurt." The solider smiled showing her teeth that had been filed into points making her look like some sort of monster.

"It's not us that will be hurt. Turn back now and tell Raphe that Klara will be staying here with us. She is not interested in his… hospitality."

"That's King Raphe! How dare you speak so disrespectfully. Take her!" the soldier signaled her men and they sprung forward. Kenna shot her light orb in their direction but it was quickly blocked by one of the soldiers. Chip lunged for the solider with the sharp teeth, slamming into her. Klara raised her hands and shot a stream of water at one of the soldiers but all it did was startle him. The other soldiers were already closing in on her. There were too many of them. Dante and Kenna had been overwhelmed and Chip was still struggling with the pointy-toothed woman but there was no way they could win. Klara tried to focus and aimed her hands towards the oncoming soldiers, she managed to knock one of them down when she heard Chip yell out in pain. The pointy-toothed soldier had bitten into his neck like a feral animal. Before Klara knew what she was doing, she had refocused her energy on the woman and the water came flying out of her palms. With a startled scream the woman was yanked up into a small whirlpool of water and was thrashing about, struggling to breathe. Klara was deep in concentration when she felt the arms go around her waist and pull her sideways toppling her to the ground. Her focus broke and the woman was freed from her watery prison. She struggled to break free from the soldier's grip and another one stepped forward grabbing her arms and pulling them behind her back, they slammed her down harder into the ground and began to bind her hands. She felt a hard kick of a boot in her side and cried out in pain. It was the pointy-toothed witch. She couldn't see Chip but she heard him yell in rage.

"Get your hands off her!" he was hissing and growling but Klara knew he couldn't get to her. They had all been overwhelmed now by the group of soldiers, they were sorely outnumbered. She could feel the desperation coming from Chip and she felt so guilty. If only she had tried harder in her training, why was she such a failure? Tears were streaking down her face now.

Klara gave up and stopped struggling for fear they would hurt her friends further.

"Much better. I don't want any more trouble out of you. Do you understand." The woman sneered.

Klara was nodding her head in submission when she heard it. It sounded like the rush of a waterfall slamming down over rocks. Screams broke out and she felt the soldier's grips loosen, she broke free of them and jumped to her feet, hands still bound behind her back. As she turned, she saw a huge hurricane forming above them, one by one it was swallowing up the soldiers. They struggled but it was useless. Klara was confused, only a Maithar could direct the elements, who was doing this? Then she saw her...a woman standing in the shadows her hair a red blaze of fire atop her head, her eyes shining in the darkness. Power surrounded her, engulfed her, embraced her. She was spectacular, fierce, magical. She looked like a *true* water goddess.

The woman stepped forward from the shadows and let the hurricane cease. The bodies of the soldiers fell to the ground. And they gasped for breath, staring at the woman in fear.

"Leave now and I will spare your lives for I take no pleasure in harming my own people. Send a message to Raphe...his invitation has been declined."

The woman spoke with authority, her voice was strong and sure. The soldiers stood and fled quickly, only the razor-toothed woman was bold enough to speak.

"This isn't over Maithar." And she followed her soldiers into the darkness.

The woman turned toward Klara and began her approach, it was then that Klara realized she wasn't alone. Trailing behind her were two figures, the first a small girl, eyes wide in fear, her hand clutching the fur of her large canine companion. The large dog looked more like a wolf.

Chip had made his way to Klara's side now, Kenna and Dante followed behind him.

It was Chip that broke the silence.

"Queen Karenia, an honor, your timing couldn't have been better." Chip took a knee before the woman.

"Please stand, I am no longer your Queen, you needn't bow to me, young man. I'm glad I arrived when I did. I saw the message Raphe transmitted and feared the worst. Such a blessing that I arrived in time and now I have two of my granddaughters safely at my side. A good day indeed." Karenia turned towards Klara now.

"Klara I'm so happy to find you here."

"I don't know what to say? I...I've heard so much about you over the past few months, we have been looking for you...wait did you just say two of your granddaughters?" Klara was confused, her eyes lingered on the girl but how could this be? The girl looked to be maybe twelve or thirteen years old and Klara knew her sisters were triplets so she should be her age.

"Yes, don't let her neglected appearance fool you, Miss Rosie here is quite the spitfire."

"Rosie? So, this is my sister?" Klara stepped closer to the girl.

She felt a feeling of relief flood over her...she wasn't alone anymore...she had a sister who from the looks of it was just as new to this world as she was. Klara couldn't help herself she lunged forward and wrapped her arms around the girl embracing her tightly.

"I'm so glad you here!"

"What the hell!" Rosie yelled and pushed Klara away.

"I don't know what the hell is going on here but you promised me some answers and some food for my dog. I already thought I was losing my mind jumping through a freaking waterfall with you and now we arrive in this medieval-looking village and you shoot a hurricane out of your hands…" the girl kept babbling on and then collapsed in a heap on the ground. Her dog whining and nudging her side.

"Don't take it personally Klara, she has been through a lot and knows nothing of our world at all."

Karenia turned towards Chip. "Is your father here? May we take sanctuary at the academy tonight?"

"Yes, my father will welcome you, of course, my queen…I mean Lady Karenia." Chip bent down and scooped Rosie up into his arms.

"Please follow us." Chip and Klara lead the way to the academy and the group followed suit. Karenia moved forward to walk beside Klara.

"I'm sorry we have to meet like this. Rosie will come around just be patient with her, you two will need each other going forward more than you realize."

Klara nodded her head.

"Karenia…Grandmother…what should I call you?"

"Whatever you are comfortable with but when you were still growing in your mothers' belly, I used to tell her I hoped you girls would call me Grams." The woman smiled softly and Klara could see the pain in her eyes, her age showed in that moment. Klara didn't feel right reaching out and reading her emotions, it felt like a violation of privacy but she didn't need her powers to see the pain was there. Klara took Karenia's hand in hers and held it there as they walked. Klara couldn't explain it. She hadn't met this woman until today but she loved her. She could feel to the core of her soul. This was her Grams, her family and she loved her. It was sudden and instant and the purest most natural thing Klara had ever felt.

"Grams it is then." Klara smiled at her and saw a small tear sneak its way down Karenia's face.

Chip interrupted their tender moment. Even cat boys are still as clueless as regular boys Klara thought to herself.

"Lady Karenia, is that who I think it is?" he nodded his head toward the dog walking ahead of them.

"Yes, its Daisy, she has been in the human world this whole time, at Rosie's side can you believe it?" Karenia answered.

Karenia turned her attention towards Kenna and Dante now.

"Thank you both for what you did back there, you could have run and saved yourselves but you stood by my granddaughter. It means the world to me, truly." She stopped and hugged them both.

"Oh, it was nothing" Dante said.

"It was more than nothing, and we will never forget it." Chip chimed in this time.

"Would the two of you mind running ahead and letting Mystic know we are coming? I don't want to part from my granddaughter's side and I don't think Chip can run with Rosie in his arms." Karenia asked.

"Yes…of course we will, come on Dante." Kenna grabbed Dante's arm and they ran ahead towards the academy.

"How much do you know about the night your parents were killed, Klara?" Karenia's face was serious now, pained even. They began walking again.

"Not a lot. Mystic felt it was better to hear it from you. All I know is that they were murdered by Raphe and you sent my sisters and me to the human world for our own safety." Klara answered.

"Yes, Raphe murdered my daughter and her husband, brutally, and he will pay for that one day soon. I didn't reach them in time to stop it but I was able to get you and Rosie to safety. Or what I thought was safety at the time. Many others were lost to us that night. Let's get to the academy and get Rosie settled, there is so much to tell you both."

Chapter 11

When they reached the academy, Mystic was waiting for them. He ushered them inside and took them to a suite of rooms on the first level. Klara had not explored the entire Academy yet as it was so vast but she knew the area that they were in was connected to the medical suites.

"I sent for a healer and some food, Karenia, my how it's good to see you again." Mystic embraced Karenia as old friends.

"Thank you for taking care of Klara in my absence Mystic, I can never repay for it but I know you are glad to have your son back home. Too much sorrow you and I have had to endure these past years."

The healer entered the room, Klara had seen him around the academy before but hadn't had the opportunity to meet him yet. He was a tall, thin man, spindly but graceful like a deer, his hair was dark and wound into long dreads that fell down his back. His skin smooth and caramel-colored, a few shades darker than Klara's. He wore a simple tunic that had an array of instruments tucked into every pocket. He had a kind face and a gentle touch. His most striking feature though were his eyes, they were a bright almost glowing shade of purple. If Klara didn't know better, she would have thought him a shifter with those eyes but since he was currently standing over Rosie, hands glowing with healing powers, she knew that couldn't be the case. From what she had learned so far you were either a shifter or a wielder, never both.

The man finished his work and turned towards the group.

"She will be just fine. She is very malnourished and dehydrated. Regular well-balanced meals and some TLC will have her better in no time." The healer approached Klara.

"May I?" he pointed to her abdomen.

With everything that had happened Klara had forgotten about the soldier's kicks to her side. She gently lifted her shirt.

"How did you know?" Klara asked in wonder.

The healer chuckled. "That's what I do."

Klara's side was already turning a deep purple color. Chip inhaled deeply when she lifted her shirt. She could see the anger in his eyes.

The healer quickly went to work and soon the bruised skin was back to normal.

"Thank you...?" Klara didn't recall having heard his name.

"Names Brian, and it was my pleasure." Brian turned to Mystic now.

"If you need anything else please let me know." The healer bowed his head to Karenia and then Klara and swiftly exited the room.

Rosie began to stir on the bed and Daisy climbed up next her ever the watchdog. Klara was pretty certain Daisy was a shifter but why she was still in animal form escaped Klara.

"Son, let's give them some time alone." Mystic motioned for Chip to go with him.

"I'll be in the dining hall if you need me." Chip squeezed her hand and left with Mystic.

Rosie opened her eyes and stared at the ceiling for a moment.

"Rosie, sweetie, how are you feeling? Karenia sat down in a chair by the bed. Klara followed and sat at the foot of the bed, keeping her distance, trying not to crowd Rosie.

"I...where am I?" Rosie sat up and held her hand to her forehead.

"You are safe. Are you thirsty? Hungry?" Karenia asked gently.

"Yes."

Karenia reached for the bedside table and passed Rosie a cup of tea and a raspberry cookie. Rosie snatched them quickly for Karenia's hands, she drank and ate quicker than Klara thought was humanly possible.

"You have anything for Daisy?" Rosie asked expectantly.

"Yes of course but Daisy needs to show you something first. It is going to come as a shock to you but I need you to think about all that you have seen today and everything we talked about in the car on the way here, can you do that for me?" Karenia reached out and placed her hand on Rosie's shoulder.

Klara watched Rosie closely. Outwardly she put off this tough girl persona but Klara could read her emotions and the girl was terrified.

"I can try, I guess." Rosie stated.

"Ok, Daisy I think we better go ahead and get it over with don't you agree."

Daisy let out a bark in response to Karenia's statement and hopped off the bed.

Klara knew what was about to happen. Rosie probably had no idea Daisy was about to transform. Klara remembered what a shock it had been for her when Chip did it, but at least Rosie would have her and Karenia to help her adjust.

Klara kept her eyes on Rosie not needing to watch Daisy, she knew what would happen the fur would start to ripple and the energy in the air would pop and where the dog once stood a person would take its place. Klara had seen it time and time again at the academy now. Shifters transformed all the time; it had become commonplace for her now. Rosie's eyes grew huge and Klara watched her sister shuffle back on the bed pushing herself up against the wall.

"Please don't be frighten my child, I am still just Daisy, your Daisy." A soothing voice sounded from behind Klara.

Her curiosity won out and she turned away from her sister's frightened face to see a striking woman standing in the dog's place. She was built like an amazon woman, strong and sturdy. She had long flowing silver hair that reached her lower back. She looked to be in her late thirty's early forties maybe. Her eyes were liquid gold and her face was defined, exotic looking. She was incredible, the picture of a warrior woman. There was a regal quality about her that Klara couldn't quite place.

Daisy stepped towards Rosie her hands reaching out.

"No stop. Stay right there, not a step closer— "Rosie was practically melding into the wall now.

Klara thought maybe she should take the focus off Rosie and give her a minute to process everything.

"You must be Rosie's, MoChara." Klara directed her question at Daisy.

"Chip, I mean Cosantoir who was in here early is my MoChara, do you know each other?" Klara felt stupid for asking that as if every shifter knew every other shifter but she was just trying to say something, anything and it was always strange to her saying Chips given name aloud.

"Actual no, I was your mother's MoChara. There wasn't enough time for Rosie to be bonded to a MoChara before your parents were attacked. I failed your mother that night, but I vowed to honor her by protecting her daughter, so I left with Rosie to the human world." Daisy's eyes never left Rosie's as she answered the question.

"And yes, I know Cosantoir and his brother Dalonus, I chose them as MoChara's for you and your sister Katherine. Rosie was to be bonded with Cindona, but she was one of many lost to us that night." Daisy's voice was solemn.

"Chip never told me he has a brother, is he out there somewhere in the human world with Katherine?" why hadn't Chip told her he had a brother? Surely that was worth mentioning to her?

It was Karenia who answered her this time.

"No, they are both gone. I was only able to save the two of you that night…I couldn't get to Katherine…I had to make a choice…save the two of you or lose all of you…so I did the only thing I could and I escaped with you and Rosie."

Karenia was speaking so softly now it was almost a whisper. The despair and guilt were coming off her in waves.

"Are you sure, maybe they aren't gone. Maybe Raphe still has them somewhere?"

"I wish that were true but your mother was holding Katherine in her arms when he killed her. I saw it with my own eyes. I saw evil consume them one by one...Kerry, Katherine, Ruben, and Dalonus. The screams.... I couldn't..."

Karenia broke down in tears and surprisingly it was Rosie he went to her first.

"It's ok Karenia, we will get justice for them we will teach that bastard a lesson."

Karenia wrapped an arm around Rosie and reached out for Klara. With hot fat tears streaming down her face Klara stepped into the embrace...into the arms of her family.

Chapter 12

They stood there locked in a bear hug for who knew how long. Finally, it was Rosie who broke it off.

"Ok so I'm not really one for hugs and this one was really long." She gave a crooked smile.

"Rosie, can I show you around the academy, I used to teach here you know." Klara had almost forgotten that Daisy was still in the room.

"Uh…no thanks, I'm just going to go with Klara for now." Rosie took a step away from Daisy and closer to Klara.

Klara could tell the great amazon of a woman was hurt by the remark, but she only nodded her head.

"I'm going to take Rosie to the dining room, I'm sure she's still hungry." Klara started towards the door and Rosie followed closely, eyes still locked on Daisy.

"That's a good idea, I will go find Mystic and make preparations to secure the academy, make no mistake Raphe will retaliate and soon. Daisy, would you care to join me?" Karenia stood and rubbed her hands down her clothing to smooth it out.

"Yes of course." Daisy answered and then turned back to Rosie. "If you need anything, I won't be far Rosie."

"I'll be fine" and Rosie pushed past Klara and out the door leaving Daisy behind. Klara had to run to catch up to Rosie.

"Hey, where are you headed? The dining hall is the other way."

"I don't care, just far away from there."

"What's wrong? Are you upset with Daisy?"

"Nothing's wrong…you wouldn't understand anyway."

"You might be surprised Rosie; it wasn't too long ago that I went through the same thing you just did. I had no idea my furry little house cat was really a grown dude."

"Whatever, you just don't get it."

"Well I'd like to try"

Rosie stopped in her tracks and turned an irritated face towards Klara.

"Listen, I know you are trying to be miss Susie sunshine sister of the year, but I don't know you and I don't trust you. I don't trust any of you and the one person in this whole world I did trust was Daisy and now, I find out she was a lie this whole time. So, I'm sorry but I just have no interest in playing happy little family with you right now ok?"

"I…I'm sorry? I was just trying to…I thought after what you said in there to Karenia about teaching Raphe a lesson—"

"I just wanted to get the hell out of there ok? I didn't mean any of it. I'm just fine on my own."

Klara couldn't believe what she was hearing. Here she thought she finally had someone to care about and who could care about her but now all she had was this screaming banshee standing in front of her.

"Whatever Rosie, I thought it would be nice to have a sister, but I guess I was wrong."

"Yeah, I guess you were." Rosie turned back in the direction of the dining hall and left Klara standing alone in the hallway.

Klara watched Rosie storm off and leaned up against the wall. She held her head in her palms and let the tears fall. She was so frustrated. The day had started out so great, she had been so happy and now all hell had broken loose. Raphe knew where she was and wanted to do who knew what to her, any hopes she had of finding Katherine had been snuffed out and Rosie wanted nothing to do with her. What a difference 24 hours can make. Klara pulled herself together. She was not going to do this; this was not her anymore. She was stronger and smarter now and she wasn't going to stand here in this hallway and feel sorry for her-self. Klara decided she would head to her room for the night and unwind. It had been a trying day, to say the least, and maybe a good book and a warm bed were exactly what she needed.

Klara walked down the hall back to the entryway of the academy and headed towards the grand staircase.

"Hey, Klara wait up!" Kenna bounded towards her and they began to climb the stairs towards the living quarters.

"Chips been looking for you, we were all waiting in the dining hall and he got all weird suddenly."

"What do you mean all weird?"

"He just had this sudden urge to find you, said he knew something was wrong and needed to find you right away."

Klara didn't have the energy nor the desire to figure out what that meant, she was tired and quite frankly she was a bit upset with Chip for not telling her about his brother.

"Well, if you see him just tell him I went to my room to go to bed and I will see him in the morning."

"Ok Klara, Night." Kenna gave Klara a quick hug and darted off back down the stairs.

Klara knew Chip's feelings would probably be hurt if Kenna found him and gave him the message. Chip had spent every night for the past three months sleeping in Klara's room in her bed. In cat form of course. Chip had tried that first night sleeping in his old room but in the middle of the night he had come knocking on Klara's door. He told her he couldn't sleep apart from her not after they had spent the past sixteen years curled up together in her room in the human world. It didn't feel right being apart. Klara had felt exactly the same way though she hadn't said it, but she told him he could stay in her bed as long as he stayed in cat form. He was happy to oblige and now they had spent every night since curled up with each other. Klara had thought it might be awkward now that she knew what he really was, but it wasn't. In fact, it was very comforting, and she found herself chatting away to him like she used to before she knew he what he was.

Klara reached the door to her room; she went inside and locked the door behind her. Klara peeked in the bathroom to make sure

Kenna hadn't made it back upstairs yet, she just wasn't in the mood to recap the day's events. She quickly cleaned herself up and brushed her teeth. Klara pulled on her favorite pair of soft pajamas and grabbed her Keepie from her desk by the window. Klara climbed into bed and pulled the covers snug up around her.

"Hmm what to read..." Klara browsed thought the library of books she had copied into her Keepie from the academy library.

MoChara's: The unbreakable bond

"Yeah, not a good idea tonight." She continued to flip through the books

Minds of Humans and how to influence them

"Hmm, that sounds a bit creepy."

A History of Natura from the separation to the first age

"Nah."

Rare Shifter Classifications

"Nope."

Light Magic, A beginner's guide

"Ugh no."

Stories and Folklore for kids

"This will do, something light that doesn't require much thought on my part." Klara had a habit of talking to herself out loud when she was alone. Klara pressed her light pen to the page and the book opened up.

The preface of the book contained lyrics to a song written in lovely curled old cursive writing.

Song of Sages

Water moves a quiet stream
Wash away the old
Water rages like the sea
A wonder to behold

Fire warms a gentle flame
Burning in the night
Fire rages can't be tamed
Impossible to fight

Earth yields fruit a treat to keep

Mountains wonders to behold
Earth can shake with tremors deep
It swallows cities whole

The Mother holds the powers three
She keeps us safe in her caress
The evil comes again you'll see
Two worlds thrown in distress

Three mages with a force unmet
One with waters strong and sure
With one the fire burns and scalds
The last is solid as the Earth
The darkness gone
The three reign strong
Peace resides upon the Earth

Klara drifted off to sleep the song ringing deep in her mind.

Tap

Tap

Tap Tap Tap

"Klara?" a whisper came from outside the door.

Klara slowly opened her eyes still heavy with sleep.

"What time is it?" She picked up her Keepie still laying on her chest.

1:00am

Klara sat up and stood unsteadily.

It must be Chip she thought.

Klara considered ignoring him but she decided against it.

She walked groggily over to the door and opened it.

"Listen Chip I'm not—

Klara opened her eyes and saw Daisy standing before her.

"Oh, I'm sorry Daisy, I thought you were someone else. Is everything ok?"

"Klara, may I come in?"

"Uh…Sure."

Klara opened the door wide and Daisy stepped inside.

"What can I do for you?" Klara was curious.

Daisy paced back and forth, clearly in distress.

"Klara…this may seem like a very strange request but…can I

sleep in here with you?"

"Uh…

"I know, I know…its strange but I have spent the past sixteen years sleeping beside your sister and the twenty-four years before that sleeping beside your mother…I just…I can't…sleep alone. I will stay in dog form of course. Would you consider my request? I went to Rosie's room, knowing I would not be welcome there but I thought I would try, however, she was not alone, so I left."

Klara sensed there was more Daisy wanted to say and didn't. Klara felt bad for Daisy, it must have been very difficult being rejected by Rosie, Klara knew the feeling and Klara wasn't nearly as invested in Rosie as Daisy probably was. Besides Klara knew somehow her mother would want her to be kind to Daisy.

"Yes, you are welcome to stay if you want Daisy."

Daisy gave her a sad smile.

"Thank you, Klara."

She morphed quickly into her dog form and bounded over to the bed, she hopped up at the foot and curled up to go to sleep.

Klara locked the door and climbed back into bed. She lay there for a moment her mind wandering. Maybe Karenia was in Rosie's room and Daisy didn't want to intrude on that. Yes, that must be it. Klara could feel Daisy's warm body at the foot of her bed and she found herself drifting quickly back to sleep.

Chapter 13

"*N*o!!!" *A woman screams, clutching her infant to her chest. She sends a desperate surge of water towards the darkness. Black tendrils snake through the air, thick like tar, absorbing the water and passing on to claim its victim. It wraps around the man first, he struggles to break free, the tendrils expand and squeeze, suffocating him, tightening as he struggles. The woman reaches for the basinet, desperate to get what's inside but she's too late. It takes her feet first, trapping her, a fly on glue paper. The blackness slowly consumes her, she's forced to watch as it oozes over the helpless infant embraced in her arms. "Please do what you will to me but spare them, I beg you!" Her pleas fall unanswered. One last scream pierces the air…followed by a hollow, malevolent laugh…*

Klara woke in a sweat, her heart racing. It took her a moment to slow her breathing.

"It was just a dream…" She told herself.

She sat up in bed and regretted it instantly. She let her head flop back down on the pillow. The pounding felt like her brain was splitting in two. What was that? She struggled to remember the dream but was left only with an uneasy feeling of dread. She shook her head, willing away the pounding but to no avail.

"Where's the healer when you need him right Daisy?" Klara raised her head slightly to look at the edge of the bed but Daisy was gone. She tried again to sit up, this time more slowly. She reached for her Keepie still lying in bed with her from last night's reading.

10:00am

"Oh no! I'm late for class!" she jumped up and rushed around the room grabbing the first set of clothes she could get her hands on. Great fashion choices would not save her from Mistress Curchio's stern look of disapproval. Maybe she could catch some slack after the events of yesterday. She threw on the clothes not paying attention to the fact that it was jeans and a tee-shirt from her human wardrobe. It will just have to do for today. Klara grabbed her Keepie and orb pen and rushed out the door.

Klara made it to the Human History classroom in record time. She may have bulldozed through a few underclassmen on her way there but hopefully, they would forgive her. She opened the door to the classroom hoping to slip inside unnoticed. She had barely set her foot inside when she heard Mistress Curchio's voice.

"Miss Rayne, thank you for gracing us with your presence dear."

Klara fumbled to her seat next to Kenna.

"I'm sorry Mistress…I overslept, yesterday was a bit…"

"No excuses Miss Rayne, I will let it go this time but don't make a habit of being late, I do not tolerate tardiness."

"Yes, Ma'am, Thank you."

Mistress Curchio returned to her lecture regarding the human industrial age and the negative impact it had on nature.

"It's not like you to oversleep? Are you ok?" Kenna asked her, concern in her voice.

"I'm fine, my head is pounding but I'll be fine."

"Hang on, I have a headache tonic in my bag, you can have it." Kenna reached into her bag and retrieved a small vial containing a pale-yellow liquid. She handed it to Klara.

"Do I just drink it?" Klara asked, unsure.

"Yeah, it works well for me, I get migraines sometimes."

Klara uncapped the vial and held it to her nose. It smelled like lemons. She pressed it to her lips and tipped the contents into her mouth. She was pleasantly surprised, it tasted like a lemon drop candy, sweet and tangy.

"Wow, medicine in the human world sure doesn't taste like that."

"Yeah well Leeches aren't the smartest, are they?"

Klara flinched at the word.

"Oh, I don't know about that, there are some humans that are pretty great, they aren't all bad you know."

"I will have to take your word for it, I have no desire to meet any of them to find out."

Klara shrugged her shoulders. She turned her attention back to the lecture and realized her headache was already gone. She would have to visit the healer and stock up on the little yellow concoction.

…polluting the air. These advances in technology progressed rapidly from that point and led to the condition of the earth that we are faced with today—

A hand shot up in the air.

"Yes, Mr. Archwold?"

"Do they truly not understand the damage they are doing? My uncle works as a suader in North America, he says that some of the humans have produced evidence of the damage but the population as a whole ignores what's right in front of them, preferring to favor their technological comforts."

"Your Uncle is right, many humans are fighting to if not undo the damage done at least prevent further damage but the struggle is difficult. That is why suaders are so important. The power to persuade the hearts and minds of humans is invaluable in the efforts to help them save their world."

"Why should we care? I mean—

"Hand please Miss Donnely."

The girl blushed slightly and raised her hand.

"Go ahead."

"Why should we care if they destroy their world? Our world is protected from them. Even if they cease to exist won't we still go on flourishing here in Natura? Don't the leeches deserve what they get, favoring selfish comforts over the gifts of the earth?"

Enough was enough, Klara surprised herself and raised her hand high.

"Yes Miss Rayne, would you like to respond?"

"I would...It is easy for you all to sit here and judge. This world is wonderful, spectacular even, but filled with an advantage the humans don't have...Magic. There is beauty in the human world too. They have only the inventions of their own making and yes some terrible humans are existing in that world, full of greed and selfishness, some of them in positions of power able to make important decisions they have no business making but there are also amazing humans too. People who help the less fortunate, give of themselves to heal the sick and feed the hungry. People who create works of music, art, poetry, stories that would amaze even all of you with all your magic and powers. They may have changes they need to make but they don't deserve to cease to exist. We should not turn our backs on them."

"Thank you, Miss Rayne. That was very impassioned. Spoken like a true Maithar." Mistress Curchio smiled at her.

Klara could feel all the eyes on her and her face flushed. Of course, the whole academy knew now who she was after Raphe's stunt last night. Some of the students were treating her differently now, reverently, it was awkward. She sat back down quickly and turned to Kenna.

"I can't believe I just did that."

"Well, I'm glad you did. It was a good speech. I still don't like the leeches though." Kenna smiled and elbowed Klara playfully.

Klara glanced over at Jackie Donnely and saw her with her head bowed down staring intently at nothing on her desk. Klara could feel the embarrassment coming from the girl. Great way to make friends Klara, call them out in class and make them feel bad. She shook her head and looked away from the girl feeling guilty.

The rest of the day went on without incident. Klara wondered if she would see Rosie today. She figured Mystic and Karenia wouldn't enroll her in classes yet. It would be too overwhelming for her having just learned about everything last night. Klara had been so excited to see Karenia and Rosie last night and then so caught off guard by Rosie's attitude that she hadn't stopped to think about what she saw. Rosie was tiny, malnourished, and frail-looking. She must have had a very rough time wherever she had been and she clearly knew nothing about Natura or magic or any of it. Klara decided she would make another effort to connect with Rosie, be patient with her, they were sisters after all and they would need each other before this whole thing was over.

Klara made the short walk to the training gym where she knew she would find Chip waiting for her. She was starting to feel bad about last night, maybe she had been too harsh telling Kenna to tell him he wasn't welcome in her room last night. She would talk to him and explain why she was upset. Chip knew her better than anyone and he would understand and she would find out why he felt the need to keep his brother a secret from her. He must have had a reason.

As Klara approached the door to the gym, she could hear laughing coming from inside. She pushed open the door and found that Chip was not the only one waiting for her. There stood Rosie laughing with Chip as though they were old friends.

"Uh, Hey Chip...Hey Rosie." Klara approached them. Chip stepped forward to meet her halfway across the gym floor.

"Can we talk?" his voice sounded unsure.

"Yeah, I think I owe you an apology." Klara led him over to the bench only yesterday they sat and joked together on. How much had changed in those short hours Klara thought.

They sat down together and Klara noticed Rosie had wandered over to the opposite side of the Gym and was looking at the training equipment.

"Yesterday was...crazy, and I may have overreacted about something. I didn't mean to hurt your feelings."

"What do you mean? Hurt my feelings how?"

"I told Kenna to tell you not to stay with me in my room last night because I guess I was upset with you for not telling me about your brother."

Chip stiffened next to her. Klara briefly sensed anger and pain but it was gone in a millisecond.

"I misunderstood Kenna's message. When she found me last

night, I was with Rosie...I had come across her in the hallway outside the dining hall and she was in pretty bad shape emotionally. When Kenna relayed your message, I took her to mean you wanted me to take care of your sister. So that's why I didn't go to your room last night."

"Do you mean you slept in Rosie's room?" Klara couldn't help but feel the jealousy rising up inside her. Why would he think she would want him to do that? That's what Daisy had meant about someone already being there.

"Yes, I didn't like the idea of leaving you alone but I figured Rosie needed the company more."

Klara was angry now but she didn't want to show it.

"It doesn't matter, I wasn't alone anyway."

Chip's eyes grew large and Klara saw a vein in his neck begin to pulse.

"You weren't alone? Well, who—

"It doesn't matter...why didn't you tell me about your brother?"

"What about my brother Klara? It seems you may know more about him than me?" Klara had never seen Chip angry before.

"No, not really, I just know he is MoChara to my sister Katherine. You didn't think that was worth mentioning to me?"

"If I had mentioned him, you would have asked where he was or what happened to him and your sister. I didn't have those answers for you so I didn't bring it up. Besides honestly Klara I don't like to talk about him...I know logically he is probably gone and I wasn't there to help him...so yeah it's not really a fun subject." His voice was cold and detached. Klara wasn't used to this Chip and she didn't like it one bit. He wasn't there to help his brother because he had been with her and now, she wondered if he resented her for it.

Klara just looked at him, unsure what to say next.

"Listen, we can't change the past, let's just move on and get to training. Mystic has asked Rosie to join us. It seems she actually has a good handle on her powers and she is eager to test her limits."

Chip stood up and started back towards the center of the gym leaving Klara behind.

Great, of course, Rosie has a handle on her powers. Klara's mind was racing now. Chip had stayed in her sister's room. Had he remained in his human form? What did they talk about? Why would he think Klara would want that? She thought something had been growing between them but maybe she had read the signs wrong and why was Chip acting so defensive with her about his brother?

"You coming?" Chip called to her.

Klara got up and made her way over to the two of them. This was going to be fun she thought to herself sarcastically.

"Ok, so Rosie, first I would like you to sit back and observe for a moment, I am going to have Klara aim at these three targets here and then you can have a go ok?" Chip motioned to three training dummies he had positioned throughout the gym.

"Watch how Klara controls the intensity of her water stream. It can be easy when you are in the heat of the moment to just blast at a target but when you learn to control the intensity you can not only aim better but you can inflict damage more precisely. Ok, Klara when you're ready."

Klara stepped forward; she could feel Rosie's eyes burning into the back of her head. Klara thrust both her hands out and shot water jets at two of the dummies knocking one of them over, she quickly turned her left hand to the remaining dummy and aimed a controlled thin jet of water straight at its head, but she missed. She lowered her hands and turned back toward Chip and Rosie.

"Hey two out of three is great Klara and you knocked one over this time. Fantastic" Chip encouraged.

Rosie stood there with a smirk on her face, clearly unimpressed. Chip quickly reset the dummies into their places.

"Ok, Rosie whenever you're ready." Chip took a few steps back.

Klara couldn't help but be curious. Rosie's power hadn't come up in the conversation yesterday and Klara wondered what it would be. She watched Rosie walk to the center of the room and really studied her appearance. She was so thin, sickly thin, her eyes were sunken in and her face was pulled taut. Clearly, this girl had not been taken care of, she looked like the kids in the commercials Klara remembered from the human world, the kids who were starving and the commercials were asking for your help. Klara felt a pang of guilt, this was her sister and she probably had very good reasons for holding everyone at arm's length. Well except for Chip apparently, she had no problem letting him in close. Klara shook away the thoughts and turned her attention back to Rosie.

"Now don't get discouraged if you can't hit the target right away." Chip encouraged. Klara remembered how frustrating training had been for her in the beginning.

Rosie turned around once eyeing the three targets. She raised one hand and aimed it at the first dummy. She inhaled deeply and then a blazing stream of fire shot out of her hand like a blow torch, it hit the dummy square in the chest and incinerated it to ash, the tiny girl spun around and took out the other two dummies with both her hands at the same time with ease. She turned towards Klara and Chip two flames still resting calmly in her palms and she raised each hand to her mouth and blew them out like candles on a cake.

"You were saying?" Rosie said with a smug look plastered across her face.

"Wow Rosie that was awesome." Chip went over to her and clapped her on the shoulder.

She's your sister, be supportive Klara, be patient, be patient, be patient. Klara repeated the words in her head.

"Rosie that was really impressive. How long have you known about your powers?" Klara asked.

"Since I was five, I guess. I was able to use my hands to warm myself and...Daisy, it got pretty cold at night. I didn't actually produce fire until a couple of years ago."

It didn't go unnoticed to Klara the hesitation Rosie had in saying Daisy's name. She couldn't understand why Rosie was being so cruel to Daisy. She had been their mother's MoChara, she had risked everything to protect Rosie. Surely that deserved some understanding.

"What did your guardians say when you told them you could make fire? I only learned about my water power a few months ago. My fake parents were horrible people and they did not seem too impressed with me. I'm really glad to be here instead." Klara hoped giving Rosie a little bit of her story would help her open up in return.

Rosie gave Klara a look that could burn metal. "My guardians didn't say much because I didn't have any. I've been on my own since I was five. I wouldn't complain about your fake parent's princess at least you had a home to go to and food on the table."

"Rosie, I don't think Klara meant anything by that she was just taking an interest—

"No, its fine Chip. You don't have to jump to my defense. I'm sorry Rosie, I was just trying to get to know a little bit more about you but clearly, that's still off the table. Why don't we get back to training?"

Chip gave Klara a hurt look but she ignored him and went to go get some new dummies.

"Yes, let's continue training but why do we need dummies? Come on Klara let's see how we do against each other. Fire versus water. Are you up for it or is it too much for you princess?" Rosie taunted.

"I don't think that's a—

Klara held up her hand to cut Chip off.

"Sure, why not Rosie. I could use the challenge."

Klara moved to face Rosie head-on. They both took a few steps back so that there was plenty of space between them.

"Ready—

Klara began but a flash of red fire was already headed her way. She lunged to the side barley missing the blow and lifted her hand shooting a stream of water back at Rosie. Rosie dodged the shot and returned it with her own. Klara felt the anger rise up in her and power coursed through her limbs she was ready this time and sent her water to meet Rosie's flame. The fire and water crashed into each other in the center of the gym and locked in place, both fighting to gain ground but neither able to overcome the other. Klara tried to increase her intensity but Rosie met her at each attempt. They remained locked in this position for what felt like ages both had sweat dripping down their faces. Klara could feel the energy draining away and didn't know how much longer she could hang on. They both were so wrapped up in their duel that neither one heard Chip yelling for them to stop. Finally, they were interrupted by a deafening roar.

Both girls dropped their hands abruptly ending the battle and stared shocked at the sight in front of them. A gigantic, menacing tiger stood in Chips place, his eyes were blazing and his growl was terrifying. Both girls reflexively took several steps back from him. He let out a frustrated sigh and transformed with a quick flourish back into the Chip they had both ignored moments before.

"What is wrong with you two? You are sisters and you are Maithars! This world needs you and you can't put your differences aside? If not for yourselves than at least for Karenia? Don't you think that woman has been through enough watching her daughter killed and worrying about the two of you for sixteen years? What about Katherine, do you think she would want this for you? You fight each other like enemies. You have no idea how lucky you are to have each other. I would give anything to see my brothers smile one more time." Chip said his peace and turned from them to storm out the gym door.

Klara and Rosie stood there in shocked silence for a few moments.

"Did he just turn into a freaking tiger?" Klara turned to Rosie.

"Yeah, …he did."

They both burst out laughing, not really because anything was funny but because everything in the past two days was too ridiculous to believe.

"Listen Rosie…I'm sorry—

"Don't worry about Klara, I'm sorry too. This is all just…new for me. Can we start over?" Rosie held her hand out to Klara.

Klara took it and noticed it was still warm from the fire that had just burned there.

"Yes, let start over. I think we should probably go find cat-boy, err…or maybe I should call him Tiger man now?"

Rosie let a smile crack on her face. "You know your jokes suck right?"

Klara laughed. "Yeah, come on."

Chapter 14

Rosie followed her sister out of the gym and into the busy hallway. Her sister...that was going to take some getting used to. Rosie had always been alone and now all of a sudden, she has a grandmother and a sister. Klara seemed alright though, she had been pretty patient with her so far considering Rosie had just tried to light her on fire. Rosie had to admit she was impressed with her sister's water power though. She wouldn't want to get caught off guard and pulled into one of those whirlpools. What was worse she wondered? Drowning or burning? She hoped she never had to find out.

"So, water power? That's pretty cool." Rosie tried to make conversation as they trekked about the academy looking for Chip. She was used to the silence when it was just her and Daisy but now it was different. She felt her throat tighten up at the thought of Daisy. She wasn't sure why she was so upset with her. Logically she understood that Daisy hadn't really done anything wrong, but her heart still felt betrayed. Daisy was the only one she had ever trusted or depended on and now all that seemed like it was a lie.

"Yep, water powers are pretty cool. I like your power too though. Fire that's brutal but very handy I bet."

Scary as well.

Rosie knew Klara had only thought the last part. Since she had arrived in Natura, she had been able to hear everyone's thoughts loud and clear. It was extremely overwhelming and was probably a big part of why she had been so temperamental. She was scared to tell anyone because as far as she could tell no one else could read minds so even in this magical, fantastic world it looked like she was still a freak.

"It's come in handy a time or two. I killed someone once you know."

Why had she just spat that out? Geez Rosie, way to bond with your sister and earn her trust she thought to herself.

Poor thing. What must have happened to her to lead to that? Rosie looked at her sister surprised by that thought. She had expected her to run away screaming.

"How old were you when you had to do that?" Klara asked.

"I was fourteen, it was self-defense. Two masked men showed up and held us at gunpoint. I took one out and D…Daisy took the other one out." Rosie said quietly.

Klara was quiet for a moment.

"You know with everything I've learned here; I wouldn't be surprised if those masked men weren't human. It sounds like something Raphe would do…send assassins after us in the human world."

She's lucky she's alive.

"I hadn't thought of that but you could be right. If they were Raphes men, they never made it back to him."

Good.

Rosie looked at Klara confused.

"What? Is something wrong? Oh no, do I have something in my teeth again? "Klara started picking at her teeth.

Rosie laughed. "No, you're just…not what I expected, that's all."

"Is that a bad thing?"

"No, I don't think it is. Hey, look—

Rosie spotted Chip sitting in the dining hall by himself.

"I should have known he would come here where there's food." Klara grabbed Rosie's arm and pulled her along.

They approached Chip and sat down in two chairs across the table from him.

"Hey Chip." Klara started.

Chip looked up from the plate of pasta he had been rolling

around on his fork absently.

"Hrhmp…so you didn't kill each other I see."

"No, we didn't do that. We came to find you so that we could say we are really sorry."

Rosie felt Klara elbow her lightly in the side.

"Oh, yeah, we are really sorry Chip." Rosie offered.

"It's not me you should be apologizing to, its each other, you don't know how lucky you are to have one another. Don't throw it away." He looked so sad. It must be awful for him to not know if his brother was alive or dead. Rosie watched as Klara reached across the table and took Chip's hand in hers.

"Chip, you are right, we know that now. We are sorry and we promise to make a better effort with each other going forward." *Please don't be angry with me Chip, I can't bear it.*

Rosie heard Klara's thoughts crystal clear. She wondered how long Klara and Chip had been in love with each other. How nice that must be to have someone like that. She couldn't help but feel a pang of jealousy. She thought she had something like that with Daisy…not the romantic part but the devotion at least.

She watched Chip and Klara the sparks flying between them.

"So, I am pretty wiped out from training, I think I'm going to head to my room. I will see you guys later ok?" Rosie thought they looked like they needed some time together and quite frankly Rosie needed some time to clear her head of everyone else's thoughts.

"Ok, see you later Rosie."

Rosie made her way out of the dining hall and back towards the living quarters.

She walked along the halls of the academy mindlessly. She was exhausted, the fight earlier between her and Klara had taken a lot more out of her then she was willing to let on. She couldn't show her weakness to anyone, not even her sister. How strange that sounded to her…sister. She knew Klara's intentions were genuine, after all, she could read the girl's mind but Rosie still felt uneasy letting her guard down with anyone. Last night with Chip had been a one-time moment of weakness. She was overwhelmed and hurting, he was there and knew just what to say so she opened up to him without thinking about it. He had such an easy way about him that she didn't even realize she was spilling her heart out until it was too late. They had stayed up talking until she fell asleep and when she woke in the morning he was there at the end of her bed, albeit as a small orange tabby cat, but he was there nonetheless. She had told him her whole life story so far and the only detail she had left out was her ability to read minds because even here in this crazy magical place it seemed like that was not a normal ability. She had spent her whole life being a freak and having to hide her true self. It looked like not much had changed for her on that front.

Rosie sighed to herself, fatigue and stress weighing on her as always but at least she had a full stomach. That was one great reason to stick around. She had never seen so much food in her life and to not have to worry about where her next meal would come from was a welcome thing. She couldn't help but think of Daisy. It stung to even say her name in her mind. How could she have kept such a major secret from her? Chip tried to tell her last night that he was forced to do the same thing to Klara but there was one major difference. Chip had no way to tell Klara in the human world. Daisy, on the other hand, knew Rosie could read minds and she had even slipped up and spoken to Rosie in her mind before. Why would she have let her think she imagined that all these years? Why wouldn't she have talked with her, everything could have been easier, different somehow if they had been able to communicate. Didn't Daisy ever think that Rosie had been lonely? Scared? Even if all they had were voices in each other's head it could have been a comfort for her. Daisy hadn't been forced to keep the secret like Chip had, Daisy chose to keep the secret and that was what hurt Rosie.

Rosie felt tears forming in the crease of her eyes but she wiped them away.

"Rosie, right?"

Rosie's path was blocked by a very perky looking girl with her hand extended out wanting to shake. Rosie recognized the girl from last night. One of Klara's friends. She held her hand out to the girl and shook it.

"Yeah, and your...Connie?"

"No, it's Kenna but that's ok, we haven't been officially intro-duced. I'm your sister's BFF. I'm a light wielder. I heard you can make fire. That's so cool. Can I see it sometime? You have such pretty hair too. Hey, I would love to style you if you want some time? We could go shopping. I know you will be needing some new clothes because it didn't look like you brought anything with you last night."

Kenna was rattling on a mile a minute it was hard for Rosie to keep up.

"I don't know if I can really go shopping with you thanks though."

"Oh no, why? Is it because you think you don't have any money? You have lots you know. Klara thought that too when she got here but your parents were king and queen and your grandma has money stashed away for you and your sister. Klara hardly spends it though she is so tight with the purse strings, I hope you won't be that way, will you? We can have so much more fun if you're not—

"I'm sorry but I'm really tired. Some other time ok."

Rosie walked off leaving Kenna in mid-sentence. Jeez, that girl could talk. She seemed really materialistic, what did Klara see in her Rosie wondered to herself. She finally reached her room, went inside and slammed the door shut behind her. When she looked up, she jumped startled to find Daisy in dog form sitting on her bed.

"What are you doing here? I don't want you here."

Daisy let out a pitiful whine.

"Did you think if you came here like that, I would forget the truth? Forget that you lied to me all these years? I trusted you and you couldn't trust me back? Just go please, I'm tired and I can't deal with this today."

Rosie opened the door and held it there. Daisy gave her the most pitiful sad dog face in the world but she hopped down off the bed and slowly walked to the door tail hung between her legs.

Rosie slammed the door behind her and leaned against it, sliding to the floor where she finally let the tears fall alone where no one would ever see. Rosie cried until she finally just fell asleep there on the floor by the door.

If she had not been so tired and distracted, she may have heard the soft whine on the other side of the door where Daisy lay and stood guard the rest of the day and night.

The next morning Rosie woke feeling refreshed. She stretched her arms and felt her head laying on a soft pillow. She must have woken up and climbed into her bad at some point last night. She rolled over and pulled the bedside drawer open. She pulled out the schedule Karenia had given her yesterday morning. Karenia had told her then that she didn't have to join in any of the classes until she was ready. She made it clear no one was forcing her to stay here but the truth was Rosie wanted to stay here and she wanted to take classes to learn about who she really was. She just wasn't going to let anyone else know that. She didn't want anyone to know how much she truly wanted all this to work. To finally belong somewhere and have people to care about. She was scared to get her hopes up.

She got out of bed and went to the armoire in the corner. Karenia had stocked it at some point yesterday and it was now full of clothing, shoes, scarves, and bags. Rosie had never had so many choices before. Her usual outfit was ragged dirty clothes that were too big or too small. Things she could dig out of the goodwill bins. She admired the clothes making a note to thank Karenia when she saw her. She chose a pair of fitted black pants and a red blouse. She had always liked the color red. She wondered if Klara had always liked the color blue or if it was just a coincidence. Rosie opened the drawers of the beautifully carved mahogany dresser and found undergarments and a small pewter box. Rosie opened it to find a selection of jewelry inside. Everything was handmade and lovely. Most of it had red or orange gemstones or had little flames patterns on it. Rosie smiled, it seemed Karenia may know her better than Rosie gave her credit for. Rosie took out a necklace, the chain was silver and it held a pendant that was the size of a dime. The pendant had an engraving of a woman with her arms stretched toward the sky and in between her hands floated a sparkling red gemstone. The woman looked powerful and free. Rosie thought it was beautiful. She put it around her neck and went to the bathroom to change.

She was running the water to brush her teeth when she thought she heard something coming from the adjoining room. Mystic had told her there was no one living in there, he assured her she would have the bathroom to herself and the privacy that went with that because she wasn't used to being around other people. He thought she would need the space to herself at night to process everything and she hadn't argued that with him. She turned the handle to the other room and stepped inside, she was met with a flash of light in her face causing her to throw her hands up and shield her eyes.

Crap.

Rosie heard a voice in her head. She stepped further in the room and the light was gone. There was a window against the far side of the wall and the sun was shining through it but the room was empty.

Strange. She could have sworn she heard someone. She shrugged her shoulders and went back to the bathroom to finish getting ready.

Once Rosie was cleaned up and dressed, she grabbed a bag from the armoire and packed it up with the strange little device Chip had shown her yesterday. It was pretty neat; she had never owned a computer or tablet or anything like that in the human world but she had seen them before. This thing seemed like it put those devices to shame though. She would have to get someone to show her how to use it. She checked her schedule and saw that she still had enough time to grab some breakfast before her first lesson.

She opened her door and almost fell over Daisy's furry body, sleeping on the floor.

"What are you doing?" Rosie asked aggravated.

Daisy got to her feet and shifted in a flash to her other form. Now the unfamiliar woman stood in her place and Rosie couldn't help but feel uncomfortable. She didn't think she would ever get used to that.

"I came here last night to tell you something but you were so tired. I thought if I came to you in my dog form you would feel more comfortable."

"There is no such thing as comfortable anymore."

"Rosie, I didn't lie to you, I couldn't tell you in the human world."

"Yes, you could have, you knew I could hear your thoughts, you spoke to me once that night we almost died. The more I think about it I believe you spoke to me when I was younger too. Tell me how did I know to call you Daisy…just a coincidence that one?"

"You don't understand, it's just not that simple—

"Whatever Daisy, I need to get to class."

Rosie turned to walk away and Daisy reached out and gently grabbed her elbow to stop her.

"I'm leaving today, I'm going home to my village to meet with the canine leader Luna and I don't know how long I will be gone but there is something I must do and I can tell you need some space from me. Perhaps when I come back you will hear me out."

Rosie looked at Daisy and stared into her eyes for a brief moment. Her eyes were the only familiar thing left. Rosie felt the hurt well up again and she turned from Daisy and walked away, leaving her standing there in the hall.

Chapter 15

As winter began to approach the academy was bustling with activity. Raphe had been suspiciously absent. He had made no further attempts to contact or capture Klara. Karenia and Mystic were certain he was unaware of Rosie as of yet but they were making preparations none the less. Added security was surrounding the academy. Klara and Rosie weren't allowed to visit the village without guards anymore. Klara understood the precautions but Rosie had voiced her objections multiple times already. It seemed to Klara her sister was determined to argue anything and everything. You could say to her; Rosie the sky is blue and she would say it wasn't. Klara found it so frustrating but she took comfort in the fact that Rosie was warming up to her slowly.

Actually, right now everyone seemed to have a slight pep in their step because the winter jubilee was approaching. Klara couldn't help but be swept up in the excitement and take advantage of the distraction from Raphe and what he was planning next. From what she could gather the Winter Jubilee was very similar to the many winter holidays back in the human world she was never allowed to participate in. Decorations were going up all around the village and people were discussing the various feasts and surprise gifts they would be giving to their friends and family. The one major difference was that here people genuinely preferred handmade gift giving and there was not even the slightest hint of consumerism. Klara had already been brainstorming on what to do for her new-found loved ones. She rattled off the list in her head of people who mattered to her now... Chip, Rosie, Karenia, Mystic, Kenna, and Dante. She was baffled at how much her life had changed. Once not too long ago that list had consisted of Chip and that was it. Now, however, the list had grown and her heart had grown along with it. For the first time in her life, the future looked appealing. Sure, there was a psychopath out there who wanted her dead or worse but it didn't matter because now she finally had a life worth fighting for. She had a real family. Even though she and Rosie got off to a rocky start, things were getting better. Rosie was starting to warm up to everyone and she was beginning to let her guard down. She had confided in Klara some of the horrors she had faced growing up on the streets and it stung Klara's heart. How she wished they could have been there for each other, how unfair it was that they were ripped apart and she couldn't even bring herself to think about Katherine, think about what might have been, the life Katherine had stolen from her before she even had a chance to live. Klara was jolted from her thoughts by the most unusual sight she had ever seen. Standing in front of her in the middle of the dormitory hallway was Dante but the bottom half of him had been replaced by talons and feathers. He had a very distressed look on his face and was hopping in place trying to...well, Klara wasn't sure what he was trying to do.

"Umm, Dante? Is everything ok?

Dante turned an exasperated look in Klara's direction.

"Oh yeah, sure, I'm just hopping around here like a feathered freak for the fun of it"

Klara approached him and grabbed on to his shirt just as he was about to topple over. She helped guide him back through the door to his dorm room and on to the chair in the corner. Klara plopped down on the floor in front of him.

"Ok, start from the beginning."

Dante slumped his shoulders and put his face in his hands.

"I woke up like this! I don't know what is going on. This is so humiliating. First, I'm the oldest student here to not have gone through the transformation and now it finally happens but it's some sort of messed up half chicken creature and I don't know how to change back. I don't want to be a freaking chicken!"

"You're not a chicken, calm down, it's going to be ok. Now how does the transformation usually happen? I haven't seen anyone go through it for the first time before? Are you sure this isn't normal?"

Dante sighed and shook his head. "Honestly Klara I don't know. Shifters don't really talk about it with each other. The knowledge is generally passed down from parent to child but my mother died when I was young and my father and I don't talk much. The only thing he ever says is how proud I should be to carry on the family line. Boy, will he be surprised by this."

Dante gestured toward his feet or rather talons.

"Why? What's wrong? I mean other than your half transformation, which by the way I think is probably not as bad as you think."

"What's wrong?!? Well, the fact that I have bird feet and not canine paws that's what's wrong. My family has always been canine for generation after generation. In fact, my family can trace its lineage back to the first canine leader. My father sent me here to the feline academy because he is already ashamed of me for not being like my brothers...strong and aggressive. I've always preferred brains to brute strength. When he sees this, he will hate me even more!"

Dante lifted a sleeve to his eye and wiped away a tear that had started to form.

"Dante, that's ridiculous! It shouldn't matter what you shift into, it should only matter what kind of person you are inside and you are one of the smartest, kindest and generous people I have ever met."

"Thanks, Klara, that means a lot, truly it does but I just don't think my father will see it that way."

Klara stood up and embraced Dante tightly.

"Well then your father is an idiot and you should tell him to go chase his tail."

Dante smiled a little at Klara's silly joke.

"Klara you know your jokes are pitiful right?"

"I know." She smiled. "Listen you sit tight and I'm going to go get Chip ok? He may not be a canine but he is a shifter and I know he will help."

"Thanks, Klara, don't worry I'm not going anywhere, I think if I try to stand again on these chicken legs I will topple over."

Klara turned and hurried out the door. She started to make her way towards Chip's room but didn't have to go far. He was headed up the stairs just as she turned the corner.

"Chip! Just who I need, can you come with me really quick?"

"Sure, is everything ok?"

"Well I'm not sure but you will have to see for yourself because I'm not sure how to describe it."

"Now I'm intrigued, Klara at a loss for words?"

She gave him a playful shove.

"Very funny Chip, I'm not that bad of a motor mouth."

Klara smiled to herself. She had become much more open and talkative over the past few months. It was like she had been silent her whole life and now someone had pulled the cork out of her mouth. For once in her life people cared what she had to say and she was no longer invisible.

"Where are you two rushing off too?" Kenna's voice sounded behind them.

She hurried up to fall in step.

"Oh. Nowhere important, listen, Kenna are you busy right now could you go find Rosie and give her a message for me?"

"Why can't you just call her on your pocket orb?" Kenna looked skeptical.

"Umm well Rosie doesn't have one yet, I would go find her myself but Chip is feeling sick so I was going to walk him down to the healer's wing."

"Ok, what's the message?"

"Ah, just tell her I won't be able to make it to our practice session."

"Yeah sure I will go find her; I hope you feel better Chip." Kenna turned and darted off towards the training rooms.

"What was that all about? I'm not sick and you don't have a session scheduled with Rosie today?"

"I know but I didn't want Kenna to follow us. Dante needs your help and I know he would be embarrassed if Kenna was there. You know he has a major thing for her."

"Really? I didn't know Dante has the hots for Kenna?"

"Wow, guys are so dense, it doesn't matter if they are human or magical cat slash tiger boys, they are still so dense."

"Hey, I resent that comment, I am not a boy...I am a man." He puffed up his chest like King Kong and beat it with his fists making Klara double over with laughter.

"You are such a dork!"

"I know, that's why you love me.... I mean um that's to say... that's why you love being around me. I didn't mean..."

"Agggghhhh." A loud bang and groan came from Dante's room interrupting Chips awkward ramble.

They ran into the room to find Dante on the floor. Now where he had earlier had two talons, he had only one and his other leg had returned to normal.

Chip rushed over and helped Dante back into his chair. Klara closed the door behind them giving Dante some privacy.

"Hey Dante, rough morning?" Chip pulled a box from beside the bed and placed it next to Dante's chair so he could sit down.

"You could say that."

"So, did you wake up like this or did it happen after you woke up?"

"I woke up like this but at first it was two legs and just before you got here one shifted back."

"May I?"

Chip pointed to the leg that was still shifted.

"Sure"

Chip lifted the leg onto his lap and began to examine it.

"Dante, I know your dad is canine but what was your mom?"

"I don't know, my father doesn't talk about her around me, I just assumed she was canine because, well you know, it's very uncommon for the races to mix."

"Yes, it's uncommon but not unheard of and not forbidden." Chip looked at Klara as he said the last part.

Klara could feel her cheeks redden. Did he mean that last part for her benefit?

"Dante, your leg appears to be avian. Are you sure your mother's shift wasn't some sort of bird?"

"I don't know, I mean I guess she could have been but I would have thought my father would have told me that."

"Me too. I mean avian shifters are extremely rare. Currently, there is only one living avian shifter in existence that I know of...."

"Morrigan." Dante and Chip spoke at the same time.

"Who is Morrigan?" Klara asked.

Chip and Dante looked at each other for a moment and then Chip answered.

"Morrigan is a shifter of legend. They say she is immortal because no one alive seems to know how old she is, but then again no one that I have ever met has ever seen her and lived to tell about it. She shifts into the form of a crow and is said to be able to see the future. Many have journeyed to her isolated lair in hopes of learning their fate but never return."

"I always thought she was just a tall tale told to kids." Dante said.

"Ah but there are many truths to be found in tall tales, my friend." Chip smirked.

"Besides, I am almost certain you are avian so now we know avians are not tall tales, are they?"

"Well, I guess not...clearly."

"Ok, Dante I want you to close your eyes and take a deep breath." Dante did as he was told, inhaling slowly.

"Now picture something that makes you happy, peaceful even. Something or someone that grounds you."

Chip was speaking to Dante but his eyes were blazing into Klara's.

"Are you picturing it?"

"I am." Dante said.

"Ok now let that feeling wash over you starting from the top of your head, down your neck, your arms, your torso…."

Klara watched Dante's posture beginning to relax as Chip spoke.

"…now your legs and lastly down to your feet."

Dante's leg rippled softly and returned to its original form.

"Ok, Dante open your eyes."

The relief washed over Dante as he looked down and saw the bird talon was gone.

"Thank you so much Chip. I don't know what to say."

"It's nothing man, listen everybody's shifting method is different but it's all tied to emotions. It's easier to shift down when you are calm and relaxed. On the flip side of that, it's easier to shift up when you are full of adrenaline, whether from fear, protective instincts or competitive natures. Understanding that makes the whole thing a lot easier."

Chip gave Dante a big slap on the back. Dante winced but Chip didn't notice.

"Listen, guys, can we keep this between us for now? I'm not ready for the whole school to know yet at least not until I get a handle on things."

"Sure Dante, secrets safe with us right Chip?"

"Right."

Chapter 16

"Hey, Rosie!" Kenna's chirpy voice sounded from behind.

Keep walking Rosie, act like you didn't hear her. Rosie was not in the mood for Kenna today. She had tried, she really had tried to like this girl. Klara loved her and Rosie whether she would say it out loud or not was beginning to love Klara. So, for her sake, she really was trying but something about this chick just really rubbed Rosie the wrong way. She was just so fake.

"Rosie! Wait up!" Kenna had caught up to her now and there was no way Rosie could pretend she didn't hear her.

"Hey Kenna, what do you want… I mean what is it?"

"Klara asked me to give you a message. She said she isn't going to be able to make the training session today she had scheduled with you."

"She must have her days mixed up because we don't have a session today but thanks for the message."

"I don't know, that's just what she said. She and Chip were headed to the hospital wing. Chip doesn't feel good. They were acting kind of strange come to think of it and…"

Rosie could see Karenia up ahead and decided she would use her as an out of this tepid conversation with Kenna.

"Sorry, Kenna gotta go. I need to see Karenia." Rosie dashed off leaving Kenna in midsentence which was not an uncommon occurrence.

Rosie reached Karenia in a flash and practically knocked the woman over.

"Rosie, my goodness. Are you all right?" Karenia reached out and grabbed Rosie's arm steadying her.

"Yeah, sorry I'm fine. I just had to escape."

Karenia gave her a slight smirk. "Well, regardless of the reason I'm always glad to have a moment to chat with you. How are things going for you?"

"Things are fine."

"Do you like your lessons?"

"Sure"

"Have you made some friends?"

"Uh-huh"

"Oh, my Rosie, you are a girl of many words, aren't you?"

"No, guess not." Rosie didn't mean to be rude she just wasn't sure what to say or not say yet. This was still so new.

"I heard from Daisy yesterday." Karenia glanced sideways at her as they walked.

"Ok." Rosie tensed up. She was still battling inside between being angry at Daisy and feeling guilty about how they left things.

"She asked how you were doing."

"What did you say?"

"I said you were doing well. Filling out now that you have some food in your stomach. Your teachers say you are keeping up in class which I was surprised to hear since you had no formal education in the human world."

"I'm a quick study. I picked up the basics in and out of my foster homes. I can read, write and do math that's about all I really needed to be able to do wasn't it?"

"Well, your teachers say you know a lot more than just the basics. They say you are well-read in human history and have a flair for science as well. Now how does that happen living on the streets?"

"I had a lot of free time, I guess. I would sometimes visit libraries because they were warm but I couldn't bring Daisy inside. The past few years these little outdoor book bins started popping up all over the place. Take a book, lend a book. I took a lot of books. I put them back though when I was finished." She added quickly. "There was one near the community college in my last town. A lot of students would put their old textbooks in there."

"I see, very resourceful of you. I'm sorry Rosie. I'm sorry you had such a hard life. I tried to find you…"

"I know Karenia, it's fine ok? It's not your fault. Its Raphes fault."

"Yes, indeed it is most definitely that sorry excuse for a living creature's fault." Karenia had a strength about her Rosie respected but she could also see her pain. It was like a cloud that clung all around her. It occurred to Rosie in that moment that she had never heard Karenia's thoughts. Her power had been on full blast since coming here. She could hear way too much all the time but when she was with Karenia…silence.

"Karenia do people here ever have any unusual powers?"

"Unusual? What do you mean?"

"Well, I've heard people talk about suaders. What exactly is their power? Can they say…read minds or something?"

"Read minds? No not at all that invasive. They can simply make a feeling grow…I suppose? The human has to already be thinking it and the suader can push it along…make it stronger."

"Why the interest in suaders?"

"No reason. Just curious."

Invasive. That's what she had said. That's what she would think, what everyone would think if they knew about Rosie's powers.

"Of course, Maithars are different you know."

A little spring of hope leapt in Rosie.

"Different how?"

"Many Maithars are empathic. Surely Klara has talked to you about this?"

"No, she hasn't. Empathic…meaning the ability to sense emotions?" Rosie knew that hopeful feeling was fleeting.

"Don't feel bad Rosie, not every Maithar has the ability. It usually goes to the first-born daughter. You girls were triplets but Klara came out first, then Katherine, then you, so technically you are the youngest."

Rosie didn't feel bad that she wasn't empathic. She felt like a freak, that she was—*invasive.*

"What's going on in that head of yours Rosie?" Karenia prodded.

"Nothing, I'm glad I'm not empathic. I don't want to feel everyone else's drama anyway." She lied.

"I didn't have the ability so I wouldn't know." Karenia said.

"Really? So, you are not the oldest daughter?"

"No, I had an older sister but she passed away early in her reign as queen. It was a hard time. Losing my sister was difficult and I was—hesitant to be queen."

Rosie could tell there was so much more behind those words but she wasn't good at this whole talking through your feeling's thing. She could barely deal with her own crap and she didn't know how to make other people feel better about theirs. That was more Klara's speed. Everyone seemed to open up to Klara. Maybe this explains why. The whole empathic thing was news to her. She wondered why it hadn't come up in conversation between them yet? They were growing closer after all but then again Klara was really good at getting people to talk about themselves and she rarely spoke about her own issues. Come to think of it, Rosie couldn't recall Klara telling her much about her own past other than that she had been raised by two Naturians. She had gathered from Chip that they were cruel to Klara but that's all she knew and she hadn't bothered to learn more. She felt a pang of guilt now about that.

"I'm not surprised Klara has that ability. It suits her." Rosie said.

"Yes, it does but it can be a difficult thing to deal with. It took its toll on my sister. Rosie—I know you have been through a lot but remember that there are many different ways in which a person can suffer inside and Klara I suspect keeps a lot of that to herself. You two need each other more than you are probably willing to admit."

"I don't need any—"

Karenia looked at Rosie and pursed her lips, one eyebrow raised.

"Alright, alright, I get it. I'm working on it ok?" Rosie shrugged her shoulders.

She really was working on it. She wouldn't go so far as to say she needed anyone. At least not out loud but she did *want* to need someone. She wanted to feel connected to people. Trust people.

"I need to get to class. I'll see you later?" Rosie questioned.

"Sure sweetie." Karenia reached over and gave Rosie a hug not really giving her a chance to accept it or not.

"If you hear from Daisy again…"

"Yes?"

"Tell her I'm fine and I'm glad she's Ok."

"You could tell her yourself you know!" Karenia called after her as she walked briskly away.

Rosie could have sworn she heard Karenia say "Teenagers" under her breath as she was walking away. She hurried down the crowded hallway, everyone trying to get to their classes and start the day. Rosie decided she was going to take a quick detour to the hospital wing and see if Chip was alright. She thought it had been odd that Klara would get confused about their training times because the schedule had been the same for weeks but if something was wrong with Chip that would definitely explain Klara being out of sorts. Unless of course, Kenna didn't relay the message right which also wouldn't surprise her as she thought the girl was an idiot anyway. She was laughing to herself when she rounded the next corner and saw Kenna looking side to side before slipping into the storeroom where all the ingredients for the elixir's class were.

Rosie continued up the hall and paused just outside the storeroom to listen. She could hear Kenna's voice in a whisper.

"I don't see any…No I am looking where you told me to and I don't see it…I'm sorry…I wasn't getting an attitude… No of course not…yes, darling you know I would…anything of course…"

Rosie tried to peek through the crack between the door and the wall. She could make out Kenna's form and she could see the soft glow of one of those light orb things people talked on like telephones. Rosie had never had a cell phone in the human and world and these little magical devices here in Natura bewildered her even more. She tried to listen closer but could not hear the voice coming from the little orb.

"I will keep looking I promise...I better go before I get caught... when can I see you again...hello?..hello?..." Kenna turned toward the door frame. Rosie jumped and continued up the hallway quickly not wanting to be caught eavesdropping.

That was strange she thought to herself. She knew that girl was up to something but what? Rosie was almost to the hospital wing when she came across Chip, Klara and Dante walking together.

"Hey, guys." She called to them.

Klara answered first.

"Morning Ro" it was one of many nicknames. This group seemed to enjoy nicknames. Tiger boy, Water Goddess, Fashion Queen, Einstein, they all changed all the time. Lately, hers alternated between Ro or Fire Cracker not that she minded it. Nicknames made her feel more a part of the group.

"You look healthy enough to me?" Rosie questioned Chip.

"Huh?" Chip looked puzzled.

"Oh yeah, the message from Kenna. Sorry I'll explain it later but yeah Chips fine." Klara gave Rosie a look that read, can't talk right now. Message received sis she thought to herself. That was another thing Rosie was starting to like too she and Klara had gotten really good at nonverbal communication. Mostly they used it for looks of *did that person just say that* or *is that person that naive* but sometimes it was handy for *can't talk in front of the boys* too.

"It's been an unusual morning" Dante said looking a bit embarrassed.

"We need some unusual. I'm so tired of being cooped up inside this place." Klara said.

"Me too." Rosie agreed. "Let's skip today. Let's just get out of here and do something else."

"I don't know if that's such a—"

"What did you have in mind?" Klara eagerly cut Chip off.

"I don't know, what about the woods behind the academy? I just want some fresh air and a change of scenery." Rosie offered.

"There are some old caves in the woods you know? I used to spend some time there before you all came to the academy when I wanted to get away from the crowds." Dante was staring down at his legs very intently as if they may disappear. Rosie looked away from him back to Klara.

"That sounds perfect to me." She said.

"Yeah let's do it." Klara agreed.

"I don't know. Karenia said we aren't supposed to leave the grounds without guards." Chip cautioned.

"First off, we aren't technically leaving the grounds, the woods are still academy property, aren't they? Secondly, we have you and Dante as our guards." Rosie winked at them playfully.

"Come on Chip. I need to get out of here and reconnect with nature. Don't you remember how much we loved our little walks through the woods back in the human world? Besides we haven't heard a peep out of Raphe in months and I really don't think he is sitting in the caves behind the academy waiting for us to randomly show up there." Klara had a good point Rosie thought.

"Still..." Chip started.

"Listen, Chip, Rosie, and I are going so you can either come with us or not but I hope you come." And with that Klara grabbed Rosie's hand and pulled her along with her towards freedom.

Chip hesitated only a moment before he and Dante came running behind them.

Chapter 17

The woods smelled divine. Klara found herself twirling around as they walked down the tiny winding trail. On either side of them were moss-covered stones that towered just above the heights of their heads making the path seem as though it were carved down into the rock. The gnarled old trees grew from the tops of the stones, and in between, them crisscrossing the path from time to time causing the group to have to climb over and under them. Flowers speckled along the edges like delicate little butterflies waiting to take flight.

"Oh, this is exactly what we needed." Klara breathed it all in deeply and ran her fingers along the sides of the stones, the soft moss cushioning her touch.

"Can you feel it, Rosie? The forest? It's like its buzzing beneath my fingers." Klara had her eyes closed as she walked. Her feet knew the path even though she had never been down it before.

"Yeah, I can feel it." Rosie answered quietly.

Klara opened her eyes to look at her sister. Rosie was walking slowly looking all around her, gently touching the flowers as they passed. Klara noticed that Rosie had the charm bracelet on that she had given her. The one from the mysterious old woman in the market. Klara smiled to herself. Rosie hadn't put it on at first but surely this was a sign that things between them were going in the right direction.

Klara looked down at her wrist where her bracelet and Katherines both sat. She had decided to wear Katherines as a way to keep a part of their sister with her. She wished so much that

Katherine could have survived along with them. That she could be walking this path with them today. All three of them together, the way it should have been. What would she have been like she wondered?

"Do you wonder what her power would have been like?" Rosie's voice broke her thoughts. Klara looked up and saw Rosie looking down at Katherine's bracelet sitting delicately on Klara's wrist.

"Yes, I do." Klara linked her arm through Rosie as they continued to walk. The boys were walking up ahead of them laughing and conversing with each other.

"I wish things could have been different. I wish she was here with us. "

"Me too."

"Rosie, I've been thinking and do you feel like there is still more that Grams hasn't told us." Klara said it carefully, not wanting to sound like she was accusing Grams of anything.

"Probably. I mean that's what adults do, don't they? Keep secrets from us for our own protection?" Rosie said the last part making quotations in the air with her fingers.

"My fake parents did. They kept everything from me but not for my good. I think it was because they just didn't give a damn. Grams isn't like that though."

"Nah, if she is keeping something from us, I think it's because she thinks it's the right thing to do. That's what my social workers back in the real world used to do. They meant well I guess."

Klara understood that sentiment. "Real-world" sometimes this world didn't feel real to her either and she knew that's what Rosie meant, they understood each other a lot more than they could really verbalize yet.

"Why do you think Raphe did what he did? I mean people here are so peaceful. How does someone like him happen?"

"I've been wondering that myself, it just doesn't all add up yet." Rosie answered.

"Hey, we're here!" Dante called back to them.

Klara and Rosie jogged ahead to catch up to them.

"I don't understand?" Rosie said looking around confused.

The path ended but there was no cave ahead of them. Only stone and trees and more stone and trees.

"I only found it by accident myself." Dante explained and he climbed up the moss-covered stones in front of them.

"I was following the path out of curiosity and when I got to the end, I decided to climb up here to sit and read when I found it."

"Found what? I don't see anything?" Chip added. One by one they each climbed up the stones following Dante and stood waiting.

Dante was leaning against a very large very odd-shaped tree that was growing from between the stones.

Dante smiled. "Let me show you, it's really cool."

He began feeling around on the tree with his hands.

"Ah, here it is." Dante pressed hard against what looked like a knot on the tree and suddenly the stones beneath them began to rattle and shake.

Chip crouched protectively near Klara and growled. "What's happening!"

Klara felt both excited and scared.

As the stones were shaking the large tree started to tilt sideways slowly. The rattling continued until the tree was completely on its side now revealing a stone staircase that lead down into the ground below.

"Amazing!" Rosie exclaimed and started straight for the staircase. Klara went to follow her when Chip grabbed her arm.

"Are you sure about this?" He asked, a worried expression on his face.

"Chip, come on don't be such a worrywart. Live a little." She dragged him along behind her.

Chip rolled his eyes at her and gave an exasperated sigh. "Dante, what's down there? Are you sure it's safe?"

"I don't actually know. I've always been alone when I came here and, to be honest, was too afraid to go inside by myself." Dante blushed a little, embarrassed.

"Chip what do you imagine might be down there the boogie

man? Come on your not afraid of the dark, are you? If so, I've got you covered." Rosie teased as she lit her palms with two small flames.

"Show off. Let's go." Chip said defeated.

Rosie lit the way and they all followed her down the dark staircase in a single file line. As they made the descent the air around them became noticeably cooler.

Klara could see her breath as she exhaled. "It sure is cold down here."

Chip shrugged off the light jacket he had been wearing and wrapped it around her. "Here take this."

Klara thought about protesting but knew she wouldn't win that battle so she just accepted it. "Thanks."

The stairs seemed to go on forever, diving deeper and deeper into the earth. It was hard to see clearly with only Rosie's fire to light the path but the stairway seemed as though it had been untouched for a very long time.

No one spoke on the way down, each lost in their thoughts of excitement for the adventure but fear of the unknown. After a good ten minutes of silence, Rosie spoke suddenly causing the group to jump startled.

"I see something!"

"What is it?" Klara squeaked.

"It looks like some sort of doorway, hang on we are almost there."

A few more steps and they had reached level ground.

"Does anyone have any diamond light with them? There is a lamp holder on this wall." Chip asked.

"Where's Kenna when you need her?" Klara joked. She thought she heard Rosie whisper something under her breath about *"Not here, thankfully"* but she wasn't sure what she heard and she didn't want to have yet another argument over Kenna and Rosie's dislike of her. She couldn't understand why Rosie couldn't just give Kenna a chance. Sure, she could be a bit chatty and overexcited but she was a good friend.

Dante was examining the lamp on the wall closely. "Chip I don't think this is meant for diamond light…I think it's meant for fire. See? There is a small well of oil in here."

"That's strange, isn't it? No one uses oil or gasoline or things like that here, right?" Klara asked puzzled.

"Well no, we have always used renewable resources only and of course things we can power with our people's different abilities. I don't even know where you could get oil in Natura?" Chip answered.

"Well, it works for me." Rosie walked over to the wall and lit the lamp with her hand. When she did the lamp came alive and the room was revealed with the gentle glow of firelight.

It was a small space, maybe ten feet long on each side, the ceiling was low and Dante with his tall stature could probably stand on his tippy toes allowing his head to touch the ceiling. There was a beautifully carved wooden door directly in front of them much like the door to the academy but much much older. The depiction of Maithar was also carved here with her arms pointed up to the heavens and there were three spaces hollowed out where the three stones were on the door at the academy.

"This looks like the door back at the academy, except someone has taken the stones." Rosie said as she lightly brushed her fingertips across the space where the red stone should be.

"Why would someone take them I wonder? Let's see if we can open it." Klara pulled on the big wooden handles but it didn't budge.

"Let me try." Chip offered but strained as hard as he could and it still didn't move.

"What the heck, we came all the way down here for nothing?" Rosie complained.

"Maybe not." Dante called from the wall near the lamp.

"There is writing here…it says *the wisdom of Maithar, a secret to share, only she may pass here, only her burden to bare.*" Dante read the inscription out loud.

"Ok so that explains who this was built for but how do we open it?" Klara was more eager than ever now. Something told her she and Rosie must enter, there were answers here she could feel it.

She looked at her sister and saw the same determination in her eyes. *We have to get in there.* She thought to herself and Rosie nodded her head. Klara's suspicions were confirmed, she had suspected for some time now that Rosie could read thoughts but she had wanted Rosie to feel comfortable enough to tell her on her own terms.

"There's more…" Dante's voice interrupted her thoughts.

"The powers of old, one green, one blue, one red, turn gold. In the unity, your pathway revealed but beware trespassers should fear for only Maithar may tread here."

"Ok so opening it has something to do with our powers. The original Maithar had all three powers, we have only two so without Katherine we can never open it?" Hearing Rosie say Katherine's name sent a little sting of sadness through her. She instinctively reached for the little green stone around her wrist, the bracelet meant for Katherine.

"Maybe it's not that literal though? Maybe we don't need to use our powers. I don't think the stones were stolen; I think they are right here." Klara held up her wrist displaying her and Katherines bracelets and reached out to hold up Rosie's wrist as well.

"Yes of course! Your brilliant sis." Rosie's excitement radiated. They both walked back to the door and gingerly took off the bracelets. Klara held up hers first and carefully fitted the small blue stone into its rightful place. As she did so it snapped into place and began to glow a blinding blue color.

"Yes, you are so awesome!" Rosie grabbed her bracelet and practically slammed the red stone into place. This time they were met with a fiery red glow.

"Klara please be careful…I don't think we will be able to go in there with you if the writing on that wall is accurate."

Klara could feel the worry permeating off of Chip and Dante as well.

She turned to him and looked into his familiar glowing orange eyes that she was so easily lost in.

"Chip, there is nothing to worry about. We are meant to find this; we are meant to go in there. I can feel it." She tried to reassure him.

"I feel the same way, it's almost like we have to go in there, there's this pull, this urge that has to be met" Rosie couldn't have explained the feeling Klara was having any better.

"Let's do this one together" Klara held out Katherine's bracelet and hand in hand they placed the little green stone into place.

They were met with a green glow and then all three stones grew so bright that they appeared golden in color. Klara and Rosie reached forward and each pulled a door handle. The doors sprung open easily for them.

As soon as the doors were open the glowing stopped and the stones fell to the ground. Rosie reached down and scooped them up, passing Klara the blue and green ones. The girls both placed them back on their wrists and stepped forward through the threshold hands clasped in each others. As they passed through, the doors slammed shut behind them blocking the boys from following. They could hear Chip and Dante banging on the doors. Klara could feel the worry coming from them.

"It's ok!" She called to them. "We are fine, I promise." The boys stopped their assault on the door and the girls turned their attention back to the adventure ahead of them.

The room was dark and Rosie lit her hands again. "Look for another torch, feel along the walls."

Klara started near the left side of the door and felt her way along the cold stone until her hands found what they were looking for. "Over here!"

Rosie approached her hands still lit. Klara wished Rosie could see herself right now. She looked so fierce walking towards her in the dark, hands-on fire, casting light into her eyes, making them glow like they too were ablaze. *I wish I had your fierceness; I wish I had your resilience.* Klara thought to herself. *It's not real if you only knew how scared I really am.* Klara heard another voice in her head, not her own but No that couldn't be right. She could not hear words only feel emotions. She was overexcited and probably just muddled her own thoughts in her head.

Rosie was looking at her with a strange expression on her face.

"Klara are you Ok? Did you say something just now?"

"What? No, I mean yes, I am ok. I'm just excited, here is the lamp lets light it and see what we've found."

Rosie hesitated a moment and then reached out to light the lamp. As soon as her flame touched the device it spread across the walls instantly lighting lamp after lamp until the whole room was revealed.

The room was large and open. The ceiling was high but roots from trees growing in the world above were dangling down, reaching for the lake that seemed to engulf the whole floor of the room in front of them. The giant pool of water rippled softly from some unseen source. The landing they were currently standing on was merely large enough to encase the doorway and access to the lamp they had previously lit. If the girls had fumbled around in the dark any further, they would have easily fallen into the deep pool. Large stepping stones started at the edge of the landing and led many feet out to the center of the lake where a structure stood. It was hard to make out exactly what was inside from where they stood but the outside of the structure was a combination of stone and wood.

"Well, that looks interesting." Rosie stated.

"Do you think it's safe?" Klara could hear Chips warnings in her head like little alarm clocks you tried to ignore.

"I think we are meant to go there, and I think we can handle anything that's waiting. I mean it's a big pool of water, that shouldn't scare you of all people, right?" Rosie countered.

"No water doesn't scare me but the thought of drowning does." Her mind brought up the terrified face of Mallory gasping for air that wasn't there.

"Klara, I don't think that can happen. If your power is anything like mine then it can't hurt you." Rosie said matter-of-factly.

"Wait what? Your fire can't hurt you? I mean I know it doesn't hurt your hands where you control it from but surely it would burn you if you say tried to walk through it or something?"

"Nope, it doesn't. I've tried it. After what happened at my foster home, I was pretty messed up. I had killed someone and the one person I thought loved me thought I was a monster. My head was in a really bad place. I had been on the run, just trying to get as far away as I could. I had been hitchhiking a lot and one night I had been riding with an old truck driver. He was nice enough but he was a complete drunkard. He ended up pulling the truck over at a rest station because he couldn't drive any further and he passed out. It was cold and rainy so I decided to stay in the truck and wait until he woke up. I was wallowing in my guilt and feelings about everything and made a stupid decision to start drinking his bottle of brandy. I had never had a sip of alcohol in my life so of course, it didn't take much to set me over the edge. It's all very hazy, I remember Daisy barking at me a lot, she kept trying to nudge the bottle away from me. At some point, I got out and locked her in the truck. The man had been kind to her and in my drunk, muddled brain I thought he would take care of her if I were gone. I took the bottle with me and went into the bathroom at the rest station and lit myself on fire. I thought I deserved to feel the pain that I had caused. "

"Rosie, it wasn't your fault, you were defending yourself. You didn't do anything—

Rosie held her hand up. "I know that now, really I do, I've come to terms with what happened. The point of my story though is that it didn't work. The fire burned, I lit up like a birthday candle but after it burned out, there wasn't a mark on me, not a single one, it didn't hurt, it didn't do anything to me. Since then I have experimented in all different ways, never again to hurt myself mind you. After I sobered up, I realized how stupid I had been. I've not touched a drop of alcohol since and never will, but I have played around, testing myself with fire, sometimes fire I've made, sometimes fire that was already there but none of it hurts me."

"That's crazy, so you are essentially fireproof?"

"Yep, guess so, and I'm willing to bet you are waterproof so to speak."

"Well, I don't really want to find out today." Klara said. "I think I will still watch my step on these stones."

"I could just push you in and we can find out?" Rosie reached out like she was going to shove Klara and Klara squealed.

"No, you better not!"

Rosie laughed. "I'm only teasing." And she gave Klara a playful nudge on the shoulder.

"Yeah yeah tease all you want, let's just go." Klara smiled at her sister and then stepped toward the stone pathway.

The girls carefully stepped from stone to stone with no issues. The stones were spaced conveniently. They were large and pretty flat making it simple to balance on them.

They reached the shore of the little island in no time and were now standing face to face with the enchanting structure. It was truly beautiful and ancient-looking.

Klara gazed up at it in awe. The wood and stonework were so delicate, it looked as though it took centuries to carve it all there. The structure consisted of four tall columns. Each column was a combination of stone and wood that seemed to twist together as if it grew that way. The patterns carved into each were a variety of decorative flowers and animals but there were also some symbols there that Klara didn't recognize. Another language perhaps. The four columns held up a roof also made of stone and wood but gold detailing could be seen all along the edges of it. More roots and vines were cascading out of the earth above and dived down through the structure and into the water's edge. It all looked very magical and mysterious.

In the center of the structure stood a wooded pedestal, it reminded Klara of the podium the principal at her school in the human world used to speak during school assemblies, except this one, was much prettier.

Klara and Rosie approached the pedestal, the moment their feet touched the floor of the structure something amazing happened. All the roots and vines around them came to life. They began encircling the structure, weaving in and out and around until the two girls were cocooned inside. The inside roof of the structure was alight with thousands of tiny stars brightening the inside of the cocoon making it shimmer and sparkle all around them.

"It's so beautiful." Rosie said softly.

Klara wanted to answer but couldn't seem to form the words so she just nodded her head in agreement.

They circled the podium until they reached the other side where they found a book laying on top of it. The book cover was made of tree bark and the binding was vines. It had that same depiction of Maithar on the cover and above her, the three little stones shone brightly.

Klara ran her hand over the top of the book and it jumped at her touch. She withdrew her hand startled and the book flew open the pages flipping quickly on their own. As the pages settled to their chosen spot blinding golden light shown from the center of the book causing the girls to shield their eyes.

A voice rang out. It was the most pleasing sound Klara had ever heard in her life, it was like her ears were being wrapped in pure love and joy.

"My children, my precious beautiful ones, let me show you our truth, let me show you our path, let me show you our purpose and our duty...come with me my little ones.... into the past...."

The light began to brighten even more and the girls were forced to close their eyes. They felt the air around them begin to swirl and their hair was whipping back and forth as if in a current.

"It's ok Klara, Rosie, Open your eyes, my children."

Klara opened her eyes and gasped. She was no longer in the little cocoon underground. She looked to her sister and saw Rosie's eyes were as wide and shocked as hers. They were standing in a meadow. The sun was shining down on them, a million different butterflies all varieties of colors were fluttering all around them. Flowers filled the meadow as far as the eye could see and the smell was intoxicating. It was like they were in a dream and in the middle of it all, stood the most breathtaking creature Klara had ever seen. She was a woman but she wasn't. She looked as though she were made of the earth and the sun and the wind and the water and the fire all in one. It almost hurt to be in her presence it was so overwhelming. She was pure light and power and joy.

"Come closer, there is no reason to fear me girls" She held her arms out to them. As if in a daze they both went to her and let her encircle her arms around them.

"My darlings, I know your path has been hard so far, it hurts me to see my children suffer but I must prepare you for what is coming. You know who I am don't you, young ones?"

Klara broke the embrace and spoke first. "Yes, we know who you are, you are Maithar aren't you? Mother Nature?"

"Yes, I have been called many things over the eons but you are correct and you also understand who you are to me right my loves?"

It was Rosie who answered this time. "You are our like great great great great great times a lot grandmother."

Maithar laughed and it was like little bells, her smile as radiant as a sunset.

"Yes, a great many greats dear one."

"Why have you brought us here Maithar? Do you bring all of your descendants here?" Klara wondered if Grams had done this and if so, why hadn't she shared it with them?

"No, my darlings, dark times are upon our precious world and it will be up to you to save it. I speak not just of Natura but of the human world as well. All the creatures of this earth are special and blessed. It will be up to you girls to unite them against the darkness."

"Do you mean Raphe? The man who killed our mother and sister? Is he the darkness your talking about? That horrible excuse for a man?"

"He may have been a mere man once but he has been consumed by an evil as ancient as myself. To understand this, I must explain our past to you." Maithar waved her hands and they were all transported once again. The scene in front of them played out and they were like invisible watchers passing through it.

"Long ago when the earth was still young, new and pure all the creatures of the earth existed in harmony, living off the earth but respecting it at the same time. I walked among the people then, helping the fields to bloom and the waters to run. Many seasons came and went and all was well but there is a balance to the earth and to

all life that cannot be forgotten and where there is light there must also be darkness. The sun and the moon. The night and the day. The warmth and the cold. I am the peace and the joy upon the earth to help things bloom, grown and nurture all things. Thus, there is also a being that is the scourge upon the earth, that wants nothing more than to see all things wilt and wither away into darkness. This creature has no name for it is nothing but emptiness and evil but make no mistake its power is strong and it feeds off of hatred and anger. The more our worlds fight each other and destroy our earth the stronger it becomes."

"So, are you saying Raphe is not a man he is this creature?" Rosie asked.

"Just like I can no longer walk the earth neither can this scourge. It must have a host to house its powers. It seems Raphe has become that host. He may have been just a man once but now he is consumed by this creature."

"Well, couldn't one of us just be your host? Then you could fight him and put an end to all of this?" Klara asked. The thought of something taking over her body was frightening even if that someone was Maithar but the thought of fighting Raphe as this scourge was much more terrifying."

Maithar reached out and stroked Klara's face. *"Oh, how brave and selfless you are to offer yourself in that way my darling. I wish I could bare this burden for you. I truly wish I could fight it myself but as I am made from love and respect and purity, I cannot violate a living being that way, even a consenting one. It is against nature to take away free will from a creature and I can never go against nature, I am nature."*

"How can we fight him? How can we defeat pure evil? We are just kids? We don't have your power and one of us has already been killed by Raphe or the creature or whatever. He's taken Katherine from us already." Rosie said.

"All hope is not lost little ones. I may not be able to help you in the way you have requested but I will be able to help you. Listen closely, children. There are three temples of power. This one here in Natura in which you have found is the water temple. There is a fire temple in

the human world and an earthen temple in the Meadowgate. Travel to each of these temples and collect my powers hidden there, once combined with your own you will have the power to defeat Raphe and the creature. I must leave you now but remember my precious ones all is not lost. That which was taken from you will return and I am always with you...."

"No, wait! Maithar don't go we have so many more questions! Maithar!" Klara scrambled forward trying to reach for her but she was gone and they were once again standing in front of the little book on the podium.

"Look..." Rosie pointed towards the water; something was glowing blue beneath the rippling depths.

"I think you need to go get it Klara; I think it has to be you. It's a water temple after all you can do this." Rosie encouraged.

"Ok. Ok. Deep breaths. I can do this. I can do this." Klara focused on the water in front of them. She imagined its cool refreshing feel on her skin and dove in headfirst. She felt the water all around her and started swimming towards the light. It was a lot further than she thought it would be but she kept swimming anyway. She was holding her breath and could feel the pressure starting to build, that desire to exhale consuming her. Rosie hadn't been burned by the fire so she had to let go and trust that the water wouldn't hurt her. She closed her eyes and exhaled expecting to feel the water come rushing into her nose and mouth but it didn't. She opened her eyes and saw that a small orb had formed around her form-fitting and so close to her skin that it was almost invisible. She inhaled and exhaled and realized she could breathe normally. The rush of relief flooded over her and she started kicking harder, swimming towards the light. When she reached it, she put her hand out to grab it and it glowed brightly then floated toward her bracelet and settled itself into the small blue stone. Klara felt its presence there and turned to swim back to the surface.

She reached the top and climb out onto the little platform by the door. Rosie had already made her way over and knelt down beside her.

"Are you ok? Did you get it?"

Klara lifted her arm to show Rosie the little bracelet. "It's inside the stone, it just kind of merged into it when I got close."

The doors behind them swung upon with a bang and the boys were standing there waiting. Klara was bombarded with their feelings of relief.

"What happened? Are you ok?" Chip was in her face the minute she passed through the doors.

"We are fine, really Chip. Everything is ok I promise." He hugged her and held her close a little longer than was normal and she felt her cheeks begin to blush. Klara wiggled free from him and looked him in the eyes. "We really are fine. It was amazing actually. We met her, we met Maithar. The Maithar."

"Incredible, are you serious?" Dante moved closer now.

"Hey guys let's get out of here, we can talk about it on the way back but I'm starving, aren't you?" Rosie was holding her stomach.

"Yeah me too." Klara suddenly realized she was also famished.

The group made their way back up the stairs and out into the open air. The afternoon had disappeared on them and the sun was low in the sky now, dusk approaching. Crickets were starting to wake and sing their songs.

"…she told us where we could find the temples, or at least what world they are in but honestly I don't know how we can find them. One is in the human world. Well, the human world is a pretty big place. That's not much to go on is it?" Rosie was finishing up the story of what had happened in the temple. Relaying the info to Dante and Chip.

"We could talk to Grams or Mystic, maybe they know where the other temples are?" Klara suggested.

"That's a good start. I think it may be worth checking the library as well. There are some ancient texts there that talk about Maithar's origins. There could be some info there too." Dante added.

"Ok after we eat why don't Rosie and I go talk with Grams, Chip you speak with your dad and Dante you get started in the library and then we can all meet there later?" Klara suggested. They all agreed and headed towards the academy and towards the dining room to silence their growling bellies.

Chapter 18

"**I** can't believe you actually spoke with her." Karenia sat down shocked on her chair in the plush comfortable room Rosie had grown very fond of.

Rosie and Klara had filled their bellies with Chip and Dante in the Dining room. Much to Rosie's dismay, Kenna had found them and before Rosie could stop her Klara had relayed the whole adventure to Kenna in great detail much like they were now doing for Karenia. Something inside Rosie had screamed at Klara to shut up and not tell Kenna a thing but how could she have justified that. So, she sat fuming and frustrated while Kenna oohed and ahhed over the whole thing and then whined that they had left her behind.

Now they sat telling Karenia who was taking it all in with unwavering attention.

"The stones opened the doorway?"

"Yes, and Maithars water power now lies in my blue stone." Klara handed the stone over to Karenia who examined it closely.

She held it in the palm of her hands and closed her eyes. "Yes, I can feel the power there. Astonishing."

"Klara where did you get these bracelets?" Karenia asked.

"The first day I came here there was an old woman in the village square selling her trinkets. I stopped to admire them and she gave me these bracelets. It was a strange interaction she grabbed my hand and said something about strength and the light?" Klara sounded frustrated. *What did she say?* Rosie could hear

Klara thinking to herself.

"I remember now! She said *Though there is strength in the one, only united as three can the answers be found, and the light set free.*" Klara had practically yelled it at them.

"There it is again the power of three, united as three, three temples, but we are no longer three. We are two now. How can we defeat Raphe without Katherine?" Rosie said.

"I don't know, but we have to try, don't we? We owe it to Katherine and our mother and father and the people we are meant to protect. You heard what Maithar said. The creature wants to swallow the world and plunge it into nothingness. We can't let that happen." Klara sounded so sure of herself. Rosie wished she felt the same.

"I know, I know, I do but I'm still afraid we just won't be strong enough without Katherine." Rosie was biting her bottom lip and sitting on the sofa next to Karenia.

"So, it wasn't really Raphe who did all this? He was taken over by this creature?" Karenia's face was unreadable. Rosie tried to read her thoughts but she had never been able to with Karenia. It was like there was a barrier there. She hadn't really minded. The silence was refreshing when they were alone together. It was beginning to be like that with Klara too. She was reading her thoughts less and less, lately, they only seemed to come through in moments where Klara was over-emotional, excited, scared, angry that kind of thing. Maybe she was losing the power. That wouldn't bother her a bit. If she couldn't read minds then she wouldn't be a freak anymore.

"I wouldn't go that far. I mean Raphe must have had a pretty dark side for the creature to choose him as a host don't you think?" Klara stated.

"He was a good man once. I really think he was...once..." Karenia was far away now, lost in memories.

"Is there something you're not telling us Karenia?" Rosie was suspicious now. "Why in the world would you of all people have any compassion for that bastard?"

"I don't...of course I don't. It's just once your mother and I both believed him to be a good man and it's hard to accept that we could have been so wrong." Karenia looked away as she spoke.

Klara and Rosie looked at each other both wondering what secrets Karenia still had locked away but the mission at hand was more important right now.

"So, have you heard of these temples? Do you know where they might be?" Klara asked.

"I don't but I know someone who might. If anyone knows where they are it will be her." Karenia stood now, the wheel turning in her head.

"I will make arrangements for us to go pay an old friend a visit. We will leave first thing in the morning. Bring Chip and Dante with you." Karenia said.

"What about Kenna? If we ask Dante, Kenna will be hurt." Klara interjected.

Karenia considered this for a moment and Rosie noticed the indecision. Maybe she wasn't the only one who had hesitations about Kenna.

"Chip must come because he is your MoChara and well I didn't want to talk to you girls about this yet until I spoke with Dante but I was hoping he would agree to train as a MoChara for Rosie. I know he hasn't made the shift yet but he is the son of the Canine leader and as Chip is the son of the Feline leader it seems a fitting alliance to have. With the current situation being as dangerous as it is Rosie should not be without a MoChara."

"What about Daisy?" Rosie said her voice catching in her throat a little.

"It was Daisy's idea. She was your mother's MoChara, she stepped up for you out of love for your mother but she was not bonded with you so she began aging the moment your mother died. No shifter can be bonded to another and as she will continue to age. She will not be able to protect you forever and she should be free now to live her second life. She went to speak with Dante's father to seek out a replacement for you and this is what they came up with. I know you are angry with her Rosie but she cares for you very much and wants to see you safe." Karenia reached out and took Rosie's hand.

"I…ok I'm open to the idea of Dante as my MoChara, he's a good friend and a clever person." Rosie was genuine in saying that about Dante but she felt a sting of regret about Daisy. A part of her had thought maybe they would work things out and everything would go back to the way it was but that was naïve of her and she shook the thought out of her head. She would not show her pain, not now, not while Klara and Karenia were counting on her to step up.

She noticed Klara staring at her, sympathy in her sisters' eyes. She looked away.

"Come on let's go tell our friends the plan and get to bed I have a feeling we have another long day ahead of us tomorrow." Rosie and Klara said goodnight to Karenia and headed back to the library where they had agreed to meet up with the boys.

"There is something she's not telling us about Raphe" Rosie said matter of fact.

"I agree, I sensed it too. She will tell us when she's ready I think." Klara answered.

"Listen, Rosie, about Daisy—

"No, I don't want to talk about it ok. I'm fine."

"Ok well let's talk about something else I've been meaning to bring up."

"Sure, what's up?"

"You know you can tell me anything right Rosie?"

Rosie shifted uncomfortably. "Yeah sure I know"

"Well you know how I can sense people's emotions; I think you can do something too can't you?"

Oh no, she knows, she knows I'm a freak. Rosie thought to herself. She felt the panic rising up inside her. She was finally settling in here she couldn't bare the thought of it all falling apart on her.

"You're not you know…a freak" Klara said softly. She stopped walking and grabbed Rosie by the shoulders forcing her to face her.

"You're not a freak. You can read minds, that's a gift, it's an amazing gift."

"You can do it too? You can read thoughts?" Rosie asked, scared to hear the answer.

"I couldn't before today. I've been able to feel emotions for as long as I can remember and I started to suspect a few weeks ago that you could read thoughts. You've slipped up a time or two and answered me when I hadn't said things out loud. I figured you just weren't ready to share yet, I didn't realize you thought it was a bad thing, I just thought you wanted to keep it to yourself for some reason. Then something happened in that temple today. I felt more powerful than I ever have and now it seems I can read your thoughts, but only your thoughts. I've tried it on the others already."

"It's not a gift, it's a curse. Hearing what people really think about you is terrible." Rosie felt relieved that Klara knew and didn't seem to care but she didn't share her sister's enthusiasm about the ability.

"Once you learn to control it, it won't be so bad, you can learn to turn it off and on like I do with the emotions. I can try and help you if you're not ready to tell anyone yet. Mystic taught me a lot and maybe it will help you too."

"Ok, I'm up for that. I would love to be able to turn it off and leave it off." Rosie said dryly.

"You might feel differently about it after you learn to control it."

"Yeah maybe."

Rosie stopped Klara before she could pull the door to the library open.

"Don't tell them yet ok? I'm just not ready."

"I won't, I swear but you've got this ok? You're the toughest person I know." Klara squeezed Rosie's hand.

The library was a creature all in its own. It seemed alive in that diamond light glittered all over the ceiling and isles. Illuminating row after row of all manner of literature. It was an impressive collection. Some books were older than the academy itself. Older than Rosie could even really process. She had spent a significant amount of time here since Klara had shown it to her.

Klara loved to copy volumes into her Keepie but Rosie preferred the feel of a book in her hand and had fallen asleep in the cozy arms chairs here many times.

The library consisted of two levels, the bottom level containing all volumes pertaining to or from Natura. The top-level had a limited selection of human literature and several rows of volumes that were off-limits to everyone except Maithars and of course the historians who cared for the library. The same deep natural tones of wood and earth that decorated the academy continued in this room yet it somehow had a more fairytale feel to it than anywhere else. It smelled of paper and dust but it was lovely nonetheless.

The girls found their friends huddled together at a table in the backmost corner of the first floor. Dante had several stacks of books piled around him already and he was lost in them. A look of determination on his face. Chip and Kenna were whispering quietly to each other next to him.

Klara and Rosie headed in their direction but were interrupted by the historian on duty. She was a short stout woman with a warm smile and stunning curly brown hair. Her eyes had the glow of a feline shifter that was common to see at the academy.

"Klara and Rosie, my sweet Maithars. So nice to see you tonight. If you need anything please let me know ok girls?"

"We will thank you, Mrs. Bell."

"Hey guys, did you find out anything?" Rosie asked the group.

"Sorry, my dad didn't know anything." Chip shrugged his shoulders.

"I haven't found any mention of the temples anywhere either. Sorry." Dante closed the book in front of him with noted frustration.

"Karenia didn't know anything either but she seemed to think she knew someone else who might. She wants us to leave in the morning." Rosie found herself staring at Dante. What would he think of Daisy and his father's plan about being her MoChara? She supposed he would be honored, everyone at the academy believed that being a MoChara was the greatest honor that could be bestowed on a shifter. She wondered if it would change the way he looked at her now? The only thing she had to compare it to was Klara and Chip. Their relationship had moved past friendship whether they could admit it or not. It could never be that way for Rosie and Dante. He wasn't her type, not in the least.

"Wonderful an adventure!" Kenna squealed and clapped her hands together.

Rosie rolled her eyes. "No cheerleaders allowed."

Klara elbowed Rosie in her rib cage.

"What Rosie meant to say was, unfortunately, Karenia said we can only bring Chip and Dante."

Kenna's face fell into a pout. "But why does Dante get to go and I don't? Does Karenia hate me or something?"

Rosie couldn't stand the girl's whinny voice another minute.

"Ugh, no Kenna calm down. Chip goes because he is Klara's MoChara and Dante goes because apparently, the adults have decided he will be mine." Rosie instantly regretted spitting it out like that. She knew she should have spoken to Dante about it privately first but she had just wanted to shut Kenna up.

Everyone's eyes turned to Dante and he had never looked more like a wide-eyed, shocked owl than he did now.

"Wait-t-t...she wants me...t-t-to be your M-M-MoChara?"

Klara sat down next to him and put a hand on his shoulder.

"It's a great honor, Dante. Daisy and your father felt no one was more suited than you to be Rosie's MoChara."

"No! I can't. I won't. I'm not the right person." Dante stood up and rushed out of the library leaving the group with jaws dropped.

"Umm Ok. Well, I feel pretty crappy about that now." Rosie knew she didn't break the news in the best way but why didn't Dante want to be her MoChara? Did he think she was a freak and was only nice to her because of Klara? Yes, that must be it. She felt tears welling up in her eyes and she tried to push them away.

"I'm suddenly really tired. I will see you guys in the morning." Rosie fled the room just as quickly as her would-be MoChara had.

————

 "He will come around. He's just scared he can't do it. You know how much Dante doubts himself." Kenna said softly. "He would make a great MoChara."

"You should tell him that Kenna. It would mean a lot coming from you." Klara said.

"Nah, it would mean more from you I think Klara, you being Maithar and all. I'm just a friend."

"Oh, for Pete's sake Kenna don't you know by now he's got it bad for you?"

Chip laughed.

"What? No, he doesn't."

"Yes, he does, he's had a crush on you forever, he's just too scared to say anything. Plus, he's scared you will reject him since you are always crushing on other guys."

"I'm not really though, I don't really like anyone that way. I just like to flirt and have fun. I never really thought about Dante like that till now." Kenna smiled to herself. "I think I will go find him."

Kenna hurried out of the room.

"Well, Klara you sure know how to clear a room quickly." Chip teased.

She laughed. "Come on let's go to bed. Something tells me we may not be getting much sleep in the next few days."

Chapter 19

elp me…I'm here…

Klara woke up covered in sweat. She had tossed and turned all night again. So much for getting a good night's sleep, she thought to herself. The dreams were happening more and more frequently. She would wake up with a sense of foreboding, and a feeling that there was something important she should remember but she could never hang on to the dream. The minute her eyes opened the dreams would slip away leaving her uneasy. Uneasy and tired. Then other times she would dream of Raphe murdering her parents and sister. Either way, she would wake with a horrible headache.

Klara yawned and stretched her arms. Who knew when she would be back at the academy and have access to a healer again? The search for the temples could take a while. She made up her mind that it was time to go see Brian in the hospital wing, maybe he had a tonic or something to help her. The last thing she wanted was to be off her game with the threat of Raphe looming over everyone's head. Who knew when he would make his move? Grams and Rosie were counting on her to be at her best and she couldn't bear the thought of letting them down.

Klara got out of bed quietly so as not to disturb the sleeping orange kitty boy at the bottom of her bed. She took a quick shower to wash off the sweat of yet another restless night and got dressed for the day. She observed herself in the mirror for a moment and smiled. She had changed quite a bit. Her hair had a shine to it that wasn't there before and her body had begun to firm up from all the training. She looked strong and healthy but what was better is she felt strong and healthy and capable. That was a new feeling for her and she liked it. Now if only she felt that confident when it came to Chip. Her feelings were undeniable to her now. She was falling in love with him but she was terrified of the thought. She knew he cared for her but in a way, one cares for their little sister or something. He was her MoChara and he took that very seriously but anything beyond that Klara just couldn't see happening. She looked over at him still sleeping soundly his fur rippling softly as he breathed in and out. She let out a soft sigh and slipped out of the room as quiet as a mouse.

It was still early yet and there weren't many people out and about. Even though the academy was huge it felt so homey to her now. Everywhere you looked there were signs of life and community. It was so different here in Natura. People just inherently trusted each other. Doors were left unlocked, belongings left out in common areas. People here didn't steal or destroy things. They respected each other and valued meaningful moments with each other over material things. Although this way of life was so foreign to her it seemed to fit her like a glove. She could honestly say that although she was in more danger than she had ever been in by being here in Natura, she had never felt safe crazy as that sounded.

She smiled to herself as she entered the archway that led to the hospital wing. The large sterile-looking room was empty. Beds lined both walls, separated by curtained partitions. The room was a mish-mosh of Natura and Human world objects. Monitors with all the bells and whistles you would expect in a human hospital but then shelves of shimmering tonics and brews Klara had grown accustomed to seeing in Natura.

Klara took a seat in a chair near the front of the room. She figured someone would be along soon so she laid her head back against the wall and closed her eyes to wait.

As she lay there, she became aware of hushed voices coming from behind a door to the side of the room. Klara stood and walked over to the door intending on knocking....

"We can't, it's not right." A female voice pleaded.

"Can't you see what's not right is you being trapped and treated like less than you are?" Klara recognized the second voice to be Brian's. His voice cracked as he spoke and he sounded distressed, angry even.

"Brian, I know you mean well but you can't save me, no one can."

"Fine, save yourself! You are a strong, incredible woman, free yourself from this. I have stayed silent for too long. I know you know how I feel for you. I can't deny my feelings but even if they are never reciprocated, I still would want to see you happy and free from him."

The woman was crying now. Klara felt guilty for listening but exchanges like this did not often happen here and she just couldn't help herself. If someone was in trouble maybe she could help? At least that's what she told herself so she felt better about standing there eavesdropping.

"Brian, please stop, I can't leave him. I am his, he owns me. There is no changing that. There is so much you just don't understand." The woman was sobbing now.

"Katie, please don't cry love. I can't bare it. Tell me the truth, I want to understand. I know if you went to mystic or Karenia, they would help, they would understand."

"No, please promise you won't say anything...please! You have to swear it." Her voice was full of panic.

"Calm down Katie, your hands are glowing, I promise I won't break your trust, you know that."

"I know, I know. Just hold me for a moment. I know we shouldn't but just a moment."

Klara could hear the woman's muffled sobs now.

"Shh, it's ok. I'm here. I will always be here."

The gentle sound of a kiss. Klara stepped closer and tried to peek through the crack in the door.

Brian held the small frame of a woman in his arms. She was breathtakingly beautiful. Long flowing brown hair, she was dressed in a delicate purple fabric that draped around her like a cloud, she was fairy-like and as fragile as a porcelain doll.

The kiss grew heated, desperate, Brian's hands went to Katie's waist pulling her closer to him. Katie wrapped her arms around his neck and melted into him. Klara exhaled deeply and stepped quietly from the door. She walked back to her seat and laid her head back against the wall.

Who was this Katie and what kind of hell was she trapped in? Klara didn't know Brian very well yet but she trusted the feelings she felt from the forbidden couple in that room. Brian was exuding frustration, love, fear, anguish for Katie and Katie was dripping with pain, guilt, fear, and love for Brian. Klara wondered what the story was? She was not quick to judge. Yes, she disapproved of someone cheating on someone else. This woman was clearly married but it also sounded like there was a lot of drama going on. How awful it would be to be trapped with someone you didn't love.

The door swung open breaking Klara's thoughts.

Katie immediately noticed Klara sitting there and her eyes grew wide. Brian, his attention still fixed on Katie followed her line of sight to Klara.

"Ah, Klara! I'm so sorry to keep you waiting, I didn't realize you were out here." Brian quickly distanced himself from Katie and walked over.

Katie stared at Klara for a moment before fleeing from the room.

"So, my friend, what brings you here today?" Brian tried to divert her attention and led Klara over to a chair next to what she assumed was his desk.

"I haven't been sleeping very well for a few weeks now. I keep having these disturbing dreams and I wake up covered in sweat with an awful headache. Brian, I don't mean to pry but who was that woman?"

"She's just a friend of mine. What kind of dreams?"

"That's just it. I don't know. They slip away as soon as I wake up. It's so frustrating and exhausting. I'm afraid it's starting to affect my training sessions. Do you have a tonic or something that can help me sleep?"

"I do have some very effective tonics and I am happy to give you some but that will only put a Band-Aid on the problem so to speak. I am more concerned about what these dreams are and why you are having them. I find that many dreams, especially recurrent ones are usually important."

Klara chuckled. "Band-Aid? Do you even have those here?"

Brian smiled. "Yes actually, we do. I spent some time in the human world and found that many of their advancements in medicine are effective and useful. Mystic has been gracious enough to allow me free reign of this clinic to incorporate the best of both our worlds. I don't actually like using band-aids much but the children like them, especially the colorful ones."

"Yeah, I noticed when I walked in here that it looks a bit different from the rest of the academy."

Brian stood up and walked over to one of the shelves and retrieved a shimmering grey tonic.

"This should do the trick. It will help you rest at night. One drop for the headaches in the morning and two before bedtime to help you sleep. This vial should last you a few weeks. Drinking too much could cause you to go into a deep sleep that could last for days so do not abuse it. Also, I want you to go see Sabine this afternoon. I think she may be able to help you with deciphering your dreams. You should be able to find her in the tall tower on the cliffs behind the academy."

"Thank you, Brian but I'm actually leaving with Karenia today, perhaps when I get back, I can go see her." Klara took the vial and stood to leave.

"Yes of course. Klara, out of curiosity, how long were you waiting here?"

Klara felt nervous and a bit guilty. She knew he was trying to tell if she had heard or saw anything.

"Oh, not long at all. Thanks again!" Klara darted out of the room before he could question her further.

She was in such a hurry to get out of there that she slammed smack into Chip.

"Ow! What's the hurry water goddess?" Chip grabbed hold of her to keep her from falling down.

"Chip! Oh my gosh sorry, I wasn't paying attention."

"Were you coming out of the hospital wing? Is everything ok?"

"Yeah, it's no big deal, I've just been having trouble sleeping lately."

"That's not normal for you. I seem to remember you sleep so deep that you snore quite loudly. Sometimes you drool too."

Shocked Klara looked up at him to find him fighting back laughter.

"You're just messing with me Chip! I don't drool!"

"Well, maybe not but you do snore. Luckily house cats don't sleep much at night. I used to watch you and just listen to the rhythm of your breathing."

"Um ok, creepy much?"

Chip shrugged his shoulders.

"Yeah I guess so but I was a cat for so long I didn't pay too much attention to politeness anymore. So, what did Brian say? About your lack of sleep?"

"He gave me a sleeping tonic and wants me to go speak with Sabine in the tower."

"Really? So, you are having bad dreams as well then?"

"I guess I am but I can't remember them, just the feelings they leave with me. So, who is this Sabine? Some kind of psychiatrist or something?"

"No, not exactly. She is more of an interpreter or a guide. She can help you sort out your innermost thoughts and feelings but in a much deeper way than a psychiatrist could."

"Sounds interesting. I may go see her when we get back but we have bigger problems right now."

"Agreed, I hope you don't mind but I went ahead and packed your bag. I know how you love to procrastinate with those sorts of things."

"What? I don't procrastinate.... Ok well, maybe I do." She laughed.

"I got a message from Karenia this morning. She wants us to meet her in Mystics office and then we will all head out." Chip led the way towards Mystics office and Klara caught up beside him.

 Chip do you know a woman named Katie? Long brown hair, really really pretty and delicate looking?"

"The only Katie I ever knew was your aunt but you will want to ask Karenia about her because I will not speak of the horror she committed." Chip said coldly.

"What!?! So, I have another family member and Karenia didn't think that she should tell me this?" Klara was shocked and quite frankly pretty pissed too.

"Well, she was just here…meeting with Brian."

"That's interesting. I'll be honest Klara I don't know much about her or her relationship with Karenia but I don't think they could be very close after what she did."

"What did she do?" Klara was so tired of getting just bits and pieces of the story all the time.

"Klara sometimes people make choices out of fear. Not everyone has an iron will like you but Katie made a very very bad choice. However, it's something you really should talk to Karenia about."

Klara thought about what she overheard and the feelings she felt coming from Katie. There was more to that story she was sure of it.

A piercing scream came from the direction of Mystics office.

"What was that?" Klara's pulse quickened.

"Nothing good. Let's go!"

They ran as quickly as they could and reached the office door at the same time as Mystic.

"I heard it too." Mystic said as he shoved open his office door.

Klara gasped.

On the floor in front of them, Rosie was crumpled over a lifeless Karenia.

"Help her! What's happened? She's not breathing!" Rosie was panicked.

Klara rushed to her side and grabbed ahold of Karenia, shaking her desperately.

"Karenia wake up! Karenia what happened? Wake up! You have to wake up!"

Mystic had already sent Chip after a healer and was now kneeling beside Karenia with a vial in his hand. He poured it over her forehead and it spread out all over her body in a thin shimmering cocoon.

"This will protect her until help arrives. She is not dead but she is very close." Mystic said.

Brian came rushing through the doorway.

"Move aside please." He pushed past Klara and Rosie and began working quickly.

His hands hovered over her body, their gentle glow scanning her.

"Is she going to be ok Brian? Please say she is going to be ok?" Rosie pleaded.

For a moment Brian remained silent, his eyes closed while his hands did their work. He paused when he reached the area near her heart. His eyes finally opened and he looked intently at Chip when he spoke.

"She's been poisoned. I don't know by what yet but Mystics' quick thinking has stabilized her for now. I will need to figure out what the poison is and see if there is an antidote. Help me carry her to the hospital wing."

Klara reached forward intending to help lift her grandmother.

"No, do not touch her!" Brian reached out and blocked her hands. "We do not know what or how she was poisoned and we cannot risk another Maithar coming to harm. If the toxin lingers on her skin you could be at risk."

"I don't care, and besides we have both already touched her when we found her like this." Klara gestured toward Rosie. It was that moment that Klara noticed how incredibly silent Rosie had become. Her sisters' eyes were hard as stone and Klara felt no emotion coming from her. She searched her thoughts, reaching out, probing.

"Stop. I can feel you. Just stop."

Klara stopped abruptly and turned her attention back towards the room. Chip had lifted Karenia into his arms and was following Brian out of the office.

Klara went to follow but was blocked by Mystic.

"I think you should leave." He stated roughly.

"What?" Klara couldn't process what he was saying. She just wanted to go with Karenia and be by her side.

"Clearly someone has access to the academy, I do not think you are any safer here than you would be out there at this point. I think you should still follow the plan Karenia has put in motion and you should seek out the other temples. It is clear to me that you two will not be safe until you have found a way to defeat Raphe. None of us will be safe."

"No, we can't just leave her."

"Why can't we Klara? There is nothing we can do to help her here. We need to go." Rosie broke her silence.

"But—"

"But nothing Klara, we are no good to her here. Let Brian do his job and we need to go do ours." Rosie said coldly.

Mystic took Klara's hand. "I know this is hard but there are times when you as a Maithar must put the good of Natura before your own needs. If this were Karenia and you were the one in that hospital wing, as much as she does love you, she would not hesitate to finish the mission set before her."

Klara wiped the tears from her eyes and set her shoulders back, she took a deep breath to calm herself.

"Yes, I know you are right. I'm sorry I forgot myself for a moment. I was thinking like a granddaughter instead of a leader."

"No one would fault you for that Klara." Mystic squeezed hand before letting it drop. He walked over to his desk and picked up his keepie.

"Here is the information you will need to begin your journey. You will find contact information and maps for the people Karenia had planned to reach out to. There are three names on the list. I am not sure which of them Karenia believed had information on the location of the temple but each name must be of importance for her to have written them here."

He reached for Klara's Keepie and scanned the information to her, then did the same for Rosie.

"It is also a good idea for you to memorize the information because your Keepies will not work where you are going."

"Wait? Where are we going?" Rosie grabbed the keepie and looked down at the list.

"Oh great." She said.

"What is it?" Klara was scared to even ask.

"We are going back to the one place I think you and I both would agree we never want to go to again."

"The human world." They both said in unison.

Chapter 20

Rosie walked quietly behind the group. They were making their way out of the village. Mystic had shown them a path through the woods behind the academy that would allow them to leave hopefully unnoticed. The group was uncharacteristically quiet with everyone worried about Karenia and the threat of a spy in the academy. Kenna had caused a bit of a scene when they left whining again that she couldn't go with them. Klara had coddled the girl and calmed her down. Just watching them interact was enough to make Rosie sick if she hadn't already been feeling raw from this morning's events. Rosie felt numb. This was the story of her life, wasn't it? The minute things seemed like they were going her way it all gets torn to shreds. She had finally let her guard down and was feeling safe with Karenia. Dare she say she even felt loved by her. Hell, she had started calling the woman Grams when they were alone. Then here comes the universe charging in to take it all away.

She saw Klara break away from Chip's side to linger back. She wished she wouldn't. Her sister had been showing her concern since they left. She felt her trying to read her thoughts, trying to pry into her mind but she just wanted to be left alone. She was better alone. It didn't hurt as much.

"Rosie, you ok?"

"Yeah, I'm fine."

"I don't think you are. You can tell me you know? I'm worried about her too."

"I said I'm fine." Rosie felt a twinge of guilt as Klara's eyes welled up a little.

"Ok if you say so." Klara scurried back to where Chip and Dante were walking ahead of them.

It's not that she wanted to hurt her sister. She just couldn't let herself be sucked in any further into this fantasy world of family and friendship.

"So, what's the plan?" Dante asked.

"Well, we have three names and addresses here. All of them in the human world. I guess we should just work our way through them and see what happens?" Chip asked Klara.

"Do you recognize any of the names on here Chip?" Klara asked her voice still lined with hurt.

Rosie looked away from them to the forest. It was so beautiful here, so peaceful and yet here they were headed right back to the last place on earth she ever wanted to go to again. The dense trees with their branches spread wide above their heads forming a canopy looked as ancient as time itself. Everything in Natura looked like that. Like it had been there since the dawn of time, there was something comforting in the very air they breathed here. Rosie did not long for the polluted air of the cities and towns back home. At least she had something to offer the group though. Rosie knew her way around the streets, had fended for herself for so long. She would undoubtedly be able to help when the got there. Where was there anyway? She hadn't bothered to look at the list yet. She pulled her Keepie out of her bag and read over the three names:

Dr. Camille Hardeson
University of Georgia
Department of Ecology

Rosemary Swanson
318 Riverbend Court
Santa Rosa California

Armando Varella
Ave. Indepencia
Tlaxcala Mexico

Rosie studied the names hoping something useful would pop out at her but it didn't. She knew nothing of these people. She had spent a significant amount of time in Georgia so she knew that the University of Georgia was in Athens. Home of the infamous Bulldogs that all Georgians were obligated to adore or you could not call yourself a Georgian. She had also spent some time in California but not Santa Rosa. As far as Mexico went, she had nothing to offer. She had picked up a little Spanish over the years but not enough to be useful.

"—I agree. That's a good a place as any to start." Klara said.

Rosie had drowned out the conversation going on in front of her and decided she better catch up to them if she wanted to know what was going on.

"Sorry I didn't hear you...where to first?"

"Chip was just saying that there is a crossing into the Meadowgate not far from here and it puts us very close to a portal leading to San Francisco California." Klara offered.

"Ah Ok yeah that's not too far from Santa Rosa where this Rosemary Swanson person lives. Sounds like a plan to me." Rosie forced herself to sound enthusiastic. Just because she was choosing to not get further attached to Klara and the rest of them didn't mean she had to be mean to them either. She could fake it for their sake.

Klara smiled at Rosie's noted change in attitude.

Guess it's working Rosie thought to herself.

"How will we get past the border patrol? They will surely be on the lookout for Klara and Rosie now." Dante asked.

"I've been thinking about that and I have an idea but it may seem a bit crazy." Klara offered.

"So, when I was in the water temple, I had to dive under the water for a very long period of time. It seems that I can breathe under there. What if I use my powers to form a sort of air pocket around the three of you and we all walk at the bottom of the river to cross into the Meadowgate? Do you think it could work?"

"Can you do that? Form an air bubble around all three of us?" Chip asked.

"I think so, I mean ever since the temple I just feel so much more connected with my powers. I really think I can do it."

"Ok any objections to Klara's plan?" Chip asked Rosie and Dante.

"I'm willing to try it." Rosie said.

"That leaves you, Dante." Chip pushed.

"I um well that's to say I—" Dante was stuttering and looking down at his hands which he was nervously twisting together. "—I can't swim."

"No one is looking for Dante, what if he just crosses?" Rosie tried to come to his aid.

"No, I have to stay with you, Rosie. What kind of MoChara in training would I be if I left you? It's ok I will figure it out." Dante squared his shoulders.

Huh, whatever Kenna had said to Dante last night about the whole MoChara thing must have had an impact. Rosie thought to herself. It still didn't change that she couldn't stand Kenna though.

"You should be ok Dante; it won't really be like swimming because you will be able to breathe. It will be like walking through water that's all." Klara said.

"It's ok I can do it. I was just having a moment. I'm sorry." Dante said stiffly.

"Hey man, it's not a crime to get scared sometimes." Chip clapped Dante on the shoulder as he spoke.

"Right because a scared MoChara really instills confidence in his Maithar." Dante mumbled.

Rosie didn't think anyone else heard him. Dante put too much pressure on himself. She had grown fond of the idea of him as her MoChara before everything that happened this morning but now that was just one more bond that could hurt her later so she wasn't going to encourage it either.

Rosie felt a twinge of guilt again. She knew if Chip was feeling this way Klara wouldn't hesitate to encourage him and tell him how much confidence she had in him but that was Klara not her. Klara could build people up, make them feel special and important. Rosie didn't know how to be that way and didn't desire to be anyway. Maybe, just maybe one day after Raphe was defeated, if Raphe was defeated, she could be a different person. The type of person Klara would be proud to call sister and Dante would be honored to call Maithar to MoChara. That day might never come though, and for now, she would just stay detached. Build her walls back up, she was good at that.

"The river should be just past that ledge there." Chip pointed.

The group walked briskly until they reached the riverbank. The water was flowing but calm and crystal clear. You could see all the way to the bottom.

"Umm Klara I'm not sure this will work. Look how clear the water is?" Rosie stared down at the water, you could see all the stones lining the bottom of the riverbed and all the little fish darting about.

Klara stood observing the water silently.

"What if—" Klara spoke to herself as she approached the edge. She lifted her hands slightly and at first Rosie didn't see anything happening. There were no jets of water coming from Klara, but she could feel the buzz of magic around her like she always did when either of them tapped into their powers. Then suddenly she saw the river picking up pace. The once calm and tranquil waters started to ripple and wave, picking up speed. The little fish darted about erratically, confused at what was happening to their little haven. As the water became choppier, the stones at the bottom were obscured. Now all that could be seen was the white foam of the rushing waters.

"Well, I think this should work right?" Klara turned to them with a triumphant smile.

"Quick thinking there, water goddess." Chip beamed, clearly proud of his Maithar.

"Ok now for the hard part, I think it will be easier if everyone huddles together, as close to each other as possible. The river isn't very deep, it looks to be maybe 4 or 5 feet down so we will have to hunch down on our hands and knees to stay submerged."

Klara directed everyone to climb down into the rushing water. Klara and Chip entered first and Rosie followed. The water was cool but not freezing and the pull of the rushing water was pretty strong. Rosie had to focus not to lose her balance. Dante was still standing on the riverbank hesitant.

"It's ok Dante take your time." Klara coaxed.

Dante stepped carefully into the water and waded over to the rest of them. He was holding his breath.

"Don't forget to breathe." Rosie whispered to him and he exhaled.

"Ok, everyone, get as close to each other as you can and on the count of three go under ok?"

They all grabbed a hold of each other and huddled in close.

"One...two...three!"

Rosie shoved herself down under the water and into a kneeling position. The rocks were hard and smooth under her palms and they hurt her knees as she tried to press her weight down. The water was strong and the current was trying to force them forward. Her lungs were still full of the large breath of air she took in and her body was trying to float its way back to the top. She could feel the pressure building in her lungs and the need for oxygen was feeling urgent. She opened her eyes and the sting of the water blurred her vision momentarily but then she could see her friends clearly around her. Poor Dante's eye looked truly panicked but he was holding his ground.

Just when Rosie though she couldn't hold her breath a moment longer she felt the water around her drain away suddenly and she let out a desperate breath. She was rewarded with fresh cool air to breathe in again.

"Wow, it really worked." Klara sounded surprised.

"You mean you weren't sure it would?" Dante sounded shocked.

"No, I mean I thought it would work but I thought it may take a few tries first I guess?" Klara motioned them forward. "Let's get moving though because I'm not sure how long I can keep it up."

The group crawled forward together, careful not to break the barrier of air around them. The water was pulling them in the direction they needed to go so it wasn't too difficult to move forward other than the rocks pressing into them. The air bubble around them somehow was helping to anchor them to the bottom so their bodies weren't working against them trying to float back up to the top now.

It was a strange sight to see. Rosie looked around her and could see the fish swimming next to them.

"It reminds me of this aquarium I went to once in the human world. It was our 6th-grade field trip and the aquarium had this tunnel you walked through that was glass all around and above. It was really neat; you could see all the coral and sea life like you were walking on the bottom of the ocean floor or something. This isn't as colorful but it still reminds me of it." Klara reached a hand into the water towards a small little silver and blue fish. Instead of it fleeing from her, Rosie could swear the little fish almost leaned in towards Klara's hand let her stroke it. "It's funny, I was normally a very shy student, always trying to blend in and become invisible, but that day at the aquarium I remember feeling empowered and happy. I asked so many questions, I was so engaged, my teachers probably didn't know what to think. I guess I felt the power of my waters even then but didn't realize it."

"Yes, I'm sure that's what it was. Don't you remember our favorite spot in the forest behind the house? Anytime you were upset that's where we went to escape. We would sit in the sun next to the little stream. You have always felt the pull of the water. Me, however, as a cat, I can't see the appeal." Chip shifted uncomfortably.

Rosie chuckled. She hadn't noticed that Chip looked almost offended to be in the water.

"How much further do you think we need to go before we are safely across?" Dante asked.

He still looked very nervous but he was trying to hide it, Rosie could tell. She didn't read his mind though. This morning, Rosie was so upset, scared and angry that when they had been all standing there arguing over whether they would still go on the trip or not she became so overwhelmed with everyone's thoughts she thought she would scream. She did scream, in her head anyway and she screamed and screamed so hard that she felt like something broke. A wall had come up and suddenly all the thoughts were gone. Everything was silent and the thoughts hadn't come back. She hoped they wouldn't, she hoped she had broken them permanently.

"I don't know, what do you think Chip? We have gone about a mile now wouldn't you say?" Klara asked.

"Why don't I peek out first and see? Hang on." It was more of a statement than a question and Chip had already broken away from the bubble to have a look.

They could still see Chips lower half in the water as he crept further down the river and back again scouting out the area. He dipped his head back into the water and then popped into the bubble.

"All clear, let's go."

Dante didn't have to be asked twice, he broke from the bubble and climbed out of the river in record time. The rest of them followed and soon they found themselves back on solid ground.

"Well, that was interesting." Rosie said as she tried to squeeze the water out of her shirt.

"Let's take cover in the trees, just in case any border patrol guards are close by." Chip suggested.

The sun had begun to set and it would be dark soon. Karenia had intended for them to leave early this morning so presumably, they would have made it to the human world before dark but with everything that happened, they were late heading out.

"So, it's going to be dark soon, should we try and find somewhere in the Meadowgate to make camp or should we try and cross the portal at night?" Rosie asked.

"I feel safer making camp here. We have our full powers here and Chip can shift here if needed. Once we cross back into the human world, I'm not sure how reliable our powers will be?" Klara looked concerned.

"Ok, that's fine with me. I never had trouble using my powers there but I'm in no hurry to get back so camping here works for me." Rosie added.

"Chip what do you think?" Klara asked.

"I follow your lead Water Goddess, always." He smiled.

"Yes, but is it what you would have suggested?" Rosie could hear the uncertainty in Klara's voice. So, her sister wasn't as confident as she seemed these days.

"I would have suggested the same but I do think we should go further into the forest and find somewhere to camp." Chip pointed toward where the trees began to grow thicker and closer together.

The group slipped away quietly into the dense foliage, wet and cold but hopeful.

Chapter 21

"Any changes?" Mystic asked as he took a seat next to Karenia's bed in the medical wing.

"No, I'm sorry Mystic. I've been able to identify what was used to poison her, however." Brian handed Mystic a small vial of thick black liquid.

Mystic studied the vial. The liquid inside was slimy and disgusting in appearance. There was something malevolent about it and he handed it quickly back to Brian, wishing it to be out of his touch.

"What is it?"

"I can't be entirely sure but It looks like some sort of Tar residue. You will recall that during part of my training as a healer I spent some time studying human medicine. While working in a hospital in the human world I was able to observe some of their more dangerous habits. Many humans enjoy using tobacco in an unhealthy manner. They take something nature has created and they turn it into an abomination by smoking and inhaling it. It creates a toxin when used this way and the toxin often builds up in the smoker's lungs creating a sort of tar that can cause cancer and many other ailments. This substance resembles that toxin but in a much more concentrated way."

"So, are you telling me Karenia has lung cancer?" Mystic asked shocked.

"Yes and No. Whatever this toxin is, it is so potent that when she consumed it, it started to shut down all her organs instantly. Your quick thinking with the stasis shield is the only reason she is still alive. The toxin has spread through her body and attached itself to her heart, lungs, kidneys, liver, and brain. The shield has frozen it from doing further damage but if I remove the shield she will die in a matter of seconds."

"Can you remove it, detach it somehow?"

"I am trying to find a way. If you'll come with me, I'll show you what I'm working on."

Brian led Mystic into the room adjoining the clinic that held all of his research equipment. Mystic never felt comfortable here surrounded by all of this technology. It was so foreign so unnatural but he trusted Brian and Brian felt strongly that there was some merit to some of the human technology. If Brian felt that these things could be useful to his people then Mystic indulged him.

"As you can see here, I have infected this bovine heart with the toxin."

Mystic held a hand to his mouth to keep from gagging. There on the table was a cow's heart surrounded in a stasis field. The organ was still beating.

"Where did you get this Brian?" Mystic asked appalled.

"I'm sorry Mystic I know it is a gruesome sight but a necessary one if we wish to heal Karenia."

"Yes, but Karenia would never wish for an animal to come to harm for her benefit, it goes against everything we stand for in Natura."

"Oh no you misunderstand, I did not harm this animal, it died of natural causes. I have an arrangement with Gilem the dairy farmer. I tend to his animals when they are ill and in trade, he allows me to use what I need for research from his animals who die from natural causes that I cannot heal. Old age or sickness beyond my healing abilities. The animal does not suffer in any way. As soon as the moment of death is upon it, I use the stasis field and remove what I need. When possible, I heal the organ just enough to use it productively."

"Ok, I still don't love the idea but I am not a healer and I am not the farmer. If you and he believe that the animals do not suffer and this is necessary than I trust your judgment on such matters."

"Thank you. So, as I was saying I have infected the organ with the toxin but so far every attempt I have made to remove it cause's it to shut down instantly."

Brian held his hand over the heart and used his power to heal. The tar began to recede off the organ for a moment but then quickly came back spreading worse than before.

"Hope is not lost though. There is something I wish to try. It is extreme and risky but if it works…"

"What is it?"

"There is a treatment used in the human world. Under normal circumstances, I would call it barbaric and ineffective. They use a harsh chemical to eradicate the cancer. It is called Chemotherapy. Of course, normal cancer here in Natura is rare but when it does occur, we healers can use our power in combination with some healing tonics to rid the patient of it so we would never even consider using something as unnatural as chemotherapy. In this situation though I think it is the only thing left to try. I would need to use so much of it though that the treatment itself may kill Karenia. I am hoping that the moment the chemo eradicates the toxin, I can then use my powers to heal her from the effects of the chemo but I can't be sure."

"Ok, what do you need to do it?"

"I will need to make a trip to the human world, I can use some of my old connections there to get what I need." Brian hesitated a moment. "Also, I will need someone else to come with me and I don't think you will like who I suggest."

Mystic looked questioningly at Brian. "Who?"

"Karenia's daughter. I need Katie."

Chapter 22

"You're shaking." Chip reached out and rubbed his hands up and down Klara's arms. His touch lit her on fire and the cold she had been feeling was gone instantly. She felt herself blush and pulled away.

"We all are cold; we need to find a way to dry our clothes," Klara said.

They had found a perfect spot to make camp. Deep in the woods, they came across a thicket. The bushes had grown together and served to camouflage the little hideaway. It was large enough for them to sit upright but not to stand. It was long enough that the four of them fit comfortably although they were in very close proximity to each other. They were all shivering from the wet clothes and the cool night air.

"Here I can dry our clothes just pass them all to me." Rosie held her hand outstretched and gave Klara a sly smirk.

Did she mean for them to strip down? In front of each other?

Chip and Dante had already pulled their shirts off and handed them to Rosie. Both boys shimmied out of their pants and sat there in nothing but their boxer shorts.

"Here line everything up on this branch here and I will get to work." Rosie started draping the clothes over the branch. She then pulled off her own shirt and pants and sat there in her bra and panties like it was no big deal.

"Klara?" Rosie smiled at her. She glanced over at Chip but he wasn't paying her any attention he was instead focusing on the food he and Dante were attempting to put together for them.

"Umm yeah ok." Klara quickly slipped out of her shirt and pants handing them to Rosie. She wrapped her arms around her body trying to cover herself from view.

"Just like wearing a bathing suit." Whispered Rosie.

"I don't wear bathing suits that look like this." Klara snapped. Rosie laughed.

Klara wished she had Rosie's confidence. There she was sitting in nothing but her underwear and it didn't seem to faze her in the least. Of course, Rosie didn't have feelings for someone in the bushes with them only two feet away.

She watched Rosie set to work using her glowing hands to dry the clothes hanging up. She wished Rosie would hurry up before Chip noticed her.

Klara felt a warm, sort of energy suddenly forming. She looked over a Chip again and this time he was staring at her intently. His orange eyes burning a hole right through her. She sensed his emotions loud and clear. Hot, nervous desire. Klara felt pressure building up in her throat and she swallowed. She tried to look away but her eyes were stuck there staring back at him.

"Ahem…Here you go, Klara." Rosie's words interrupted them and Klara saw that her sister was handing her pants back to her. Klara grabbed them and quickly slid them back on followed by her shirt.

"Quit staring at her you pervert." Rosie said sternly.

"What? Oh, no…I'm sorry. I didn't mean to. I—" Chip fumbled with his words.

Rosie laughed hysterically. "Oh my god, calm down, I'm only joking."

"What's so funny?" Dante had noticed them all now.

"Nothing, nothing just these two weirdos." Rosie handed everyone's clothes back to them.

"So, what's on the menu." Rosie changed the subject.

"Klara, can you add a little water?" Dante handed her four small cups.

"I didn't pack any water because I assumed Klara could make it when we need it and that was one less heavy thing to lug around." Dante offered.

"Good idea." Chip held his cup out to Klara and she filled it with water. She proceeded to do the same for each of them.

"Now Rosie if you wouldn't mind giving us all a little heat." Dante asked.

"Sure." Rosie took each of their cups in between her hands and heated the contents up. Soon they all sat eating their soup and the warm broth warmed the chill Klara had been feeling. Now that she was warm and her stomach was no longer screaming at her she began to feel the exhaustion set in. Her eyes began to droop and she felt her head start to fall forward slightly start-ling herself.

"I'm tired, I think I'm going to go ahead and get some sleep. Should we take shifts keeping watch?" Klara asked.

"I'm wide awake so I'll go first, I'll wake one of you in a few hours." Dante offered.

"Ok works for me." Rosie lay down on the ground and curled herself up into a little ball closing her eyes.

Klara thought she looked so tiny in that moment curled up like that. So petite and helpless but Klara knew how untrue that was. Rosie was far from helpless. She turned to find that Chip was already laying down next to her.

"Here, lay down you don't need to lay your head on the hard ground." He held his arms open to her and motioned for her to lay her head on his chest. She hesitated.

"Or would you rather I shift? I'm sure my cat form would make a great soft furry pillow." He was teasing her.

"Ha-ha, cat boy." Klara snuggled in close to him and let her head rest on his warm chest. She could feel his heartbeat under his shirt and his pulse was racing. He pulled her in close and wrapped his arms around her.

"Goodnight my water goddess, sweet dreams." He kissed her gently on the top of her head.

She wanted to savor this moment. Laying there in his arms but she was so tired that she couldn't force herself to stay awake a moment longer and soon she had drifted off into oblivion.

∞∞∞∞

"No!!!" A woman screams, clutching her infant to her chest. She sends a desperate surge of water towards the darkness. Black tendrils snake through the air, thick like tar, absorbing the water and passing on to claim its victim. It wraps around the man first, he struggles to break free, the tendrils expand and squeeze, suffocating him, tightening as he struggles. The woman reaches for the basinet, desperate to get what's inside but she's too late. It takes her feet first, trapping her, a fly on glue paper. The blackness slowly consumes her, she's forced to watch as it oozes over the helpless infant embraced in her arms. "Please do what you will to me but spare them, I beg you!" Her pleas fall unanswered. One last scream pierces the air...followed by a hollow, malevolent laugh...

"Klara! Wake Up! It's just a dream! It's ok wake up!"
Klara opened her eyes and grabbed Chips outstretched arm.
"What...where am I? What happened." She felt disoriented, confused. She looked around and saw her friends concerned faces staring at her. It all came rushing back. They were in the woods in the Meadowgate, in a thicket, in Chips arms.
"You were having another nightmare." Chip's voice sounded worried.
"You were screaming." Rosie added.
"I'm sorry, I didn't mean to scare everyone." Klara sat up and held her hand to her head. The headache that followed her dreams came as sure as the sun sets. She reached into her bag to retrieve the tonic that Brian had given her.
"What is that?" Rosie asked.
"That's Narmium, isn't it?" Dante said.
"I don't know what it's called but Brian gave it to me to help with the headaches and help me sleep, in all the excitement last

night I forgot to take it. I'm sorry I disturbed everyone."

"Klara, that's strong stuff, are you sure everything is ok? These dreams what are they about?" Chip watched as Klara uncorked the vial and took a single drop of the tonic.

"Sometimes they are about the night my parents were killed, and sometimes they are about—"

"What? What is it?" Rosie asked.

"That's just it…I don't know. The other dreams leave me when I wake up but I'm left with this nagging feeling that whatever it is…it's important." Klara was biting her bottom lip, trying to make the dream come back to her but she just couldn't grasp it. It was always right there just out of reach.

Help me…

She shook her head. "Anyway, they are just bad dreams, let's not waste any more time on them then we already have." Klara began gathering her things. "It's dawn now so why don't we go ahead and head out if that's ok with everyone?"

They all made sounds of agreement and after a few minutes of shuffling around and scooting out of there little makeshift camp, they were back on their way.

"So why didn't anyone wake me to take a shift last night?" Klara asked.

"Yeah me either?" Rosie added.

"Dante did most of the night, he didn't wake me until maybe two hours before dawn." Chip stretched his arms and arched his back as he walked.

"Yeah, I just couldn't sleep, I figured there was no sense keeping someone else awake if I wasn't going to sleep anyway." Dante looked worn and worried. Klara had noticed that Dante had been looking pretty rough for a while now. She knew he was dealing with a lot. He was still having trouble with the shift and wasn't sure what was going on there. Now he had the added pressure of being Rosie's MoChara. She knew Kenna had spent time with him last night and from the brief conversation, she had had with her before all hell broke loose this morning she knew Kenna told Dante she knew he liked her and she wouldn't mind going out some time, Klara suspected that had a lot to do with his newfound confidence and acceptance of MoChara status. She was happy her friends had a chance at love, they would make a cute couple but she was a little jealous too. She wished she had the courage to just tell Chip how she felt.

"You should tell him, you know." Rosie whispered in her ear.

Klara started and then glanced back to see if Chip could hear them. Luckily, he and Dante were busy goofing off a few feet behind and well out of earshot. They had found sticks and were using them as makeshift swords. They looked like two little boys playing around. Klara rolled her eyes. "Stop listening to my thoughts, Rosie."

"I wasn't, I don't have to read your thoughts to know what you were pining away about. You always get the same sad look on your face when you are thinking about your forbidden love." Rosie drug the words out for dramatic effect.

"So, you think it would be forbidden too?"

"No, I was just teasing you. I don't see why it would be? Have you asked?"

"Of course not, how would I do that. Hey, Chip is it against the rules for a MoChara and a Maithar to date? Why do you ask Klara? Oh, I don't know because I've been in love with you for months now?"

Rosie laughed. "Sure, why not ask it just like that?" What are you so afraid of?"

Klara shrugged her shoulders. "I don't know."

"He feels the same, you know." Rosie said softly.

"Did he tell you that?"

"No, but I know it."

"Sometimes, I think I know it too but I'm just scared that if I say it out loud, everything will change."

"It could change, who knows but isn't it worse to never know what you could be to each other?"

"Since when did you become such a romantic Rosie?"

"Ha, I'm far from it. I have an idea." Rosie stopped and waited for the boys to catch up.

"Hey Chip?"

Klara felt her heart leap into her throat. Oh my god is Rosie about to tell him?

"What are you doing." Klara said through her teeth.

Rosie ignored her. "Are MoCharas and Maithars allowed to hook up?"

Chip looked at her and then looked at Klara and then back at Rosie.

"Uh...why do you ask?" He was nervous. *Crap Crap Crap, Klara was going to kill Rosie.*

"Well, I was thinking that Dante here is kind of a hottie and I don't know maybe I want to keep our options open?" Rosie reached over and elbowed Dante in the side playfully.

Klara felt the panic start to subside but poor Dante looked like he might have a stroke.

Chip's eyes were huge. "Well, uh, it's not exactly against any rule or anything—"

Klara felt hope spring up.

"—but it's not exactly encouraged either."

"Oh, and why is that?" Rosie sounded genuinely disappointed.

"The whole aging thing makes it complicated. The Maithar will age the MoChara will not, at least not until the Maithar dies. So, relationships could get difficult that way I suppose."

"Sorry Rosie, I'm already seeing someone but I'm very flattered that you are interested." Dante was fifty shades of red.

"Let me guess? You are seeing that twat, Kenna?"

"Rosaline!" Klara said.

"Yeah Yeah sorry. I mean that's great Dante...I'm sooooo happy for you and her royal highness Kenna. I guess I missed my chance with your tall sexy self." She winked at Dante and he walked a little faster. Chip gave them both another odd look and went to catch up with Dante probably to talk about how strange girls are.

"What the hell was that?" Klara exclaimed.

"I know I know Kenna's your friend blah blah blah."

"No... I mean yes, Kenna's my friend but what was that? Saying you had the hots for poor Dante."

"Oh, I knew he already has it bad for Kenna so I figured it was a good cover to ask the question without Chip knowing it was for you. Besides I wasn't lying Dante is a cutie, I wouldn't mind getting my hands on him for a minute or two." Rosie gave Klara a sly smile.

"Your terrible."

"I know but that's why you love me." Rosie reached over and wrapped her arm around Klara's waist.

"He said it's not encouraged." Klara whispered.

"He did…but he also said it's not forbidden, so there's hope."

"Yeah…hope."

Chapter 23

It took every ounce of self-control Brian had not to run towards Katie when she arrived at the academy. Mystic had lost it at first when he told him it was Katie, he needed to bring with him but after much debate and insistence his old friend had given in.

Desperate times call for desperate measures he had said. Mystic had no idea how right that statement was. Brian planned to solve more than one mystery on this trip. He would hopefully be able to help Karenia and also save Katie in the process.

Katie was walking towards them now. Ever the beautiful ethereal creature that she was. Long flowing hair that almost floated around her as she walked. Brian could lose himself at the sight of her. He had always considered himself a logical man…a man of medicine had to be after all. The minute he met Katie though all that disappeared, he found himself daydreaming about her when they were apart. The more time went by the more risks he took to try and be close to her. If he didn't know any better, he would say she had cast a spell on him but if she had he didn't care. He had to save her, he had to be with her no matter what it took.

"You took a great risk summoning me here Mystic." Katie's sing-song voice was like soft bells.

"Yes well, it was not my idea. Brian insisted that you and you alone were the only one who could help him."

"Yes, you mentioned that someone important to me was in peril?" Katie was looking into Brian's eyes now. He saw the worry there, the fear.

"Yes, it's your mo—" Brian began.

"Wait. How do we know you won't just bring this information right back to your *beloved* husband?" Mystic said with disgust.

"I will not, you have my word, but I cannot guarantee he doesn't already know. His spies are everywhere. Even here."

"Is your word supposed to mean something to me then?"

Katie's eye welled up with tears. "It did once my friend."

"Do not call me friend for I trust you not. That was lost to us long ago but I do trust Brian and so I will leave you to it." Mystic turned from them and left the room.

As soon as they were alone Katie ran into Brian's arms.

"What were you thinking my love? Every time I come here; we risk him finding out. He doesn't watch me like he once did but he is not a stupid man Brian." Katie took his face in her hands.

"I know, I am sorry darling but it's your mother, she is dying and I need your help to save her."

"What…where is she can I see her?"

"Yes of course" Brian led Katie into Karenia's medical room.

As soon as Katie saw her mother she ran to her bedside.

"Mother…no…please no…I'm so sorry…"

The tears were pouring down her face like raindrops.

"What happened? What's wrong with her?"

"She's been poisoned."

"That bastard, he swore…he swore to me that if I did as he said he would spare her."

"He is vile, you know this, it was only a matter of time before he broke his word."

"Yes, I know and he is more dangerous than ever. He is desperate now that my nieces have returned."

"Niece's? So, he knows then about Rosie as well?"

"Of course, he knows…not much happens in Natura that goes unnoticed by him. You and I…we have been tempting fate…he thinks me weak and broken and so he hasn't watched as closely as he should have but one wrong move…one mistake and he will kill us both."

"He won't hurt you...I won't let him." Katie turned from him and then turned back.

"And what will you do my love? How will you stop him?" She pointed to Karenia. "My mother is one of the most powerful Maithars in Naturas history and she couldn't stop him. Look... Look what he has done to her! My poor innocent nieces. Why did they ever return..." Katie turned back to Karenia now.

"What were you thinking mother. Why would you bring them back here? They were better off in the human world."

"No Katie, you're wrong." Brian grabbed her arm and made her face him. "I've seen their powers; they are young and untamed but I've never seen anything like it. They can beat him. They can."

Katie stood on her tippy toes and kissed him gently.

"For all our sakes my love, I hope you are right."

Chapter 24

"Here we are." Dante pointed at a cave a few yards ahead of them. It was set into a sloping hill covered with moss and greenery. Branches from the trees surrounding it acted as a screen shielding the cave from direct sight. It could easily be missed if you didn't know where to look. It was small and dark and looked like an animal probably lived in it.

"Huh, that's not what I was expecting the portal to look like." Rosie puzzled.

"What were you expecting?" Chip asked.

"I don't know...something a little grander, I guess. The waterfall I came here through was much more impressive."

"If someone paid attention in class she might know that when the portals were first made, they were placed at points of high natural magic concentration. They can be anywhere and any-thing, waterfalls, caves, giant trees, there's one said to be made out of an enormous fossilized beehive. Some are magnificent and some are ordinary." Klara said smugly.

"Not all of us are teacher's pet dear sister." Rosie snipped.

"I'm not teach—"

"Oh hush, yes you are." Rosie said. Chip and Dante both nodded in agreement and laughed.

Klara crossed her arms. "Whatever."

"Well, who wants to go first?" Rosie asked.

"I guess the teacher's pet will!" Klara stuck her tongue out at them and pushed forward towards the entrance of the cave.

Rosie laughed at her and followed suit. It was so easy to get her sister wound up but Klara knew she was just toying with her. It was nice to have a sister to bicker with and have fun with. It was going to be a lot harder than she thought to detach from the relationships she had formed here but she had to if she was going to protect her heart from further pain.

The group hunched down to enter the dark cave. The entrance was only about five feet tall so Rosie only needed to bend her head down slightly, Klara and Chip both had to hunch their shoulders down a bit, but poor Dante had to practically get down on his hands and knees he was so tall.

You could feel the nervous energy coming from everyone, they all knew what to expect from a portal in theory but going through one was different. Rosie had been so overwhelmed and out of it when she came through with Karenia the first time that she really couldn't remember much detail about the experience. One minute they were in front of a waterfall the next they were in a field.

"I think I can see light up ahead." Klara called from the front of the group.

Rosie squinted her eyes; all she could see was darkness and the very faint shadow of Dante in front of her but then after a few more feet forward she saw it. Just the tiniest speck of light growing bigger as they approached until finally, they reached a sort of doorway. Rosie couldn't make out what was on the other side it was just all light.

"Here goes nothing." Klara said as she stepped through and disappeared. One by one the rest of them followed her.

Rosie could feel solid ground under her feet for a few steps and then it was gone and she was free falling. She could hear her screams joining the rest of them as they fell. Then she felt a sudden sharp pain as she landed flat on her belly. The wind was knocked out of her and she could hear groans coming from Klara and Chip. She opened her eyes and carefully pushed herself to a sitting position, dusting herself off as she did.

"Oh my." She heard Klara whisper. Rosie looked over at her sister who was staring at something in front of her. Rosie followed the line of sight to see Dante landing gently on the ground in front of them, two extremely large outspread black wings protruding from his back. He looked like an avenging angel come to earth. Magnificent.

Rosie stood up and walked towards him. "Dante wow, that's amazing! Look at you!"

Dante looked side to side examining his wings his face just as shocked as the rest of them.

"I... I don't know what happened. I was falling and then suddenly I wasn't."

"Hey man, this is great, real progress but we need to get out of here quick before someone sees you, unless you know how to shift back?" Chip said as he looked around worried.

Rosie had been so caught up in Dante's wings that she didn't notice until then that they were in the middle of a public park. Luckily it did look as though anyone was here yet, it was still quite early in the morning but if she knew anything about humans, she knew there would be some morning joggers here any moment now.

"I'm sorry I don't know how." Dante hung his head.

"Hey, it's ok, we will figure it out." Klara reached out and put a hand on his shoulder.

"Let's go find somewhere out of sight and make a plan ok guys?" Chip lead the way and they darted off towards a building in the distance. Klara was trying to fold Dante's wings down behind him and it wasn't working very well.

"If someone sees, we will just say it's a costume, that he is getting ready for Comicon." Rosie suggested.

"What is Comicon?" Dante asked out of breath.

"It's a human thing, but it would explain the wings trust me." Rosie reassured him.

They reached the building with no incident. It was a small public restroom that was off to the side of the recreation area that held a playground and sporting fields. They darted inside and were rewarded with the smell of bleach and urine mixed together for a lovely combination.

"Ah, how I have not missed this smell." Rosie had spent her fair share of time in dingy, dirty public restrooms living in the streets and it wasn't a fond memory.

"Ok, what do we do now?" Klara was still inspecting Dante's wings, trying to make them collapse on themselves.

"Dante, I think if you just relax a little you can get them to fold up like a bird does, they will be much less noticeable that way." Klara was saying.

"Ok let me try." Dante took a few deep breaths and let his shoulders drop. The wings started to droop down behind him. Rosie and Klara quickly clutched the wings and folded them in gently. When Rosie touched them, they felt both soft and strong at the same time. She wanted to run her fingers across the feather but thought better of it. Dante might not appreciate that very much. It could be awkward after the way she had been messing with him already this morning.

"Yes, there that's much better." She exclaimed.

Dante examined himself in the gritty bathroom mirror. "Well, I guess they could look like they are part of a costume now, tucked down like this. I'm sorry to cause so much trouble, you guys."

"It's ok man, don't worry about it. You will get the hang of it and when you do…those wings of yours might come in pretty handy, just saying." Chip said.

"Ok now that that is settled, what now because from what I saw out there I don't think we are in San Francisco. The temperature doesn't feel right for California." Rosie had spent plenty of time in California and she knew that's not where they were right now.

"Does anyone know where we are? Where did the portal lead us? Chip I thought you said this one was supposed to lead to San Francisco?" Dante asked.

"I mean it's been a while since I used these portals regularly but I do remember that this one was supposed to lead to California, my brother and I used it several times before. I've never known portals to suddenly change or anything." Chip said perplexed.

"It's ok, it shouldn't be hard to figure out where we are. Let's go look around and find somewhere to eat. Then we can plan our next move ok?" Klara said positively.

Chip's stomach growled in response.

"Food is always your top priority isn't it?" Klara laughed.

"Yes…yes it is." Chip countered.

Rosie shook her head. "You two are weirdos, let's go find something to eat."

They left the smelly bathroom and began walking up the paved pathway through the park and out onto the streets. As they neared the edge of the park and the treetops began to recede Rosie could see the skyscrapers peeking out of the skyline. An impressive stone building stood out to the side of them, with a grand staircase.

"Wait, I know where we are! That's the metropolitan museum of art. This is Central Park. We are in New York City." Klara exclaimed. "Oh wow, I used to dream of going to New York City. I've always wanted to see a Broadway show and visit the statue of liberty and pay my respects at the 9/11 memorial. I never thought I would get to come here." The excitement coming from Klara was evident.

"Ah, I don't know what all the hype is about. Once you've seen one dirty, loud, city you've seen them all." Rosie added.

"I don't like it. All this concrete drowns out nature. It's stifling." Dante looked around unimpressed.

"I don't know, I'm not saying I'd want to live here or anything and you know I love nature, but there is a certain beauty to a place like this too. It's like I've been trying to say in class… Everything about the human world is not bad. Sure, there are problems, but there are amazing things too. Just because something is different doesn't mean it's wrong." Klara said passionately.

"That's why you will make a great leader one day, water goddess. Compassion and the ability to embrace differences." Chip beamed at her.

"Not me, I'd be happy to never set foot in another city for the rest of my life. As a matter of fact, I'd have been happy never to set foot in the human world ever again but to each his own so they say." Rosie said sourly.

The group walked along the sidewalk past the museum a few blocks and finally settled on a casual little coffee house where they could sit and plan out their next move. Luckily, Karenia had thought of everything. In their bags, everyone had ID's, passports, and money. Rosie had a credit card but she had no idea if there was a limit to it. They had their Keepies but they wouldn't work in the human world so they were of no use at this point. Karenia had packed them each a small cell phone in case they were separated. Klara gave everyone a quick run-through on how to use them as she was the only one in the group who-ever had. Karenia had thought of everything. The walker into the coffee shop and found a quiet corner to sit in.

Rosie offered to go to the counter and order for everyone. She didn't want to admit it but she was kind of excited to use the credit card. She had never had one before. She had rarely ever had money before either, other than what little time she had spent in the foster system. Even then no one had ever trusted her with a credit card.

"What can I get you?" the pretty girl behind the counter asked. She was cute, with short hair cut in a bob, it was dyed pink, purple, and aqua. She had a few piercings scattered across her ears and face. She had a friendly smile and pretty green eyes.

"What do you recommend? My friends and I aren't from here." Rosie said sweetly.

The girl smiled and leaned forward on the counter. "Where are you from? Somewhere they don't have coffee and sandwiches?" She teased.

Rosie laughed. "They do but probably not as fancy as your city-goers have? What do you like?"

"Besides your smile?" The girl smiled slyly at her.

"Hmm, you do have good taste, then don't you? Why don't you surprise us? Just bring us four drinks and four sandwiches. We don't eat meat though, that's the only preference." Rosie handed the girl her credit card. "Put something on there for yourself too ok?" Rosie let her hand graze the girls when she handed over the card.

"I just ate so no thanks but I'll take your number instead?" the girl said.

"Ok, I'll have it for you when you bring us our order."

The girl handed Rosie back her card. She gave the girl one last smile and headed back to the table.

"Umm, what was that?" Klara asked as she sat down.

"What was what?" Rosie asked innocently.

"Could you be any more obvious? You were totally flirting with that woman?" Klara said.

"So, what if I was?"

"Well...I mean nothing...it's just. I didn't know you like girls like that."

"Is that a problem?" Rosie got defensive.

Klara looked at her a little hurt. "No, of course, it's not, it just seems like that is something you would have told me before now?"

The boys just sat there awkwardly silent pretending not to listen to them.

"Why would you think that? Have you ever said to me...Hey, Rosie, I like boys?"

"Well no, why would I?"

"Then why would I? Because it's different to like girls?"

Klara was quiet for a moment as she contemplated this. "I'm sorry, I get what you're saying. You don't have to explain yourself; I was just surprised that's all. I'm sorry if I offended you." Klara looked down at the table.

"It's ok Klara, really it is. I know you didn't mean anything by it. To be honest my life until now never really afforded me the opportunity to explore romance but I do know that I am attracted to both men and women. I just see people and the way they make me feel. I don't care about gender. Also, I don't really know how that will go over in Natura so I wasn't exactly jumping at the bit to say anything."

Chip decided to chime in now. "Naturians are pretty much the same as humans on that front. You have a lot of people who are open-minded and a lot of people who aren't. There are no rules or laws against it and Naturians as a race are peaceful people so even the ones who may not agree with it aren't vocal about it usually. There are jerks here and there just like anywhere but you shouldn't catch much drama about it back home."

"Well, you sure got over me fast, then didn't you?" Dante asked in all seriousness.

Rosie looked at Klara and they both laughed.

"Sorry Dante, I know when I'm not wanted and I know when to move on buddy, but if you ever decide to kick Kenna to the curb you let me know." And she winked at him.

Klara kicked her under the table. "Stop messing with the poor guy." She whispered.

"Ok back on track guys come on. So, we are in New York and we need to get to one of these three locations, Santa Rosa California, Athens Georgia, or Tlaxcala Mexico." Chip pointed to the list he had written down.

"Well, Georgia is closest but it's still pretty far. If we want to be quick about this we should just fly there." Klara stated.

"Do you think we have enough money for plane tickets?" Rosie asked.

"Yeah, I'm sure Karenia would have planned for this but if we get to the airport and the cards don't work, we will just figure something else out." Klara said.

"Couldn't we just call the number on the card and see what the limit is?" Chip asked.

"We would need to know the password or social security number or something like that and I don't know that." Klara said.

"Ok well let's just take our chances at the airport then." Rosie said as she looked up her number in the cell phone Karenia gave her and wrote it down on a napkin.

"What are you writing?" Klara asked.

"My number for the waitress." Rosie answered.

Klara rolled her eyes. "I don't think you will have time for dating right now Rosie."

"Eh, you never know." Rosie smiled at her.

The waitress walked over and handed them each a sandwich and drinks.

"Cool wings, what character are you?" The waitress asked Dante.

"This looks great, good choices." Rosie said as she handed the napkin to the girl distracting her from Dante.

"I hope you enjoy." The girl smiled at Rosie and took the napkin, slipping it into her apron pocket and sashayed away.

"Anyway…. let's eat and then head to the airport. Georgia or California first? Mexico could be problematic because one thing Karenia didn't pack was passports." Klara said. "We should be able to enter the country without a passport but we won't be able to reenter the US without one so Mexico will need to be our last stop and then we will need to portal back from there."

"How will we find a portal though?" Dante asked.

"We need a portal compass." Chip said. "Karenia didn't pack one and I have no idea where we can get one, they are very rare."

"Ugh, of course…I know someone who has one, unfortunately." Klara said bitterly. "I guess we will be taking a trip back to my home town. Rosie you will get to meet my lovely fake parents if we can find them."

"Maybe they will have left some sort of clue at the house." Chip said.

"Luckily Warner Robins isn't too far from Athens, a few hours' drive so we won't waste too much time." Klara said as she finished up her sandwich.

"This food is really good." Chip said with a mouthful of sandwich.

They all shook their head and finish clearing their plates.

Klara stood first and dropped a few bucks on the table for a tip.

"Let's catch a taxi to the airport and see what we can do."

Chapter 25

Katie lay her head back against the seat of the car. The gentle vibration of the vehicle helped soothe her nerves. She felt Brian's hand; fingers interlaced with hers. His presence next to her was both soothing and disturbing all at once and for so many reasons. If only she could tell him everything. She loved that he trusted her without knowing the whole truth, that he had faith in her when no one else did. If only she could tell him what was really at stake but it was just too dangerous. She couldn't be sure he wouldn't find out she was gone. Raphe had been so preoccupied by her nieces return that the past few months he had all but forgotten about Katie. She feigned illness like he had come to expect from her, like everyone had come to expect from her, and she went to recover in the palace by the lake at east bay. Brian had been pivotal in this scheme. When the old castle healer passed away two years ago his apprentice had not been prepared to take over yet. Brian was summoned to the castle to finish the training. Katie could still remember the moment they met. There had been a grand celebration that evening in honor of Raphe's latest legislation that the Meadowgate borders would now be regulated and patrolled. He had closed Natura's borders to any and all travel without prior authorization from him. He said it was for the safety of the people because ever since the rebellion Humans were now able to cross into the Meadowgate somehow. He led the people to believe the threat of Humans coming to Natura was more important than the freedom of the Naturian people to come and go as they pleased. Natura as a whole was in support of this new act because they all still believed it was humanity to blame for the deaths of the beloved royal family and the abduction of the triplet Maithars. Natura was ignorant of Raphe's cruelty and true nature and so there was a grand celebration. Feasting and dancing and good times. The castle was full of honored guests and Raphe was occupied with being the center of attention, he had all but forgotten about Katie his beloved prisoner of a wife. Katie had been standing in the corner just watching the festivities trying not to cry.

"Such a beauty shouldn't look so sad on a night like this?" a voice had startled her from her thoughts.

He was dressed in Naturian finery and was as handsome as they come.

"Don't mind me, I don't have many reasons to smile anymore sir."

"Ah, I'd imagine not. It is a hard thing to lose those you love. My parents and my brother were lost to me many years ago and not a day goes by that I don't miss them. I can't imagine what it would be like to watch them murdered as you did."

"So, you know who I am then and what he is?" Katie asked curiously, nodding her head in Raphe's direction.

"I do. You are the queen and he is a monster."

"and yet you talk to me?"

"and yet I talk to you." He smiled at her.

"Some would say that is a dangerous thing to do."

"Maybe. Some might also say that things are never what they appear to be. You, for example, are not what they think you are."

"And what do they think I am? Enlighten me?"

"It depends on who you ask. Some say you are the queen, a poor sickly soul, weak and still mourning the loss of your family. Others would say you are a traitor who married the man that killed your family."

Katie stared at him intently. "Which of those things do you think I am? I care not for your pity or your judgment, I am just curious."

"I think you are neither of those things. You are not weak or sickly and you are not a traitor. I believe there is more to the story."

Katie let a tear fall from one eye.

"Then you are the only one to think that way. What is your name kind sir?"

"Brian, my name is Brian. I'm here to train the healer. I live at the feline academy in the great forest of vines in the north."

"It's wonderful to meet you Brian, healer from the north."

"You as well, Queen Katie."

The car rode hard over a pothole in the street jolting Katie back into the present.

"What are you thinking about over there, you're very quiet."

"I was thinking about the night we met."

Brian smiled at her and leaned in to kiss her.

"My world changed that night." He said.

"Mine too, you gave me hope that things could change."

"They will change, I promised you then and I'll promise you now. They will change."

"We are almost to JFK. Departures or arrivals? Where do you want me to drop yous guys off?" the cab drive interrupted loudly.

"Departures please." Brian responded.

Chapter 26

"That will be twenty-one bucks." The cabby looked at Chip expectantly.

"Here you go, Keep the change." Klara handed the cabby the money and rolled her eyes. Right, cause only the man is going to pay. He just assumed that and had been looking at Chip for payment.

The group climbed out of the taxi and onto the curb in front of the ticket counters at JFK airport.

"Here we are. Let's see what we can do." Klara led the way into the airport and headed to the first ticket counter she saw. It was a Delta airlines counter. Klara didn't know much about airlines but she knew Delta had a prominent presence at the Airport in Atlanta Georgia where they needed to fly to so that was their best bet at an available ticket.

"Hello, we need four tickets to Atlanta on the next available flight please." Klara said politely.

The woman behind the counter looked up from her monitor and peered at them from underneath the rim of her glasses.

"I'll need to see some ID please."

Klara's pulse began to race. She hadn't thought about the fact that they were all technically minors. She and Rosie would be 17 next month. Chip and Dante both looked a lot older than they were so they may be ok. Were there rules about minors buying tickets? Klara wasn't sure.

She handed over her ID. The woman snatched it from her and looked at it.

"Hmm. Where did you say you are traveling to again?"

"Atlanta."

"For business or pleasure?"

"Pleasure, we are visiting some old friends." Klara lied.

The woman typed into her keyboard.

"Ok, well I have four seats available on the 10:30 a.m. flight it will begin boarding in 45 minutes. I can't seat you in the same row though, it will be two of you on one row and two of you in another row. The rows are four across but there are none that have four seats available."

"That's ok we can sit separately. Can we make it through security quick enough to make that flight?" Klara asked.

"You should be able to if you don't dottle and have no issues." The woman said flatly.

"Ok, we will take them."

"You don't want to know how much first?" The woman said sarcastically.

"Oh yes of course sorry. How much?"

"For four tickets…plus tax…any checked baggage?"

"No nothing but our personal bags." Klara lifted her small green pouch as an example.

The woman proceeded to take their personal information and look at each of their IDs. Klara noted the fake address on each of them. Made sense she figured it sure would look strange for the IDs to say forest of vines north Natura on them.

"Ok, that will be three thousand two hundred and thirty-five dollars and nine cents."

"Oh geez, that's a lot." Klara said as she pulled out her credit card and handed it to the woman.

The woman took it from her and swiped it. They all glanced at each other nervously hoping Karenia had thought about this scenario and there was enough money on the card.

"Ok, here you go. Please sign here."

The group let out a sigh of relief in unison and Klara signed the paper. The woman handed her four boarding passes and pointed them in the direction of the security checkpoint.

They joined the long line of people waiting to go through security. Klara had been so worried about getting the boarding passes that she had not had the time to let it sink in yet that they were back in the human world. As they stood waiting in the insanely slow line, she looked around at the people with their cell phone glued to them and headphones on. So much technology everywhere. The variety of people was so vast as well. Business people dressed in suits with their briefcases looking hurried. Families with suitcases looking excited. People speaking different languages. Natura was amazing and she couldn't wait to get back there but she also acknowledged that the human world had its perks too. Like the Taco Bell she could see just past security. Her mouth watered; Taco bell had been one of her favorite guilty pleasures before. She could get whatever she wanted and just substitute beans to make it vegetarian. Too bad they didn't have time to stop there before they caught their flight. It would be fun to experience some human things with Chip now that he was…well…a person. She looked over at him and wondered if he felt uncomfortable here. She knew that only incredibly powerful shifters had the ability to shift in the human world so Chip was stuck in whatever form he entered in. That was probably why Dante couldn't get rid of his wings as well. People hadn't been paying too much attention to them. They had gotten a few weird looks but only briefly. To be honest Dante wasn't the strangest looking person in line right now anyway. Ahead of them, there was a man whose entire face was tattooed and he had huge piercings in his ears that made them into holes. Dante's *costume* wings were nothing.

Dante's wide-eyed face, however, was a bit out of place. His head was spinning a mile a minute looking from thing to thing, person to person.

"Hey Dante, you doing ok? I know this is new for you." Klara said.

"It's just so loud and busy. I don't know where to look." He was looking at the tattooed man right now and the man just nodded at him. Dante looked away nervously.

"I know it's a lot to take in." Rosie said.

A TSA agent was shouting instructions to the crowd.

"Remove your shoes, belts and empty your pockets into the bins. Please place any electronic devices such as laptops in a separate bin."

It was finally their turn and they all did as instructed.

"Sir you're going to need to remove those wings, they can't go through the scanner." The agent was tugging at Dante's wings now.

Klara jumped in. "He can't remove them. Can he just try and go through the scanner? I'm sure they will fit."

"Why can't he remove them? You two step over here." The woman directed Dante and Klara off to the side of the line to a holding area where other passengers were being searched and patted down.

"Wait right here." The woman instructed and went back to the line of people.

Chip and Rosie had made it through security and were on the other side looking back at them with concern.

Klara waved and shrugged her shoulders trying to look not worried. How would they explain his wings? Why hadn't she thought of this?

"Next!"

Dante stepped up toward the agent now. He was a large burly man who had a permeant scowl on his face.

"Take the wings off kid."

"I can't, they are stuck." Dante said, the fear in his voice very evident.

The man looked at him suspiciously and approached him.

"What do you mean they are stuck?" He started to pull at the wings and was looking for where they might be attached.

"It's part of his Comicon costume but we were a little heavy with the superglue and they are attached to his skin. We plan on finding a way to get them off when we get to Atlanta." Klara offered hoping she sounded convincing. It was the best she could come up with.

"Superglue? You expect me to believe that? What is going on here? Are you two trying to conceal something—"

"Oh, now why would these sweet children do anything like that?" A familiar sing-song voice came from behind Klara. She turned around to see Brian and Katie standing there.

"What are y—" she began but Brian motioned for her to be quiet. Katie stepped up close to the guard and placed a hand on his forearm.

"What an amazing job you do keeping us all safe. I bet you are the bravest agent here aren't you?" She smiled sweetly and gazed into the agent's eyes.

"What is she doing? This dude is too hardcore to fall for flirting?" She whispered to Brian.

"Oh, she is doing much more than that. You will see. No worries Klara." He responded with a sly smile.

"You just want to let these children pass so they aren't late for the plane, don't you?" Katie continued not breaking eye contact.

The man's hard face melted before their eyes into the sloppiest, silliest smile Klara had ever seen on a grown man. "Oh yes of course! Please let me escort you all to the gate?"

"Oh, that won't be necessary, you are needed here to keep us all safe, aren't you?" Katie said sweetly.

"Right, yes, I am needed here. Please don't let me hold you up any longer! Have a great flight!" The agent released his grip on Dante and motioned them through the security checkpoint.

"Goodbye!" The man yelled to Katie as they walked away and he waved to her with that same ridiculous smile. One of the other agents looked at him like he was crazy and Klara couldn't help but laugh out loud.

"What was that?" Klara squealed still laughing.

"I have the ability to change people's minds about things." Katie said simply.

"So, you are a suader?" Klara asked

"She is being humble. Katie is more than a suader. She is the most powerful sauder Natura has ever seen." Brian said proudly.

Klara looked at the two of them. She recognized this woman as the woman Brian had been within the clinic sharing a secret liaison with.

"What are you doing here?" Rosie and Chip had joined back up with them now.

"We are here to get supplies that are needed to heal Karenia." Brian said.

"How is she?" Klara asked.

"The same but I'm very hopeful for a cure if I can get what I need here." Brian said.

"That sounds promising, where are you headed and why is *she* with you?" Chip asked eyeing Katie with suspicion.

"*She* wants to help save Karenia as much as anyone if not more, and *she* just saved Klara and Dante so it's a good thing *she* is here isn't it?" Brian said clearly offended.

"Please, none of that. I know what most of my mother's circle thinks of me and I understand why but I truly do want to help her." Katie said.

"Wait…. your mother?" Klara asked shocked.

"Yes, I'm not surprised she didn't tell you about me. I am your Aunt. Kerry, your mother was my older sister."

"Why wouldn't Karenia tell us about you?" Rosie asked confused.

"It's a very long, very complex story and we all have places to be so perhaps another time?" Brian was trying to lead Katie away from them.

"Wait, where are you going?" Katie looked at Klara.

"Don't tell her." Chip said coldly.

Klara looked at Chip shocked he would be so rude. She recalled the conversation they had back at the academy when they speculated that the Katie, Brian was talking to, may be her aunt and that there was some sort of secret. He wouldn't tell her more than that then and the opportunity to ask Karenia about it never had come. "We are going to Georgia. Where are you going?"

"Well, what luck! We are going to Georgia as well." Katie

beamed. "That gives us plenty of time to talk."

Chip grunted in dissatisfaction and Klara glared at him.

"There's a lot you don't know Klara." He said sourly.

"Yes, and I can see you of all people didn't feel the need to enlighten me but my Aunt here seems willing to and I would like to hear what she has to say thanks." Klara turned from him. She was so tired of all these secrets coming out little by little. She looked over at Rosie who was just watching Katie blankly. Klara couldn't tell what her sister was thinking, not this time. Not since this morning actually. She knew Rosie was trying to shut her out. She suspected it was because she was scared after what happened with Karenia but Klara had no intention of letting her sister close herself off again.

"Splendid! Isn't it Brian? I can get to know my nieces on the way." Katie beamed.

"Yes, of course, I wouldn't think to keep you from them as long as we remember why we came here." He said solemnly.

Katie looked at him clearly offended. "Do you think for a moment I would forget?"

"I'm sorry...no... of course you wouldn't."

Chapter 27

The group made their way through the crowded airport to the gate. As luck would have it, they were all on the same flight and with the help of Katie's abilities they were able to convince the woman at check-in to make some last-minute changes to seat arrangements so that they would all be seated together. Katie's charm and powers of persuasion had the woman so enthralled that she even bumped them all up to first-class without Katie even asking her to.

They loaded on board, Chip and Dante seemed very uneasy walking into the airplane. Klara could understand their hesitation to fly through the air in a man-made contraption. Brian, on the other hand, appeared to fully embrace the comforts of first-class and technology.

"Would you look at this?" he said to no one in particular as he was inspecting the little touch screen ensconced in the back of the seat in front of him.

Katie smiled at him and turned her attention back to Klara and Rosie.

"So, tell me where have you girls been all this time, in the human world?"

Chip leaned forward from the seat behind them. "Don't answer that."

Klara jumped slightly startled. "Oh my god Chip, please stop, I'll answer what I want to answer, chill out."

He grunted and sat back. Klara sensed his frustration.

"Yes, we were both in the human world until this year, since returning to Natura we've been hiding out so to speak at the feline academy with Karenia." Klara answered.

Rosie leaned forward from the other side of Klara. "Our turn now. Where have you been and why didn't Karenia tell us about you?"

Klara had to hand it to Rosie she sure knew how to cut straight to the point didn't she?

"I'm afraid you will not like the answer but I hope you will hear me out." Katie said sadly.

"We will. I am willing to hear what you have to say. I for one am tired of all the secrets." Rosie said firmly.

Klara nodded in agreement.

"First please believe me when I say, I loved your mother, my sister, very much, I loved my whole family very much. Your mother was strong and regal. She entered a room and everyone stopped and listened. I preferred to slip into a room unnoticed and hide in the shadows. I guess because of this it was so easy for everyone to believe I would betray the family. You have to understand though…by the time I realized what Raphe was…it was too late."

"What do you mean betrayed the family?" Klara felt her throat tightening.

"Darling, are you sure you want to tell them all this now?" Brian took Katie's hand in his, clearly concerned.

"If not now then when? At least here there is a much smaller chance that Raphes spies are listening. Besides, you need to know the whole story now too. I'm tired of pretending. Meeting my nieces like this and in this moment…tells me it is fate. Now is the time to fight back." She answered.

"I did not betray our family, of that I swear, but everyone thinks I did. I don't know if you know this but Raphe was an advisor to your father Ruben. He was a friend of the family for many years. We all trusted him. He was the only one in the palace who didn't treat me like a porcelain doll. He challenged me to grow my power, he encouraged me to speak my mind, he helped me sneak out of the palace and see the world. He told me he loved me and I believed him. You know honestly, in his own sick way I think he does love me if you can call it that."

"He isn't capable of love. He is a villainous monster." Brian said softly.

"Maybe so…but I had no idea what he was planning. None of us did. He was so eloquent and always knew what to say to people."

"So, you were fooled by him just like our mom and dad? How does that mean you betrayed the family? If you didn't know what he was planning you certainly couldn't stop it?" Klara asked.

"Yes, but after it happened, she didn't have to go on and marry the bastard, did she?" Chip was leaning forward again.

Klara and Rosie both stared at Katie in disbelief.

"What? He must have forced you, somehow right?" Rosie offered.

"No…he did not force me. I married him willingly but I had my reasons and Karenia has never given me the chance to explain them. Although if she had I couldn't have told her then anyway."

"What reason could you possibly have to marry that son of a b-"Rosie started.

"Let her finish, we said we would hear her out." Klara interrupted.

"Thank you, Klara, truly. Don't you see? He had intentions of killing all of you…Karenia, all three of you girls. I was too late to save Katherine; she was in your mother's arms as I walked into the room…I watched him…I watched him…." Katie looked away, tears in her eyes. Klara could feel the pain, the heartbreak pouring out of her.

She reached out and took her other hand. "It's ok, I believe you loved them…please finish."

"When I entered the room Karenia and a guard had just grabbed you and Rosie from the bassinet and disappeared. I didn't see what happened to Ruben but I can imagine and as I said I watched him…engulf Kerry and Katherine. When I came in, he turned towards me ready to strike but hesitated."

"Could I show you? I won't show you what happened to your

parents. I wouldn't want you to have the burden of that imagery but can I show you what happened after that?"

"Don't let her in your head." Chip almost shouted.

"Chip, please! What do you mean show us?" Klara asked.

"Part of being a suader is that you can change the way a person thinks right? Well, I have been able to develop my powers to a point where I can put actual images, memories in a person's mind. It can make them think they are their own memories but I can also just show them the images while still allowing them to realize they are not their own memories. Like playing a video inside your head."

"What if she messes with your head? You can't do it, Klara." Klara knew Chip was only trying to protect her but she was beginning to get angry with him.

"Chip, I've asked you to stop. Now as your Maithar, I am demanding that you stop. Do you think me so weak that I cannot protect my own mind? I have been reading Katie's emotions since we got on this plane. What she says is genuine. I have questions and I want them answered. You may not trust her but surely you trust me?"

Chip's face dropped. Klara could feel that she had hurt his feelings. "Of course, Maithar, as you wish." He sat back in his seat and looked away from her.

"Rosie do you agree?" Katie asked.

"I do."

"OK give me your hands. Brian you too. It's time you knew the whole truth as well." Katie held her hands out to them and they reciprocated.

"It will be fuzzy at first."

Klara felt the hairs on her arms stand up and her vision suddenly became foggy, she felt herself spinning and then suddenly she was running.

She looked down at herself but didn't recognize her body. As she ran, she glanced over towards the windows that lined the hallway and saw her reflection. Katie's face stared back at her. She understood now that she was seeing this through Katie's eyes but she was aware that she was herself. She tried to stop running and take in her surroundings but she could not. Whatever Katie was going to show her would play out and she was just a spectator. She kept running until she reached a large door that was slightly ajar. She could hear screaming inside. Suddenly everything went blurry.

I do not wish you to see this part.

The memory jumped ahead in a blur and now she was standing in a room that seemed eerily familiar to her. I t was the room from her dreams. She saw the little bassinet and she saw the pool of thick black tar on the floor where the woman from her dream had been standing.

I know this place.... I've seen it before. She thought in her head.

Me too. Rosie's voice answered.

How could you remember this place, you were both only babies? K-atie's voice now.

I've dreamed this, I've seen him murder them. It wakes me up at night. Klara answered.

It does me too. I should have told you. Rosie said.

"Join me...stand by my side...I love you...you know I love you." They were drawn back into the memory.

"Raphe...what...what have you done? How could you?"

"I did it for you, my love. Don't you see? Now we can rule together. Now you can be the Maithar, the queen you were meant to be."

"I didn't ask for this? I never asked you for this! I loved them... you know I loved them!" Katie was crying desperately. She ran to the bassinet. "My nieces! Oh, no Raphe! They were only babies. How could you kill innocent little babies!?" She was hysterical now.

He stepped towards her and she backed away. His face fell in disappointment.

"I had hoped you would see things my way. I didn't want to hurt you but I will do what's necessary to build the future that Natura needs. I will find Karenia and She will not be able to hide the other two brats for long."

"You didn't kill them all? They are still alive?"

"Unfortunately, yes. I had hoped to get it all done in one fell swoop but now Karenia will have had time to tell her story and It will be so very hard to convince the people to stay loyal to me."

"Not if I help you. I can use my powers to make them believe what you want them to believe."

"You would do that? You would rule by my side? I knew you loved me."

"Do not misunderstand me Raphe. I hate you. You disgust me for what you have done but I will do what you want under one condition."

"You are in no position to negotiate with me, my dear."

"Ah but I think I am. You cannot murder all of Natura and If word gets out of what you have done here today, they will never follow you. You know I can fix all of that for you. You have seen what my power has become."

"Yes, you would be very useful to me. Very useful." He stepped forward and pulled her close to him. He pressed his hot mouth against hers and she tried to push away. He held her tightly and forced his kiss upon her lips. She bit him hard and he drew back quickly, spitting blood onto the floor.

"Do not do that again, so help me! I will do what you ask and my condition is this. You spare Karenia and my two remaining nieces. You let them live out their lives in the human world. I will use my power on my mother and make her think whatever you want. I will make the girls believe they are human and they can live out their lives in peace. I will use my power on anyone else who speaks out against you. This is my condition. Accept or kill me and fend for yourself."

"I believe I can live with this condition however; I will add one of my own or the deal is off and the rest of your wretched family dies but I will not kill you. You will live as my prisoner and suffer the pain of knowing they are all dead."

"What is your condition Raphe?"

"You will be my wife, you will marry me, you will be my queen and you will be my lover, you will do what I want when I want or they will all die and for good measure, I will not stop at your family. I will randomly kill another unfortunate soul every day until you relent and give me what I want."

"Ok Raphe, you have won. I am yours."

He reached forward and pulled her to him, he pressed his lips against hers, he let his hands wander up her sides until he reached her face. He took a fistful of her hair and dragged her to her sister and brother-in-law's bed.

"Please no...not now...not here."

"Oh no, my dear. That's not what the agreement was. What I want, when I want it, remember?"

He let go of her hair and used his thumb to wipe away the tears streaming down her face. Then his hands went to her shoulders and I one swift movement he ripped the dress from her body and shoved her down on the bed. Everything went blurry again and Klara could feel her self spinning. She opened her eyes to find that she was once again sitting in the airplane, flying through the sky towards Georgia.

She looked over into Katie's face, older now than in the memory but the same tears streamed down her face.

"Oh Katie, I'm so sorry! I understand why you did it, I understand everything now." Klara embraced her aunt tightly.

Rosie reached over and wrapped her arms around both of them.

"So, you used your power on Karenia? That's why she thinks you betrayed us all?" Klara said sadly

"Yes, Karenia returned to the palace that night to try and rescue me as Raphe knew she would. She thought she slipped into the palace unnoticed, but he wanted it that way. Karenia and Mystic came to me that night to sneak me away. I used my powers to make them believe I was involved and that I wanted to stay. I made them believe the only way to protect you girls was to send you away as I had promised Raphe. However, I added my own contingency plan. Instead of suggesting they send you away forever I made them believe they would send you away until you came of age and into your powers. That they should all remain hidden and silent about what happened that night until you girls were strong enough to come back and fight."

"So that's why Karenia has stayed hidden and hasn't spoken out publicly against Raphe?" Rosie said.

"Yes, but when Klara returned, and Raphe got wind of it he was furious. It took a lot of convincing for him to believe it was not my doing. I have played the part of a broken woman very well all these years and so he has so far believed that I did as I was told."

"How awful for you to live with him all these years day in and day out at his beck and call." Klara felt so disgusted by what he had done to them all especially Katie.

"Actually, to be honest, he lost interest in me very quickly. He moved me to a home near the feline academy only weeks after your parent's murder. I've not been allowed back in the palace since. He occasionally comes to check on me and I pretend to have lost my mind in grief."

"Why would he send you away? It seems to me he would want to keep you close to him?" Rosie asked.

"I've wondered that myself but I think he doesn't want me to see what he's up to. He worries I would use my power on his loyal guards and work against him. No one but his chosen few are allowed in the palace and those few never leave either. No chance of them telling anyone the truth about him and his doings."

"I have one question? Why have you not used your powers on Raphe?" Klara asked.

"I have tried, I have tried so many times but my powers don't work on him. I think because he helped me to develop them perhaps, he has found a way to resist them. Honestly, I just can't understand it myself." Katie said defeated. "If only they did work. I could have been so much more useful against him, maybe even stopped him."

"Don't say that Don't minimize what you have done. You saved our lives and you couldn't have stopped him. By the time you knew what he was doing he had already done it." Rosie reassured her.

"Care for a drink?" They all jumped when the flight attendant interrupted them.

"You have no idea how much I would!" Katie smiled at her. "However, I will just have hot tea."

They all sat in silence lost in their thoughts while the flight attended passed out everyone's drinks and handed everyone their choice of little bags of crackers and nuts.

"How much longer until we arrive in Atlanta?" Brian asked politely.

"Not long now, we are expected to be at the gate in twenty minutes sir."

"Thank you."

She finished up and continued down the aisle way to the rows behind them.

"I suggest we figure out what we will do when we land." Brian suggested.

"I agree, we are headed to a town called Athens to seek out a Dr. Hardeson at the University of Georgia." Klara offered.

"Amazing, fate truly is on our side if ever that were a sign of good luck. We are also headed to the University in Athens to a one Dr. Hardeson, an old colleague of mine and friend." Brian exclaimed.

"This is hopeful, isn't it? We must be going down the right path if it's all lining up like this?" Katie said.

"Could just be a coincidence." Rosie said flatly.

"I don't believe in coincidences." Klara said hopefully. "I believe in fate and when it comes to Raphe.... I believe in Karma."

Chapter 28

"Don't be so hurt Chip. She was right to listen to Katie. I saw the memories too. Everything she said was the truth." Rosie was sitting with Chip in the lobby of the hotel Brian had kindly gotten for all of them. The plane had landed in Atlanta and they realized it would do no one any good to exhaust themselves driving several hours to Athens hungry and tired. So, they had all agreed to spend the night in Atlanta, get some dinner and get an early start the next morning.

"What if you're wrong? What if she has used her powers on you?" Rosie could tell this was more about Chip's feelings being hurt by Klara pulling the Maithar card on him and less about his suspicions of Katie.

"Chip, if that were the case, wouldn't she then also use her powers on you to win you to her side as well?"

"Yes, I suppose that's true." He said sourly. "It's just that the stronger Klara gets the more I feel as though she doesn't need me anymore and I am losing her."

"I've never met two people who are more stupid. Why don't you tell her how you feel? It's obvious to everyone else but the two of you." Rosie shook her head.

"What is obvious?" Chip blushed.

"That you two are in love with each other." Rosie said exasperated.

"Did she say that? Did she say she loves me?"

"Oh, Chip anyone with eyes can see that. She doesn't have to say it."

"I don't know...I don't want to hold her back...If she did really love me and we tried to make a go of it...I would be a liability for her...she would put herself in danger to try and protect me and it's supposed to be me protecting her. This is why MoCharas are not meant to be together in that way."

"Do you honestly think she wouldn't already do just that? Whether you tell her how you feel or not it won't change that she already loves you and would put herself in harm's way for you....for any of us truly...this is Klara we are talking about... she would put herself in harm's way to save a turtle crossing a highway."

Chip laughed. "That is so true. You know your sister well."

"I'd let the damn turtle get squished, shouldn't be in the road anyway." Rosie said sarcastically.

"Now who is lying to themselves? You aren't as closed off as you pretend to be Rosie and that is also something, we can all see."

Rosie turned away. She had resolved after what happened to Karenia that she wouldn't invest her feelings any further with everyone. She was tired of losing the people she let herself care about. Then she heard or saw rather everything Katie had been through and it made her realize who was she to whine about being hurt. Katie had been hurt and let everyone she cared about believe she was evil. If she could do that all these years then Rosie owed it to her family to be present and invested. She couldn't promise she wouldn't be sarcastic at every opportunity. Personalities don't really change, do they? But she would be there for her sister and the rest of them.

"Yes, I know, it's a work in progress. How about we make a pact right here that we will both work on opening ourselves up to the people we love and being honest?" She held her hand out to Chip and he took it.

"It's a deal." He smiled.

"What are we shaking on?" Klara appeared next to them.

Chip blushed. "Umm nothing just playing around that's all."

Klara looked at him suspiciously. "Ok...well everyone is ready to go eat are you two coming or would you rather continue to just play around?"

"Eat? When would I ever turn down a meal?" Chip hurried past them.

"Are you going to tell me what that was really about sister?"

"Ah, don't worry it was a step in the right direction for all of us." Rosie said.

"How cryptic."

"You know me a lady of mystery and intrigue." Rosie looped her arm through Klara's and they headed after the group.

Dinner had been a quiet affair, everyone lost in their thoughts about one thing or another they had learned that day. After bellies had been filled, they went back to the hotel and everyone said their goodnights.

Rosie thought it was very telling that Katie and Brian had shared a room. She suspected something was going on between them already just by the way they interacted but there was no denying it now. I suppose there was no point in hiding anything now anyway they all had agreed Raphe will have noticed Katie was gone by now and would be onto them.

There was some discussion about who would room with whom as Klara and Chip were used to sleeping in the same room together but everyone could sense Dante's discomfort at the idea of spending the night alone with Rosie and they had agreed the girls would share a room and the boys would share a room.

Rosie was tempted to push the issue and insist her MoChara in training room with her just to spite Kenna and see the look on her face when she found out but she decided to be a better person for tonight at least. Plus, she really wanted to talk to Klara privately about all they had learned that day.

They were curled up under the covers now facing each other.

"So, we have an Aunt." Klara said.

"Why didn't Karenia tell us? Do you think that was part of the plan Katie put in her head or did she choose not to tell us?" Rosie asked.

"I don't know. Karenia has only given us bits and pieces this whole time. I think she thinks she's protecting us but I also think there is more she doesn't want us to know."

"I get the same feeling. She is holding back…she is holding something important maybe even vital back."

"So, what do we do about it? How do we find out?"

Rosie thought for a moment.

"Do you think Katie knows whatever it is?" Klara asked.

"I don't know…In a way, I hope she doesn't because I don't want to have yet another family member who keeps things from us."

"I agree but I just can't get a great read on Katie. I mean I sense her emotions and they feel genuine but then that could be what she wants me to feel."

"Do you doubt what she's told us today?" Rosie asked surprised. She had thought that like herself Klara believed Katie.

"No, I don't think I doubt her…I just don't want to be made a fool of either…Chips right there is always the possibility that she could be manipulating us…it's just my heart so strongly tells me that she is telling the truth. Am I being naive?"

"No, I don't think you are and If anyone would tell you that it would be me. I believe her too. It's just all too horrible to be made up don't you think?"

"Besides she couldn't have planted that dream in our heads, could she? It all matches up to what she's told us."

Rosie considered this for a moment. "True, Karenia took us away immediately, Katie never would have had a chance to do anything to us. The dream must be real."

"Your right. Why can't I hear your thoughts anymore?"

"Well, that was subtle."

"Don't be sarcastic Rosie, why are you shutting me out?"

"I'm sorry. It's not easy for me to let people in, to begin with. After what happened with Karenia I went to a bad place for a moment and turned it all off. I don't know how to turn it back on."

"Can you still hear other people's thoughts?"

"No, I haven't been able to."

"It's ok, you just need time that's all. It will come back. Our powers are tied to our emotions so it's only natural that they would suffer when we suffer."

"I hope you're right."

"Let's get some sleep, I think we are in for an eventful day tomorrow. Goodnight Rosie."

"Goodnight."

∞∞∞∞

"How are you holding up my love? It's been a day for old memories hasn't it?"

"Yes, but it is such a relief to finally be able, to tell the truth. To finally have a reason for hope." Katie took Brian's hands in hers and pulled him close.

"You have been the only light in my dark world for so long. You have kept me going so I could make it to this day and finally have a reason to fight again." She lifted up on her toes and kissed him gently on the lips.

"Oh, my darling, there is nothing I wouldn't do for you, you know that right?" Brian's words were breathless in her ear.

"And I you, my love." Katie let her kisses trail down his neck.

"One day when all of this is over and you are safe, we can finally be together." Brian held her like she would disappear from his arms.

"Why wait my love. We are here in this room with no one to spy on us." Katie whispered.

"Are you sure?"

"I've never been more sure of anything in my life."

Chapter 29

The next morning Klara felt renewed. For the first time in a long time, she had slept with no dreams to awaken her. There was a sense of hope and determination among the group now that hadn't been there before. She suspected that though no one wanted to admit it the fact that there were now two full-grown adults among their number they all felt a little more secure. Brian had found a rental car place and they were all now safely loaded into a minivan headed towards Athens.

"I feel like we should be saying are we there yet?" Klara laughed. They all looked at her confused.

"Don't tell me none of you understand that reference?" she asked surprised.

"Next you're going to tell me you don't understand Luke I am your father."

"Who's Luke?" Dante asked in all seriousness.

"Really? Beam me up, Scotty? No? You're a wizard Harry?... Nothing?"

"What on earth are you talking about?" Rosie said.

Chip laughed to himself.

"Chip I know you know what I'm talking about." Klara squeaked.

"I was a cat; I didn't pay much attention to anything other than you and my next meal sorry."

"Not much has changed then." Rosie teased.

Chip hissed at Rosie in jest.

Klara was laughing and they were all joking around. Anyone

watching would have thought they were a normal group of teenagers out on a road trip with their parents. The only thing maybe a little odd was the giant wings attached to the back of Dante but Katie had been able to handle that with everyone they had come across so far.

If only their lives were as simple as this. In this moment she was happy. She could forget the nightmare looming over them and as with any nightmare, it was beginning to creep back in. First, she felt one of the group's emotions had changed. She searched their face until she reached Brian's. He was driving and checking his rear-view mirror too much too be normal. She felt the worry starting to build in him.

"Brian, what's wrong?" When Klara asked everyone in the group grew silent and looked at him.

"I think we are being followed." He said calmly.

They all turned their heads behind them.

"Well don't everyone look at once." He cried but it was too late. The black SUV behind them started to speed up until it was right on top of them. Klara could see to figures in the front seat, definitely Naturians, definitely shifters from the glow of their eyes.

"Go Go Go they are Shifters!" Klara yelled.

Brian sped up and raced down the interstate, swerving in and out of cars. The black SUV stayed on them like glue.

"I can't lose them."

"Turn off at the next exit maybe we can find somewhere to take a stand. There are too many innocent people here for us to use our powers." Klara said.

Brian continued to speed along and made a mad dash for the nearest exit. The SUV hot on their tail. It sped up and slammed into the back of them making everyone scream.

"Hold on tight everyone."

Brian swerved quickly making a last-minute left turn into a parking garage. The SUV flew past them and slammed on the breaks to turn around.

"Now's our chance everyone, get ready!"

The group piled out of the van and faced the oncoming SUV.

"Ready on my count hit them with everything you've got Rosie."

"One…"

The SUV was getting closer.

"Two.."

They could see the two figures in the front seat.

"Three…Now!"

Klara sent a surge of water flying towards the SUV flipping it over. Rosie ran forwards and shot it with a flaming stream of hot fire. The SUV caught up in ablaze. They could hear screaming as one of the men burned. The other managed to crawl out through the broken glass of the window and was stumbling toward them.

"Stay back. You've lost already." Chip called to the man.

He kept approaching and, in a flash, pulled something from his waist belt and Klara heard a loud pop. Everything happened so quickly. Pop, flash of wings, Rosie screaming, the roar of a cat, another scream.

Then Brian's voice. "Move aside Rosie let me see him."

Klara stood and took in her surroundings. The SUV was still ablaze, one charred body inside. She slowly walked up to it and used her water to put the fire out. She turned and Chip was shifting back into his human form and a mauled corpse was beside him. How had he shifted here? Her thoughts were cut short by the sound of her sister in distress. A few feet away Rosie sat crying, and Katie was holding her.

"Is he going to be ok? Please say he is going to be ok?" Rosie was pleading.

Klara snapped back into the real world and rushed to Brian's side. Dante lay on the ground unconscious. A bullet wound in his shoulder.

"Brian, is he going to be ok?" She asked.

"Yes, it went straight through and it's only a shoulder wound. I can heal it. He will be sore but he will be ok." Brian set to work his hands glowing over the wound.

"Oh, thank goodness. What an idiot...why would he do that... why would he jump in front of me like that...he could have died." Rosie was yelling.

"Rosie he is going to be your MoChara it's his job to protect you. He was doing his duty." Chip tried to comfort her.

"Screw duty. I won't have anyone risking their lives for me like that."

"That's not really for you to decide now is it Rosie. Any one of us would do the same and you for us as well. It's what comes with caring about people. Get used to it." Klara said.

"I don't know if I can." Rosie said quietly her eyes still locked on Dante.

"We need to get him in the van and move. If they found us there are sure to be more coming." Katie said softly.

"Yes, your right." Brian said and he motioned for Chip to help him lift Dante into the van.

"Hey Look...His wings are gone." Rosie pointed out.

"The trauma of the gunshot must have made them shift back." Brian explained.

"Well at least when he wakes up, he will be relieved by that anyway." Klara said as they all settled into their seats and Brian headed back out onto the highway.

"How did they find us?" Rosie questioned.

"I don't know but I wish we had a way to get a message to my father and let him know what's happened maybe he can report on Raphes movements too us as well. Brian, do you have any way to get in touch with him?" Chip asked.

"No, unfortunately, there was no time when I left to set up any sort of communication means. Karenia doesn't have long and time was imperative. Communication between the two worlds would require human technology in both combined with magic. Our Naturian forms of communication don't work across the Meadowgate." Brian answered.

"I may be able to help with that actually." Dante chimed in.

"You're awake! Oh, Dante! You crazy bird brain! Why did you do that! You could have died!" Rosie punched him in the shoulder.

His wounded shoulder.

"Oww. Geez. It hurts bad enough already." Dante said.

"Oh, I'm sorry I'm sorry I didn't think." Rosie pleaded.

"What do you mean you can help Dante?" Chip asked.

"Well, you all know I have a fondness for human things and at the last fair I bought a pair of what the humans call walkie talkies off of a peddler. I made some modifications with a magical assist and before I left, I gave one to Kenna and I have the other right here so we could see if they worked and they did." He pulled a slim phone from his pocket. "She was so sad that she couldn't come with us and I wanted to be able to let her know we are ok so I've been calling her at night before bed."

"What? That's great! Ok, we can call her and ask her to bring the walkie talkie to Mystic." Klara said excitedly.

"Are you all stupid?" Rosie said sourly.

"Really Rosie, you don't have to be mean." Klara rebuffed.

"Don't you see? That's probably exactly how he found us. Kenna." Rosie said.

"What are you saying, Rosie? That's my girlfriend you are talking about. Are you saying she would betray us to Raphe? What's wrong with you?" Dante was clearly angry and offended.

"Let's all calm down a moment." Katie suggested. "I don't think anyone is accusing anyone of anything. We are all just worked up after what just happened. I'm sure Rosie isn't accusing your girlfriend of anything."

"Maybe I am, maybe I'm not. I'm just saying how did he find us? If we had been followed this whole time we would have known by now and what are the odds they randomly found us here in Georgia a plane ride away from where we entered the human world? Did you call her last night? Did you tell her where we were?" Rosie said harshly.

"Well...I. Yes, I did call her last night and I may have mentioned the hotel. I was excited, I've never been in a hotel before and... why am I explaining myself to you...Kenna didn't rat us out... she wouldn't do it and I can't believe you would be so jealous as to accuse her of something that horrible." Dante was shaking with anger.

"Jealous. Jealous. Are you kidding me? Why the hell would I be jealous of that little bi_"

"That is enough. Really are we all twelve here? We don't have the time nor the energy for this petty mess. The reality is that he found us and now we need to get to the university, get what we need and get out of there without being killed. Nothing else matters right now." Klara was frustrated. Why did Rosie have to be so…so difficult sometimes?

"I agree. However, I don't think it is worth the risk to contact Mystic at this point. I'm not saying Kenna has done anything wrong but for all, we know Raphe has found out about the devices and is monitoring them somehow without her knowledge." Katie suggested.

"Yes, I suppose that could be true." Dante conceded. "I'm sorry it was stupid of me; I've left us open to attack."

"It's not your fault Dante, Raphe has spies everywhere we don't know for sure it was the devices but using them does open Kenna up to risk, as well as us, so I think you should get rid of it." Chip reached his hand out for the walkie talkie.

Dante handed it to him and Chip opened the window and hurled it out of the van.

Klara could feel all the tension festering among them in the van. Dante was fuming mad at Rosie and with good reason. Chip has concerned and worried which had been his pretty much constant state of being since they encountered Katie and Brian at the airport. Brian was worried but it had a much more reserved feel to it. She supposed that came with age. Rosie was a firecracker full of emotion like she always was. Klara was just thankful she was starting to be able to read her again. Katie was the one that was curious to Klara. She felt some worry there but mostly she felt this elated feeling of freedom and excitement. Klara guessed she couldn't blame her. The truth was finally out and she was working toward justice against Raphe. Klara supposed there was some freedom in that.

"We are almost there. This is the campus now up here on the

left. I believe I know what building to go to, not much looks to have changed since the last time I was here." Brian said with a touch of nostalgia.

"So, this is what everyone was always going on about?" Klara said wistfully.

"What do you mean?" Rosie asked.

"Well I grew up in Georgia you know and everyone at my high school pretty much had their sights set on coming to this college after graduation. The Georgia Bulldogs are quite a thing in this neck of the world." Klara thought all of that seemed like a lifetime ago but in reality, it was little over a year ago that she was a mousy, invisible, girl trying to survive high school and cruel parents.

Chip reached over and took her hand and gave it a little squeeze. Funny how he always knew what she was thinking.

"Alright, here we are." Brian parked the car in front of one of the massive brick buildings. They made their way inside passing a few book laden students chatting with each other. They all seemed so carefree, only the worries of college exams and what party to go to this weekend on their minds. While Klara and her group had the weight of the world on theirs…two worlds really.

"Here we are, this should be the one." Brian had stopped them in front of what looked to be an office door on the first floor of the building. The hallway was busy but not overcrowded. The walls lined with bulletin boards loaded with brightly colored paper announcing one thing or another.

He knocked firmly on the door.

"Come on in but my office hours are nearly over so this better not be another request to go over the material from yesterday, if you don't know it by now then you better be prepared to face the music on the test today." A woman was saying to them in a lovely British accent as the entered the room. Her back was to them and she was going through some paperwork as she turned to face them. She was an older woman maybe in her late sixties. She wore her brown curly hair pulled back into a French braid. She had slim bifocals laying low on her nose which itself was a bit pointy. Her skin looked as though she had spent a little too much time in the sun over the years but her eyes were a bright blue and full of surprise at seeing Brian.

"Brian old chap is that really you? It's been ages." She hurried over and took Brian's hand to give it a firm handshake.

"I know, I know, it's been too long but you know me, Camille, I get lost in a project and shut out the world." Brian answered. It was clear they knew each other well.

"Yes, some things never change, then, do they? How rude of us. Who are your lovely companions Brian? Please have a seat everyone." There were several chairs spread out around a conference table of sorts on one side of the large office and Camille motioned for them to sit.

"Of course, so sorry, these are friends of mine from home. Let me introduce you to Dante of the canine clan, Chip of the feline clan, son of Mystic, Klara and Rosie Maithars and heirs to Karenia, and lastly, this is Katie, daughter of Karenia." The group stood shocked.

"Umm Brian are you sure you meant to introduce us that way?" Klara asked quietly.

Camille laughed slightly. "Oh, dear Brian I think you've shocked them. Did you neglect to tell them I am Naturian?"

Brian looked around now realizing their reactions. "Oh, I'm sorry I assumed Mystic would have told you but of course he may not have known with Karenia in the state she's in and Camille being her old friend after all."

"You are a friend of my mother?" Katie asked.

"Yes, my dear although I haven't seen her nor heard from her in many many years. Not since before your sister...well not for a long time that is. Brian here has been my sole source of news from Natura and I thank him for it. Now, what's this about Karenia being in a state?"

"Yes, I wish we had time to catch up but Karenia has been poisoned and I believe you may have what I need for a cure. Also, I believe the girls here have some questions you may be able to answer for them?" Brian answered.

"Oh no, my poor dear Karenia. Poisoned. I guess I can assume by who. Our lovely King of course?" Camille said sarcastically.

"Yes, one and the same." Brian handed Camille a list of what he needed.

"Let's see here. Yes, I can certainly help. I have all of these things. Though I will need this one back when you are finished, or I will have some explaining to do to the university." She pointed to something on the list and Brian nodded his head.

"Yes, of course, I will get it back to you as soon as I'm finished."

"Though I dare say if you are planning on truly integrating modern technology into your clinic at the academy you should think about getting one of your own to have." Camille suggested.

"Ahh baby steps, baby steps, Mystic has been gracious with the advancements but I don't want to overwhelm him." Brian responded.

"I understand. Naturians, in general, cling to tradition and the modern world is such a fear for them. Brian, you will find everything you need in the lab through there." Camille motioned to a door on the far side of the room. "Help yourself and I will see what questions I can answer for your young friends here."

"Thank you, I won't be long." Brian darted through the door and was out of sight in a flash.

"So, what can I do for you?" Camille asked.

"We have reason to believe you may know something that can help us on our quest to find some ancient temples." Klara was the first to speak up. "You see we came across one in the forest behind the academy and it's very important that we find them all."

"Temples you say? Well, there are many temples through both the human world and Natura. What can you tell me about the temple you found already that may help me narrow down what you may be seeking?" Camille said her curiosity evident in her voice.

"There's no point beating around the bush." Rosie interjected. "It was a temple for Maithars, we communicated with mother nature, the first Maithar and she made Klara stronger somehow. We believe there are two more temples that can help strengthen us so we can defeat Raphe and restore peace in Natura."

"Well…that is something." Camille was quiet for a moment. The group all gave Rosie a look of disbelief.

"You spat that out all at once didn't you." Klara said.

"We don't have time to waste, do we?" Rosie countered.

"No, it's fine. I appreciate the straightforwardness." Camille stood up and went to her desk. She began rummaging through a drawer until she retrieved what she was looking for and returned to the table.

"This may be able to help you." She slid a small tattered looking package toward them. It was brown and worn. There was a flap fastened tight by a spring that wrapped around the clasp. The circular clasp had an engraving on it just barely visible after years of ware."

"That's the symbol of the Maithar. It's the same one we found outside the first temple." Rosie said.

"I came across this many years ago in Ireland when I was studying some plant life there. It was hidden deep in a magnificent hollowed-out tree. I found it by accident. I had climbed the tree trying to get a closer look at one of the blooms growing on a tree nearby it and I lost my footing. I fell down into the center of the tree and was trapped there for several hours before a colleague came looking for me. Whilst in there I was feeling around for something that may help me find a way out and I found this." Camille unwound the string and opened the book.

"I showed it to Karenia after I found it, we were still in close contact back then. We never really knew what to make of it. There are some old poems in it and drawings but nothing we could make heads or tails of. We knew it was Naturian because of the symbol on the clasp and though it was very peculiar that I should find it in the human world but beyond that, we didn't really think about it."

"What makes you think it may help us.?" Klara asked as she flipped gently through the pages.

"There is a mention in one of the poems that I think may mean something to you." Camille took the book and flipped through until she found what she was looking for. "Here read this." She pointed to the page.

Klara took it from her and began to read.

Deep in the forest of stone and trees
Great power there awaits thee
If but you are the chosen three
Seek me out and you will see
Raging water pure and free
This is the key to conquer the sea
Burning lava fast asleep
I lay waiting until you seek
My fire burns fierce once set free
But caution if you should seek
The fire hidden deep
If not one of the three
One last power as old as time
I can create but I can destroy
Use me wisely or fall to the void
Hidden among the flowers that glow
As bright as starlight the path will show.
Seek me out if you be them
Three wielders of power to light the way
Push back the darkness, unite the day
Only together will the light stay

"Yes, this must be it! The forest of stone and trees and the great sea. That is the first temple we found. It must be." Klara said excitedly.

"So, what does this mean then? We know that we found the temple in Natura so that leaves one hidden here in the human world and one in the Meadowgate." Rosie said.

"They must be talking about a volcano, right? Lave fast asleep?" Dante suggested.

"Yes, that makes sense to me and since there are no volcanoes in the meadow gate then this one the fire temple must be here in the human world." Katie offered.

"There is a place in the Meadowgate that may be the flowers that glow. I use to go there as a girl with our family for picnics at night. It is very beautiful and filled with fireflies. They love the flowers there and land on them making it seem as though the flowers are glowing. I believe that must be the place they are talking about." Katie said.

"One problem though. I don't mean to be insensitive but it speaks of the power of three and with the death of your sister... well you are only two now?" Dante said softly.

"Yes, we know that but we have to try anyway. Even if we can only enhance our two powers at least that will be something. That's why I think it makes more sense to find the fire temple next. Even if you are right and we know the location of the third temple, we don't know that we will be able to gain access to it without Katherine. "Klara said.

"I agree let's try and figure out the fire temple next. So, we need to find a volcano." Rosie said.

"Yes, but there are hundreds of volcanoes in the human world. How can we narrow it down further?" Dante said.

"Hundreds? Great. That's helpful." Rosie said sourly crossing her arms over her chest and falling back against her chair.

"Let me see the list Karenia left us, maybe one of the names on there can help." Dante said.

Klara pulled it out and handed it to him.

"This name here, Armando Varella . He lives in Tlaxcala and there is a volcano there called Malinche. Maybe we should try there?" Dante offered.

"Well unless anyone has any better ideas then that sounds good to me." Klara said.

The group all shook their heads in agreement.

"Thank you so much for this Camille. It really has been helpful." Klara said earnestly.

"Not a problem at all. I only wish I could be of more help dear."

"I'm sorry we can't stay Camille but time is not on our side and we must go." Brian had snuck back in the room unnoticed and he was carrying a box full of items presumably for Karenia's cure.

"I understand. It was good to see you again even if it was a brief visit old friend." Camille gave him a pat on the shoulder and everyone stood to leave.

"It was very nice meeting you thank you again for your help." Klara held her hand out and Camille took it.

"Wait! I have one more thing you may need?" Camille ran to her desk and came back with a necklace. "These are very rare; I'm guessing you may not have one?" She held it out to Klara.

"Is this a portal compass?" Klara said with excitement.

"Yes, please take it, I have no reason to go back to Natura any time soon and you need it more than I do." Camille said.

"Thank you so much, my friend." Brian said and gave her one last warm hug.

"I wish you well, all of you. Bon Chance!" Camille walked them to the door.

They quickly pushed past the now overcrowded hallway and hurried back to the van.

"Now what?" Dante asked once they were all settled in the box tucked safely at Klara's feet.

"We head back to the airport and I'm afraid that is where we will part ways. Katie and I have to get back and work on this cure for Karenia. You all must complete the mission she set you on." Brian stated.

"Do we have any English to Spanish books in that little bag of yours Klara? Because it looks like we are headed to Mexico." Rosie said.

Chapter 30

"What do you mean you're not coming?" Brian pleaded.

"I'm sorry my love but I feel I must stay and help my nieces. We were brought together for a reason. I can be of no help with you in Natura. You didn't need me for your mission I know you used it as a way to break me free but the girls may need me in the coming days and I owe it to my sister to protect her daughters if I can. Don't you understand?" Katie was holding his hands in hers trying to soothe him.

"Of course, I understand. It's just to finally have you in my arms, only to let you run off to danger is more than I can bare." He took her face in his hands.

"I love you, Brian, I will come back to you. I will."

"You better my darling, you must." He kissed her passionately.

"Umm…sorry to break up this soap opera Aunt Katie but we gotta go." Rosie said.

"Yes of course." Katie pulled herself away from Brian and joined the rest of them. They stood there for a moment watching him board his plane.

"So, we are only two gates down. We are catching a plane to El Paso and then we have a connecting flight to Mexico City. Once there we can take a bus into Tlaxcala or rent a car, either one." Klara led the way towards the gate.

"Looks like we won't start boarding for another ten minutes. I'm going to go grab something to drink and use the restroom. Rosie, will you hold my bag?" Klara handed the bag to Rosie who took it and plopped down in a seat next to Chip.

"Ok, will you grab me a snack or something too?" Rosie asked.

"Sure, anybody else want something?" Klara asked and the others shook their heads no.

Klara pushed past the crowds of people and headed towards the ladies' room. She was repeating the poem from the book in her head trying to think if there was any clue they had missed. It didn't occur to her when she entered the restroom that it was eerily empty. If she hadn't been so distracted, tired and hungry she may have thought it was odd that in a crowded airport there wasn't a soul in this bathroom. She went over to the sink to look at herself in the mirror and everything went black.

Chapter 31

Klara opened her eyes and instantly regretted it. The light from above was piercing and her head throbbed. She lifted her hand to the back of her head and felt around gingerly until she found a large bump, it was already the size of a goose egg. She opened her eyes again slowly letting them adjust and she carefully pushed herself up into a sitting position.

Where am I? What happened?

The room was small and circular in shape. It was barren except for a dirty old mattress on the floor that Klara was currently sitting on. There were no windows and the only light in the room came from the torches burning at the top of the high walls. The room smelled of dirt, sweat, and blood.

Klara stood up slowly, her head spinning and she walked over to the door.

Locked, of course.

"Hey! Is anyone there? What is going on? Let me out of here!" She bellowed and banged on the door with her fists.

Nothing.

She reached out with her mind, trying to sense if anyone else was present nearby but again she found nothing.

Whatever, I'm not sticking around here to find out what's going on. She raised her hands and prepared to shoot the door off its hinges with her water but nothing came. She couldn't feel that familiar surge of energy pooling up inside her, as a matter of fact, she couldn't feel any energy at all.

Panic started to rise up in her chest and she ran back over to the door and began beating it wildly.

"Let me out now!"

"Klara is that you?" Kenna's voice replied from the other side of the door. The small metal window slid open and Klara could see Kenna's face staring back at her.

"Kenna? Oh, thank goodness! Kenna, how did you find me? You have to get me out of here. Where are we? The last thing I remember I'm in the airport in Atlanta and now I'm here?"

"Calm down calm down. I'll answer your questions in a minute. Let me just get this door open." Kenna whispered. She fiddled with the lock a moment and then the door swung open with a thud.

Klara lunged forward giving her best friend a huge bear hug. "I'm so glad to see you!"

Kenna hugged her back. "Me too you have no idea. Hurry let's get out of here before he catches us."

"You mean Raphe I'm assuming. Are we in some sort of prison? Why don't my powers work down here?"

"Raphe built drain stones into the walls; they strip away powers that are earth-based like yours. Remember we learned about them in class. They block you from being able to draw power from the earth."

Klara remembered her lessons at the academy. Different abilities drew their magic from different sources. Water, fire, earth powers came from the earth's core and spread up through the ground, rocks, water, and trees all around. Light magic came from the sun and Shifter magic came from a combination of the earth and the inner soul of the shifter themselves. No one was quite sure where Raphe drew his power from. After all, many of the Natura citizens didn't even know what his powers were, but Klara did, she had seen them in her dreams, her visions of the past, she had watched his sick black tendrils destroy her parent's lives.

Klara followed Kenna down hallway after hallway like a maze until they finally reached a large open room. It was dark and smelled odd…Klara pictured the vehicles parked at her old school's parking lot and the smell that came from them…it was gasoline…why would there be gasoline here in Natura?

"Kenna, where are we…and why do I smell gasoline?" It was so dark she couldn't see her hands in front of her face.

Klara didn't hear a response only silence and the hairs on her arms began to stand on end. Something was definitely wrong here.

"Kenna?"

Klara turned around in a circle and reached her arms to try and find Kenna but she only found empty air.

There was a rustling sound and Klara could hear someone breathing. The gasoline smell was getting stronger to a point it was sickening.

"Kenna are you there?"

"Yes, …she's still here." Klara froze, fear shivered through her body. She knew that voice…Raphe.

Suddenly an orb burst to light and lit up the room.

Kenna was standing several feet away with a smirk on her face and right next to her, stroking her hair like you would a pet dog was Raphe.

"Hey, bestie." Kenna sneered.

Klara was confused. What was going on here?

"Kenna? What is happening?"

"Oh, you are stupid, aren't you? Precious Klara. High and mighty Maithar. Everyone bow down to the savior of Natura." She spat and laughed in disgust.

"I don't understand? You're my best friend Kenna what are you saying? This can't be right. He's done something to you I know it." Klara pleaded with her friend. Hot tears streaming down her face. Not Kenna, not her bright, bubbly Kenna.

"You should have listened to your stupid trash heap of a sister. She knew the real me right from the start. She might be a worthless, scrawny little rat but at least she has a brain. I'll give her that." Kenna's words infuriated Klara. Rosie had been right all along. Kenna was the traitor. It was always Kenna.

"You little b- "but Klara didn't get to finish her insult. She was slammed to the ground with Kenna's light orb.

"You were saying?" Kenna laughed. Klara was shocked, she had thought light orbs weren't able to be used as aggressive powers but she had been wrong. She could feel the sting of Kenna's orb where it had hit her.

"You wouldn't dare try that if I had my powers, this isn't a fair fight and you know it. Why not take me outside and let's see what happens?" Klara mocked Kenna trying to rattle her, distract Raphe until help could get there. She got to her feet and braced herself for what she thought would be another orb headed her way.

Kenna raised her hand preparing to shoot.

"That's enough my pet, you have served me well but I can't have you harming my prize pony."

"Don't worry Klara. Your friends will all be here soon. I've set a little trap you see. Bread crumbs for them to follow. I can take care of you all in one fell swoop." Raphe circled her like a predator ready to strike.

"You underestimate my friends Raphe. What makes you think you can take them all." Klara felt the fear welling up inside her. The truth was, they weren't ready to face him. They hadn't found the other temples yet. They hadn't enhanced Rosie's powers and Karenia wouldn't be coming to save them, she lay poisoned in the academy barely hanging on.

"You won't hurt Dante though right Raphe? You promised you wouldn't hurt Dante." Kenna sounded concerned.

"Did I?" Raphe answered Kenna but he kept his eyes on Klara still circling her.

"You know you did! Don't you dare hurt Dante." Kenna raised her voice.

Raphe stopped short in his tracks and turned to face her. "Are we making demands my pet?" he said coolly.

Kenna's eye-widening, realizing her mistake. "No of course not, it's just...you promised." She whimpered.

"You promised." Raphe mocked her cruelly.

Kenna began to cry and shrunk away from him.

"Oh, my poor little Kenna? Did I scare you? Come here my pet. Let me reassure you." He held his arms out open to her.

Kenna looked relieved and ran into his arms. He pulled her in close to him and pressed his lips against hers. Klara saw Kenna relax into his embrace as though it was a familiar affair. Klara felt sick to her stomach at the sight of them but she looked on anyway afraid to take her eyes off the two of them and she watched as the embrace went from passionate to deadly. By the time Kenna realized what was happening it was too late. Raphe wrapped his oily black tentacles around her and squeezed her arms to her sides. He pulled away from the kiss and opened his mouth letting another tendril snake out like a tongue and it wrapped itself around Kenna's neck squeezing until there was a deafening crack. The tentacles slithered back into their master and Kenna's lifeless body fell to the ground, eyes wide, frozen in terror.

"I'm sorry you had to witness that nasty bit of business Klara dear, but Kenna was becoming somewhat of a nuisance for me. She was a nice distraction from the heartbreak of finding my loving wife Katie has betrayed me but I can find another distraction easy enough that is not so tepid and whimpering." Raphe walked toward Klara and she backed away.

"No, no dear, please follow me and let's talk about your future." Raphe sent a tentacle lashing out at her, she turned to run but it was no use. It grabbed her wrists and waist, pulling her after Raphe as he walked into an adjoining room. There were computers along the walls and all sorts of human inventions, that were out of place in this world. She struggled against her oily black captors but they only wrapped around her tighter, squeezing so hard she could barely breathe. The smell of oil and gasoline was overwhelming her and blurring her vision, stealing her breath.

Raphe sat down and the tentacle slammed her into the seat across from him, still wrapped around her tightly forcing her to comply but it loosened ever so slightly to allow her to take in a few breaths. She inhaled deeply and glared at him across the small table.

"Save your breath Raphe, I don't want to hear anything you have to say." Klara tilted her head down and bit the tentacle that was in reach. It shuddered slightly but did not loosen and Klara was rewarded with a horrible oil taste in her mouth.

Raphe laughed cruelly.

"How crude of you but then you were raised with the humans weren't you."

Klara spit the nasty taste out of her mouth.

"It doesn't have to be like this Klara, join me. Together our powers can restore Natura. Make it great again. We can rid the earth of the human filth and Natura can once again populate the entire planet, no more hiding."

"I will never join you."

"You say that now but what about your sister? Don't you want to be with her?"

"You leave Rosie out of this; she will never join you either!" The thought of Raphe anywhere near Rosie angered Klara beyond words. Rosie's life had been terrible enough already and she was not going to let Raphe hurt her. Klara finally had a family, a sister who she refused to be parted from.

"Oh, Rosie will come to me soon enough but I was referring to Katherine, or have you forgotten you have another sister. Tsk Tsk, Katherine will be hurt to hear this."

"Katherine is alive!? You sick bastard! Where is she! What have you done to her?!"

Klara raged against her captor, she tried desperately to free herself but without her powers, she was just no match for Raphe. Klara couldn't bare to think about what Katherine had endured at the hands of this man for the past 16 years. Her mind raced with all the gruesome possibilities. Katherine is alive…part of her always knew it. If they could get to her, find her and reunite their three powers…maybe just maybe they stood a chance against this monster. Klara found her hope renewed. She would make it out of this somehow and she would find her sister.

"She is mine…and I will use her as I see fit…soon you and Rosie will be mine as well." His voice was calm and matter of fact.

"You're delusional."

"Am I? Perhaps you need some incentive to see things my way." Raphe stood again and walked towards the computer monitors. Klara was dragged along, thrashing every step, fighting with every ounce of energy she had to wiggle free of his grip.

He looked at the screens and they sprang to life. Klara stopped moving and fixed her gaze on the bright screen glowing in front of her. It was an image of her hometown, she could see the high school and her beloved forest behind it, she could see the small suburban housing complexes surrounding the school. Everything leading to the main drag of town, the movie theater, grocery stores, skating rink…all so familiar yet so long ago. It was the middle of the afternoon and she could see people coming and going in town and cars parked at the school. Classes would be letting out soon.

"What is this?"

"Don't you recognize your home?" Raphe pretended to be surprised.

"Of course, I do but why are you showing me this?"

"I'm glad you asked. Let me give you a brief demonstration of my powers and perhaps that will help you make the right decision."

Raphe let his tendril slither back to him, releasing Klara. She thought about trying to make a run for it but knew deep down she needed to see what he was about to show her; besides he would have no problem catching her before she even made it halfway to the door.

Raphe closed his eyes and lifted his arms above his head. The computer screens began to flicker and the smell of gas and oil became even stronger. Klara watched the screen and saw people near the center of town begin to panic. The ground was rumbling and was beginning to split open like an earthquake but instead of a gaping hole, black goop began oozing up from the ground everywhere. The people were running trying to escape it but it just kept coming, swallowing them whole…one by one..men…women..children. In mere seconds the entire grocery store parking lot was a pool of black death.

"Stop! Please!"

Raphe lowered his hands and the pool of black liquid stilled. He turned to face Klara.

"You can make this stop. Join me and I will spare the rest of your town. Refuse me and I will swallow the school next."

Klara thought of all the teachers and students in the school. All innocent and going about their day. She couldn't stand by and let them be murdered. She thought of her history teacher and the last conversation she had with him about futures, he was kind and wanted to see her succeed. She even thought of Mallory, even after all the years of bullying Klara didn't want Mallory to suffer such an awful fate. She had no choice but to play along with him. At the very least it would buy her some more time and maybe she could get out of this building, get her powers back and put up a fight.

"Ok, I will do what you want."

Raphe's lips curled up into a sadistic smile.

"I knew you were a reasonable girl."

Raphe snapped his fingers and two guards appeared out of nowhere.

"Please take my guest back to her cell."

The guards nodded and grabbed Klara by both arms.

"Wait!? I said I will do what you want?"

"Yes, you did and in time you will stand by my side as we shape a new future but I am not a stupid man…you will remain here until I am sure I can trust you not to make…shall we say…an unfortunate decision? Don't worry…I will be back to help you train personally for our mission." He reached out and stroked Klara's face. It sent shudders of revolution through her and she turned her face away from him.

He grabbed her chin and forced her to look into her eyes.

"You will learn to enjoy my company in time…I can promise you that."

He gestured with his hand for the guards to carry her away.

"RAPHE!!!!"

At the sound of Chip's voice, Klara's heart leapt. Finally! Klara struggled and broke free from the guard's grips. She reached her arm back and punched one straight in the face knocking him to the ground and she ran towards the sound of Chip's voice.

"It's a trap! Be careful!" She screamed

Fire came blasting through the side of the wall, leaving a gaping hole to the outside, rendering the stones that were blocking her power useless. Klara instantly felt rejuvenated. Energy began filling every fiber of her being and she turned toward Raphe blasting him with a surge of power. It hit him square in the chest and forced him to stumble back a few feet but he did not lose his footing. Enraged he locked eyes with Klara and sent his tentacles racing for her but before they could reach her a wall of fire rose up between them. His tentacles slammed against it, sparking and angry. Klara could barely see Raphe through the fire but she could feel his anger and hatred, his emotions were pure evil. The tentacles were burrowing their way through the fire and would soon breakthrough. Klara began to run towards the opening in the wall, she could see them now...Rosie...and...Chip. Her heart exploded with relief. She was almost to them now... only feet away but she could see Rosie struggling to maintain her power...she was draining quickly and if Klara tried to shoot water at Raphe it would only diminish her firepower.

"ARGHHH!!!" Raphe let out a terrible groan and his tentacles burst through the fire. Rosie collapsed to the ground.

His tendrils reached Klara in an instant and wrapped around her midsection, squeezing tightly, pinning her arms to her sides.

"Where do you think you're going?"

He sent another tendril towards Rosie and it wrapped around her pinning her to the ground where she lay.

A fierce growl exploded from Chip and in a flash, he was racing at Raphe full speed, transforming into a mighty tiger. He lunged at Raphe and slammed a massive clawed paw at his head. It knocked Raphe to the ground and drew blood. His tentacles loosened their grip slightly.

"How dare you strike your king you filthy shifter!" Raphe stood up and was focused on Chip. He opened his mouth and a smoldering ball of black sparks came plummeting out. It hit Chip square in the face and knocked the great cat into the wall, his body slid down to the ground and was still.

"NO!!!!!!!!!!!" Klara screamed.

Raphe walked towards Chip another spark ball building up, preparing to finish him off. Chip, her best friend, her protector, her MoChara...Her love.

Klara's whole body began to pulse, her skin began to glow a faint aqua color. She could feel all the energy building in her. She wasn't sure what was happening but she knew she had to latch on to it...channel it. Her hair floated up around her and her feet lifted from the ground and she was floating in the air. Water burst from her hands...and her arms...every inch of her skin so that she was surrounded by a whirlpool of water. Raphes remaining tentacles dropped away from her like they were nothing.

Raphe turned his sight to her and began pooling his strength again, preparing to attack but Klara wasn't scared...she knew something was different this time. She wasn't Klara anymore. She was a Maithar. She was power. She was...a water goddess. She set her sights on Raphe and flew at him like a hurricane. She crashed into him sending him flying. She reached out with one arm and directed a current of water at him, enveloping him, lifting him into the air. He began to struggle and thrash, his black tentacles sprang forth from his hands and mouth and wrapped themselves around him so that he was in a black cocoon. Klara swept him up higher in the air and then thrust him down slamming him hard on the ground. The cocoon lay there still and Klara lowered herself to the ground next to him. She let the water drain away and she was herself again. Tann skinned, hair wet, just Klara again. She approached the cocoon slowly, hands at the ready. She reached one foot out tentatively and kicked Raphe to see if he was still alive. Hoping he wasn't, hoping this could all be over now. As her foot made contact with the cocoon it disintegrated before her eyes and in its place was just a small pile of ash. No tentacles and no Raphe.

A malicious laugh came from nowhere and Klara spun around expecting to find him but there was no one there.

"This isn't over…ah but you are powerful…and you will be mine."

Klara felt sick. His words chilled her to the bone. A groan brought her back to the present and Klara raced towards Chip. Rosie had regained conciseness and was standing up.

"Rosie are you ok? Can you help me with him?"

"Yeah I'm fine, just drained but I'm ok."

They both reached Chip quickly and Klara drew in a sharp breath. The fur on one side of Chip's body from his face down to his legs had been burned away and the skin underneath was scalded, blackened. It looked horrible and dead. Raphe's disgusting power had left its terrible mark.

Klara lay there beside Chip stroking his soft fur, even though he was currently in the form of a mighty Tiger he looked so frail right now.

"He is going to be ok Klara, he is one tough guy, you know that. Besides he would never leave his water goddess without her MoChara. You know that." Rosie wrapped her arms around Klara's shoulders, embracing her, holding her close. She squeezed her tightly, reassuring her.

"I'm so scared Rosie, what if he isn't ok? I can't do any of this without him. You may think I'm weak but I need him." Klara felt tears streaming down her face.

"It's not weak Klara, loving someone, needing someone…it's not weak…you taught me that. Besides Chip is too stubborn to die without finally hearing you admit your feelings."

"What are you talking about?" but before Rosie could answer help had arrived in the form of Dante, Brian, and Katie.

Chapter 32

Klara felt the relief flood over her as Brian came into view.

"Brian over here quickly! Chip is hurt and it looks bad." Brian raced to Chip's side and set to work examining the wounds.

"Will he be ok? Please tell me he will be ok?"

"Klara, everything will be fine, stand back and let Brian work. Are you ok? Are you hurt anywhere? Rosie what about you? Are you ok?" Katie pulled Klara and Rosie toward her and was looking them over, touching their faces and their hair and their shoulders erratically, she pulled them in for a hug that could squeeze the life out of a rock.

"Rosie what in the world were you thinking! You should have stuck to the plan!" Katie scolded.

"What plan? What happened and how did you all know where to find me? Raphe said it was a trap." Klara asked.

"When we noticed you had been gone too long, we went looking for you and found a message in the bathroom from Raphe. We knew it would be a trap and so Dante and I said we needed to go back to the academy first for help. I thought we were all on the same page but when we got to the Meadowgate Chip and Rosie took off. Dante and I went back to the academy anyway because we knew at the very least, we would need to bring a healer." Katie explained.

"I'm sorry Katie but Chip and I couldn't wait. Trap or not we had to go to Klara and do what we could." Rosie said.

"Well I'm grateful to you both because if you hadn't blasted a hole in that wall, I don't think we would be having this conversation right now and If you hadn't brought Brian to heal Chip…" Klara's eyes caught a devastating scene in the distance.

Dante was kneeling beside Kenna's lifeless corpse.

"Oh no, Dante!" Klara rushed to him.

"Oh, No, what has he done. That bastard has taken another innocent young life." Katie said.

"Innocent my ass." Rosie spat.

"No, Rosie, not now, not here." Klara pleaded and directed her eyes towards Dante.

He spoke now, in a whisper, just barely audible.

"Let her finish…I want to know what happened. All of it."

Klara took a step forward and placed her hand on his shoulder.

"Dante, we don't have to do this now. Please, let's all go back to the academy first."

Dante just stared into her eyes and shook his head.

"Now."

Klara hung her head, desperate to avoid the words that needed to come out next.

"It was Kenna, she was the spy we suspected. She told him where to find us. I was hit over the head and brought here to a cell. My powers had been blocked and Kenna was there. I thought at first, she was here to save me and she acted like she was but she was she was only toying with me and Raphe was waiting here. Kenna and Raphe were…together…romantically it seemed but as soon as she had served her purpose for him, he ended her life like it was nothing. She pleaded for your life Dante in the end. Whatever she may have been she did really care for you."

Dante said nothing. He just stared at Kenna's body. Klara felt nothing but emptiness from him.

"What did Raphe want with you? If he had wanted to kill you, he had plenty of time before we got here?" Rosie pointed out.

"He tried to get me to join him, as if I would ever do that but he tried to threaten and blackmail me into it by making me watch as he took innocent lives."

"That's awful. I'm sorry. He is pure evil." Katie put her hand on Klara's shoulder.

"That's not all…He implied that Katherine is alive and that he has her. Rosie…she's still alive…he has her…but she is still alive."

Rosie and Klara looked at each other.

A loud scream startled them all and they turned towards the noise.

Dante was clutching the sides of his head, screaming and pounding his fists against his own skull.

He began to shift suddenly and in an instant, an owl the size of a small elephant stood in his place. The owl took one last longing, broken, look at Kenna's lifeless body before leaping into the air and soaring away.

"Dante!" Rosie called after him.

"Let him go, he needs time to absorb this." Katie bent down and slid Kenna's eyes closed gently with her hand.

"Come on girls let's get Chip back to the academy."

Klara was surprised to find that they were not very far from the academy at all. The ruined building turned out to be only a 30-minute ride on horseback to get back home.

Once they arrived Chip, Rosie and Klara were taken straight to the medical wing. Brian had assured Klara that Chip was stabilized but he hadn't woken up yet. Brian checked them over for injuries and then made her leave with Katie and Rosie to go get something to eat and had promised her he would send word if anything changed.

The three of them were sitting in Karenia's quarters still reeling from the news that Katherine was alive. After having learned the whole story about Katie, Mystic had forgiven her and told her to stay in Karenia's quarters for now.

Brian had administered the cure on Karenia and said it was too soon to tell if it was working or not so they were all cautiously optimistic.

"We have to save Katherine; we have to get her away from him." Klara couldn't imagine what she had been through all these years at Raphe's hands.

"Did he give you any clue of where he might be keeping her?" Rosie asked.

"No. Nothing."

"He would want to keep her close and under his control. He would know she has the potential to be very powerful like you girls." Katie said.

"Do you think he has her with him at the castle?" Rosie asked.

"It's possible…actually, it's pretty likely and would explain why he moved me out of the castle and only lets a select few in." Katie was pacing the room.

"How can we get in there?" Rosie asked.

Katie stopped pacing and flopped down into the chair next to Rosie.

"I don't know just yet but we will think of something. It's late and we are all exhausted. I've discussed it with Mystic and it's no longer safe to stay here out in the open. Tomorrow we will be leaving, Luna the leader of the Canines has a secure location and has offered it to us."

"Can we trust her? After what happened with Kenna, I feel like we can't trust anyone anymore." Klara asked.

"Yes, we can trust Luna, I would trust her with my life and besides in a way she is family." Katie said sadly.

"How's that?" Rosie inquired.

"Well, Luna was my MoChara before I *betrayed* everyone." Katie answered. "This is a reunion that I both dread and can't wait for."

"I'm sure she will understand once you tell her the truth just like everyone else has so far." Klara reassured her.

"I hope you are right but keeping a secret from your MoChara is a pretty big betrayal." Katie said sadly. "Anyway, I am going to go say goodnight to Brian and go to bed. I'll see you girls in the morning." Katie hugged them both and walked them to the door.

Klara and Rosie walked down the hallway in silence. Both thinking of the day's events.

I'm sorry I didn't listen to you about Kenna.

It's ok she was your best friend.

But you're my sister I should have listened. I won't make that mistake again Rosie.

I'm glad we can talk like this again. I was scared you had shut me out forever.

Never Klara, I never want to shut you out. After today it's clear to me now that nothing matters more than family. When you went missing and I thought for a minute I had lost your forever....

Klara stopped walking and pulled her sister into her arms. "You aren't going to lose me. We are going to beat him. We are going to find Katherine and we are going to live a long happy life with our friends and family." Klara said with certainty.

"Promise?"

"I promise. You're not the only one who had an emotional breakthrough today. I'm not going to bed just yet. I have something important I need to tell Chip when he wakes up." Klara said.

"Umm Hmmm, I bet you do." Rosie said knowingly.

Klara arched an eyebrow at her and Rosie laughed.

"Goodnight sis and Good luck." Rosie darted off with a laugh.

Klara started to walk back to the hospital wing and replayed the night in her mind. She had been so relieved to see Chip there, so relieved to have back up and escape Raphe but if Chip didn't recover from this, she didn't know what she would do. She couldn't survive without him. She knew now without a doubt that she was in love with him and she couldn't let another day go by without telling him. Klara began to run towards the hospital wing with a renewed sense of purpose. She would tell Chip how she felt and give him a reason to wake up.

"I'm coming Chip...I love you...I will always love you my MoChara."

Epilogue

"Papa are you sure I have to attend the dinner tonight?"

"Kat, you know I need you by my side, if I have to sit through one more of Lady Venezia's singing performances, I will need my favorite girl by my side to elbow me when I start to fall asleep."

Katherine laughed. "You shouldn't say that Papa, she has a lovely voice."

Katherine looped her arm through her fathers and they continued to walk down the breezeway of the castle. It was such a perfect day, the sun was shining, the breeze was just enough to keep it comfortable outside. She could smell the first blooms of spring growing in the castle gardens just ahead. She and her father had been taking these afternoon strolls through the gardens for as long as she could remember.

She looked forward to them each day. Her father was such a busy man and everyone demanded his time but somehow, he always managed to meet her here for their strolls together.

"So, tell me how your classes are going? Do you like your new tutors?" he gave her a suspicious look.

Katherine was not the most behaved student. She had run off several tutors in the past. Especially once she had come into her powers. Her most recent stunt had been to wrap her language tutor up in a tangle of vines and hang her upside down from the library ceiling. In her defense, the woman had been vile. Katherine walked in on her mistreating one of the servants, she had actually had the nerve to beat the poor girl with a Latin book for simply forgetting to bring sugar with her tea. Katherine didn't like bullies.

"Yes papa, so far my studies are going well and I promise to be on my best behavior." Katherine gave him her biggest, brightest smile. She held her hand out, palm facing up, it glowed a light emerald green and a fully matured yellow rose appeared in her hand. She handed it to her father.

"Bribes will not win you any points, my dear." He said as he accepted the rose. Katherine knew he was lying to her. Yellow roses were his favorite and Katherine could do no wrong in his eyes.

"I see your getting faster with your abilities, have you been practicing anything new, anything we talked about?"

"I have...yesterday I was finally able to propel a rock forward fifty or so feet, but I much prefer using my talents for growing beautiful things...Don't you think that is a more useful way for me to contribute father?"

"I know it's hard for you to go against your instinct my love and use your gift for...defensive purposes but you need to be prepared. We have many enemies out there and there may come a time I will need you by my side for more than just flowers and dinner parties."

He sat down on their favorite stone bench. It was surrounded by yellow roses and it was secluded. He gestured for her to sit beside him.

"Why would anyone ever want to hurt us, papa?"

"There are many people in our world who do not like change and progress, they would seek to destroy us so that they may live in that past, outdated, never moving forward."

Katherine was about to ask her father exactly what that meant but was interrupted by a castle guard.

"I'm sorry to disturb you sire but Cornel Jaspin wishes to have an audience with you as soon as possible."

"Please inform Cornel Jaspin I will see him in the throne room when I am done visiting with my daughter. He knows not to disturb me during this time as do you solider."

Katherine thought her father sounded a bit harsh but it warmed her heart that their time together meant so much to him.

"Yes, King Raphe, I will relay your message, I apologize for the interruption."

"Oh, father you mustn't be so harsh with him." Katherine scolded her father.

"I'm sorry my darling. You have such a tender heart, my dear. It's one of the things I love about you." Raphe pulled her close, embracing his daughter tightly in his arms.

"I love you too Papa." Katherine let herself relax into the safest place in the world. Her father's arms.

The story contiues in...*Becoming Rayne*.

Coming Soon

www.ingramcontent.com/pod-product-compliance
Lightning Source LLC
Chambersburg PA
CBHW021959170626
46808CB00001B/214